Subject

....

Charity James

Contents

Chapter 1

I stared at the vault door ahead of me as alarms rang out and it slowly crept open. Red lights flashed around me, warning anyone in the area of the impending danger.

My mind felt foggy and my eyes blurry as some kind of shadowy smoke seeped through the opening out into the hallway where I stood. My heart was racing and I felt like I couldn't breathe as the door completely opened showing nothing but a pitch-black void.

A distorted voice from within called my name but I couldn't move, couldn't think while whatever was inside that room writhed inside of the darkness. Coming closer. I could feel it around me, suffocating me in an embrace that both terrified and comforted me but I couldn't see it.

'Ava' the voice called out once more, but this time it was closer, practically whispering in my ear.

"Ava!"

I jolted upright, started awake by my co-worker standing beside me. "hey! Were you seriously taking a nap?" jade asked teasingly. I blinked a few times confused and looked at my desk where I was sitting then around the room, slowly recognizing everything I saw. I'm in the lab?

"hello?" earth to Ava, do you copy? " Jade waved her hand in front of my face and I smacked it away gently before groaning and closing my eyes. I ran one hand over my face and tried to compose myself. "yes I copy." I mumbled in response.

"hm? You okay? You don't look so good... Did you have a bad dream?" she asked, leaning against my desk beside me.

Dream? Oh yeah my dream was... my mind felt hazy and I couldn't remember anything. Did I seriously forget what I was dreaming about, so quickly? I can still remember the feeling it gave me but. That's it.

"I don't remember..."

Jade looked at me for a moment before giving me an awkward smile. "Maybe you've been overworking yourself too much. Why don't we go to the cafeteria and get some breakfast and coffee?"

Glancing at all the papers on my desk I sighed and stood up grabbing my glasses. "sure."

"great! I'll tell Sarah and Matt we'll meet them there!" Jade beamed as she pushed herself off my desk and skipped away cheerfully. She's always been so full of energy and always seems happy. I'm a scientist and even I don't understand how she manages with the stress of work, lack of outside contact, and the insane scenarios that happen in this damn lab.

This job could drive anyone mad, it's one reason why we have to take evaluations weekly and talk to doctors all the time. The last person who had a mental breakdown nearly killed themselves.

Putting on my glasses I followed after jade, going into the hallway. She was a few paces ahead of me, nearly speed walking down the hall like a child, who wanted to run but didn't want to get scolded by adults. Sighing I looked to the wall seeing the operations logo painted on the wall.

A.C.O.R.N 'the seed of humanity' I wanted to roll my eyes at that phrase. If people really knew what A.c.o.r.n. Did down in these bunkers, the world would be in an uproar.

People think the government is shady, covering up assassinations, hiding alien ufo's, brainwashing the public...but they have no idea what's really going on behind the ocurtains. Even we don't know to the full extent what bunkers like these are hiding.

As long as we do our jobs and keep quiet, then we get paid, and that's all that matters. For most of us at least.

Walking down the hall I made my way to the cafe, passing by a few co-workers and guards, but didn't pay them any mind. I only have one thing on my mind. Coffee.

Upon entering the mess hall I could see the place was crowded with scientists, guards, doctors and a few other specialists who worked here. Across the room I could see jade waving me over to a table where Sarah and Matt were sitting with their food trays. I waved back in acknowledgment before going to the coffee dispenser and getting a cappuccino.

Taking the first sip I paused, noticing how it tasted strange and quite bitter. I usually don't do this but I don't really care right now I need my caffeine. So I grabbed a bunch of sugar packets and dumped them in before going over to the table where my friends sat.

Jade was already sitting with the others, blabbing about how many files she went through yesterday while the others ate. I on the other hand sipped my coffee still painfully aware of the strange aftertaste it left in my mouth. Why is it so bitter today?

"hey at least you get to sit around all day. Do you have any idea what it's like to be standing guard in one spot on your feet for 10 hours?!" Matt juted in on jades rant. "My feet are killing me after yesterday's shift!"

"yeah well I had to take three aspirin this morning for the massive headache those files gave me! I'm pretty sure I killed off half my brain just staring at the computer all day! I'd say try it sometime but I'm not so sure you have any more brain cells left to lose!" jade teased.

Soon enough Jack came over with his food tray and sat down. "Are we arguing over who's job is worse again?"

Matt and jade both started spouting more nonsense over who was right and who was wrong and why. And soon enough Jack also started saying how guards have it worse.

Their conversation was drowned out as I stared at my coffee seeing just how dark it really was. There was no reflection in the dark pool, just darkness almost like I was staring into an abyss...

'Ava' a familiar voice spoke up in the back of my head and images of the vault door opening flashed before me.

"Ava!" Sarah snapped her fingers in front of my face and I was jolted back to reality.

"w-what?"

"Who has it worse? Us or those dimwits?" jade pointed to Jack and Matt who glared back.

I looked between the four of them confused, and lost in this conversation before shaking my head and looking back at my coffee seeing my reflection. "i-...us, I guess..."

They all seemed to go silent simultaneously while looking at me. As I met their gazes I suddenly felt anxious.

"Ava are you alright?" Sarah spoke up looking concerned.

"yeah I think so..."

"you've been zoned out during the entire conversation..." Sarah stated.

"and she fell asleep at her desk again and wouldn't wake up." jade added.

"maybe you should go talk to the doctor you seem stressed out..."

"Maybe the doctor is the issue. I mean they have been spending a lot of time together as of late! with him keeping her up all night she's probably sleep deprived!" jade snickered and my face flushed slightly.

Sarah jabbed her in the side with her elbow earning a distinct 'ow' followed by a pout. "Leave her alone just because she has an actual sex life and someone to go too doesn't mean you should always bug her about it."

Sarah looked at me and smiled sweetly. "I'm sure you could take a day or two off of work to catch up on sleep and destress."

"yeah sleep deprivation can be a big problem in a place like this you've seen how people go crazy down here! We've had to sedate three guars in the past month because they went wild from lack of sleep and the stress!" Matt added, earning a glare from Sarah.

"not helping!" she scolded.

I was starting to feel overwhelmed not by work but by everyone's concern.

Sighing I got up from my seat at the table. "I'll go back to my room and rest for a bit. Will that make you guys happy?"

They were all a bit awkward and silent at my question but each one nodded. Resigning myself to my fate, I grabbed my coffee and dumped it on my way out of the cafe, before stuffing my hands in my lab coat pockets.

If anything, the last thing I want to do right now is be stuck in my room. I get anxious being alone and isolated, sleeping isn't much better.

At least when I'm working it distracts me from the fact im down in this bunker separated from the rest of the world, for three years at that. The isolation and such can do a lot to one's mind. Everyone down here is affected by it. Some people are more easily bothered than others. But we all handle the stress in our own ways.

Jade is a social butterfly who can't go more than 15 minutes without talking to someone, Jack likes to put himself through physical strain, Sarah is a sugar addict. Matt is a heavy drinker and I'm a workaholic.

It's a miracle this facility is still functioning. I shook my head just thinking about it.

As I walked down the hall I passed the facility logo on the wall and stared at it.

A.C.O.R.N.

Aviation control and operations relay network.

That's how the public sees us... no one outside knows what our true purpose is. What we really do down here.

Anomaly Containment and Origins Research Network. That's what we really are. A containment facility that focuses on researching things that can't be explained.

Containing strange artifacts and on rare occasions creatures that are found all around the world. This job isn't to be taken lightly, everything is top secret down here and you could be killed for revealing classified information.

Stopping in my tracks I looked over to see I had unconsciously wandered over to the containment section, and now I stood in front of the vault containing our biggest and most dangerous anomaly yet.

Subject-59.

S-59 for short.

But the main thing that caught my eye was the fact the blast door was cracked open, which shouldn't even be possible.

With all the crazy incidents that happen around here we have nearly three deaths every two weeks, and s-59 is usually deemed responsible for such deaths.

And we aren't even a red-class facility. We're yellow, which means although the things we house here are dangerous, they are at least contained easily and don't pose major threats.

It's strange considering its s-59 has the potential to kill anyone in its vicinity, and it's now forbidden to open its vault. In fact alarms usually would go off if a vault is opened, and a full security team would immediately be alerted to the breach.

I stare at the blast door in front of me and have a weird sense of deja-vu.

Subject-59 is our main research focus down here but I'm not even sure what S-59 looks like. Stepping closer to the door I reached out to touch it, even going as far as stepping past the danger lines marked on the ground.

An unsettling feeling creeped up my spine as the hair on the back of my neck stood on end and I froze. I felt Something slide across the back of my neck, and I shuddered.

"You shouldn't be here."

Chapter 2

The feeling of something trailing across the back of my neck made me gasp. Something about it felt inhuman, felt wrong. It wasn't natural.

"You shouldn't be here..." a voice seemed to whisper in my ear. Filling me with a sense of dread. Before I could look back I was suddenly grabbed and in turn I shrieked.

My sudden scream took the stranger by surprise and he quickly let go, confused by my panic. "woah hey, relax it's just me!" he chuckled, only for the smile on his face to fade into concern when he noticed the look of panic and pure fear in my eyes.

"Ava?" he questioned.

Snapping out of my panicked state I shook my head and looked up at him as he moved closer. It was the doctor.

"Are you alright?" he looked me over, seeming concerned but didn't move any closer or touch me, as if afraid I might bolt. I grabbed my head trying to get a hold of myself. I swear I felt something strange but was it just him?

Then I realized something and quickly spun around to look at the blast doors once more. Only now they were completely sealed shut.

"What are you doing over here?" he asked, but I didn't pay attention. I was too focused on the fact the door into S-59's containment cell was now shut even though it was open only a moment prior.

I should have heard it close. These doors are heavy and usually creek... Not to mention the alarm's should have been going off...what is happening?

"Ava?" he called out my name again drawing me from my thoughts.

"y-yes?" I responded, and looked up, meeting his light grey eyes. He waited a moment before cautiously reaching towards me like I was a scared animal. His hand grazed my cheek affectionately and I relaxed a bit from the sensation I felt being touched by him.

"Are you okay? You seem a bit...out of it."

That was a good question. I was supposed to be going back to my room but somehow wandered here to the containment sector. How did I even get down here?

"i-..." I glanced back at the blast doors, unsure how to explain my predicament.

"You look pale, Jade told me you weren't feeling well. On my way over to the cafe I noticed you just standing here in the hall, blankly staring at the door..." he looked at the door as well trying to see what had grabbed my attention but there was nothing out of the ordinary.

After a few moments he returned his gaze to me but I hardly acknowledged him, too deep in my own thoughts. "Ava, you're worrying me..."

I relaxed a bit, feeling like a fool for being so on edge, it was probably just the breeze from a vent or something... "im fine kerian just a little jittery from the coffee this morning..." turning back to look at him a scowl made its way on my face. "and you shouldn't sneak up on people like that! You nearly gave me a heart attack!"

A half hearted smile made its way back on his face as he chuckled nervously. "sorry I didn't think i'd spook you that bad you were just standing there..." he glanced at the door and I followed his gaze half expecting it to be open again. There's no way I imagined that right?

"So, mind telling me what's on your mind, or what has you so jumpy?" he questioned, walking over to stand in front of me.

"it's nothing... I'm pretty sure I was just daydreaming and you startled me is all."

He was silent before stepping closer. He looked down at me, seeming unsure about my answer.

"You know you can talk to me, right?" he cupped my cheek and leaned in for what I assumed was a kiss, taking me by surprise. The kiss was just a peck to the lips, small and sweet. But it made me flustered and my cheeks turned red from the simple action.

"I'm fine kerian, I just...i thought I saw the door open." he seemed to freeze at this knowledge and his expression became unreadable as he looked down at me. After a moment his soft gaze returned with a smile and he removed his hand from my cheek to grab my own hands.

"you know that's not possible. The door is sealed tight, no one is allowed to access that room without permission and if they did then the whole security team would be down here in minutes arresting you."

"I know but..." my gaze moved to the eerie door only to be disrupted by Kerian as he turned my face to look at him.

"You were going to your room to rest right? How about I walk you there?" I nodded meekly as he let go of me and we started walking down the hallways together. He often glanced down at me and smiled as we went, making me a bit flustered once more.

The entire walk back was awkward and I didn't know what to say, we were anything but strangers, yet I didn't know what to say or do at this moment, everything felt strange, and it was hard to get my mind off the doors.

We entered my quarters and he moved to my dresser grabbing a pair of clothes for me to change into. While I stood by awkwardly.

"we haven't really talked much lately bit I know you wanted to rest so, Would you rather I leave you alone?"

My eyes met his gentle gaze and I took in a sharp breath feeling guilty about how I treated him before. He's always been gentle and quite affectionate, taking my needs and wants very seriously i'm not sure if that's the doctor side of him or just how he is normally. i'm extremely lucky to have someone like him as my lover.

"you can stay..." he smiled and handed me the extra clothes before leaning in and kissing my forehead. "alright. I'm going to shower if that's okay, I've been running all over the facility today."

A blush adorned my face as I nodded and watched him walk away. He removed his coat and hung it on the wall before pulling off his shirt, revealing his toned body. I couldn't help but stare as he walked to the bathroom and set his shirt on the counter before turning the hot water in the shower on.

I meekly moved over to the open door, clutching the clothes he handed me tightly to my chest and peeked inside. He had already fully undressed and I could faintly make out his blurred form as he stood in the shower letting the hot water run over him while his back was turned towards me.

I quickly looked away feeling like a shy schoolgirl. What am I doing?! What would he think if he caught me peeping on him?!

"Ava." his voice called out with a deep undertone to it. "you're free to join me if you'd like..."

He saw me! Shaking my head I did my best not to stutter my reply. "n-no thanks! I'm just going to lay down and rest. I'm still not feeling quite right!" god this is embarrassing!

I quickly changed into my night wear and sat down on the bed. Taking off my glasses I pinched the bridge on my nose feeling even more like a fool than before.

Opening my eyes I quickly took notice of something strange. My vision isn't blurry with my glasses off in fact I could see nearly perfectly even in the dimly lit room.

I blinked a few times and tested my natural eyesight against the glasses and sure enough I could see perfectly fine?

What on earth...

The number of strange things happening to me today is really starting to bother me. Maybe I really am overworking myself.

"You know a hot shower is a good way to help relieve stress." snapping out of my thoughts I looked up to see Kerian stepping out of the bathroom, shirtless with only a pair of sweats on to cover his lower half.

He finished drying his hair with a towel before dropping it by the door and looking back over at me. I hadn't even heard him get out of the shower.

Realizing I was staring once again, I quickly looked away and responded. "I just didn't feel like washing off right now..."

He didn't say anything else and stepped over before sitting next to me. "If you're not comfortable with me staying with you tonight then I can leave..."

"n-no it's not that i'm not worried about you I just...it's just..."

He was silent for a moment thinking to himself. "We haven't exactly seen or spoken to each other for a few days so I thought you might enjoy some company tonight, but if you're not feeling up for it then I won't force you..."

"n-no i'm sorry for acting weird kerian nothings wrong I think I may actually just be stressed from work and tired...i think my insomnia has been wracking my body for the past few nights, preventing me from getting any proper rest...I Want you to stay so don't worry about me."

Looking over at him I could see a glint in his eyes as he looked at me intently and smiled. "I was thinking we could just spend some quality time together and maybe watch a movie, talk, or lay together...if you want."

He leaned forward, cupping my cheek lovingly and we gazed at each other intensely until his lips crashed into mine with a passionate kiss. I closed my eyes melting into the feeling as all my worries seemed to wash away. I fell back on the bed and he quickly climbed over me without breaking the kiss and placed both arms on either side of my head. He finally pulled away so we could catch our breaths and I gazed up at him as he hovered over me with a smile. "if your too tired ill back off..."

He leaned in and nipped at my ear before trailing kisses down the side of my neck. Closing my eyes I could feel my face heat up as he went and moved one of his hands to travel up and under my shirt. It feels good... "i'm not that tired but, K-kerian I just got changed..."

He hummed against my skin and I could feel my body practically buzzing with anticipation. "then keep the rest of your clothes on...ill work around them-"

A tingle ran down my spine at those words and I brought my hand up to my face to cover my mouth and muffle the small sounds that threatened to spill out as he started kneading my breasts with his hand. "k-kerian?!"

"you are so beautiful... You're so perfect, in every way..." he mumbled against the skin of my shoulder before sitting upright. He lifted my shirt just enough to expose my chest and smiled before removing his hand from under my bra to unclasp the front.

I instinctively covered my chest with my arms, making him chuckle at my response. "still as shy as ever..." blushing I turned my head away as he moved back slightly. I glanced down to see him hook his fingers on the hem of my shorts to pull them down. He lifted my legs in the air to completely remove them then dropped one leg back down to his side.

I could already feel the knot in my stomach growing tighter and the tingles across my skin as he trailed his hands across my bare legs and up my thighs. I bit my lip as his finger tips grazed over the top of my underwear in a teasing fashion.

"if I didn't know any better Ava. I'd say you are already wet..." he ended up pulling them to the side and I gasped at the feeling of his fingers suddenly invading my core. "oh, only two fingers and you're already squeezing me so tightly...Ava were you anticipating this perhaps?"

He moved his fingers around teasingly, making me squirm as he held one leg up in the air. The smile that adorned his face was so sweet it felt like it didn't fit his current attitude.

"your body responds so well to my touch... I can just imagine you becoming entranced by a single graze from my fingertips..." the moment he said that I could feel his palm rubbing against my clit nearly making me squeak. "I think you're ready..."

He slipped his fingers free, and the emptiness I felt nearly had me reeling as I gripped onto the bed sheets with one hand and lifted my head to look down at him. He was inspecting his fingers with genuine curiosity as they were covered in my very obvious arousal.

his gaze found mine once more and he smiled before reaching down to lower the hem of his sweats to free his erection from its confines. Had it not been for him sitting between my legs keeping them separated, I would have squeezed them shut out of reflex.

"don't worry I'll make sure you're plenty tired after this... so much so, you might not wake till tomorrow afternoon..."

"Kerian!" I scolded and his deep chuckle had my toes curling as he positioned himself closer and placed my leg over his shoulder and held the other one on his side.

"your right, I should stop teasing you..." I shrieked as he suddenly plunged himself deep inside of me. My fingers dug into the bedding as my back arched slightly from the shock.

The feeling of him being inside me, and not just his fingers was overwhelming. He groaned in satisfaction before closing his eyes with a subtle sigh. My body was given a moment to adjust and my chest was rising and falling much quicker than before. I looked back down at kerian to see him trying to compose himself before he opened his eyes to smile at me.

"I may have been a little hasty this time... Sorry."

Biting my lip I moved my hips a little, drawing his attention downward. "please... Move." his eyes met mine once more and he shook his head slightly with a chuckle before grabbing onto my legs in a secure grip once more.

"as you wish..."

He started off grinding into me before doing small thrusts in and out. I laid my head back staring at the ceiling before closing my eyes, enjoying the feeling as he filled me so perfectly.

He slowly started picking up the pace, making each thrust longer while also speeding up and I nearly mewled at the sensation. I was already stimulated by him using his fingers on me so I could feel the knot in my stomach growing tighter and tighter.

His grip on my thighs tightened as he started going for more rapid thrusts and I arched my back slightly feeling my orgasm climbing higher and higher.

Images of S-59's blast door opening, flashed in my mind and everything started feeling hazy. Kerian became rougher, digging his fingers into my legs but I couldn't comprehend anything or conjure the words that seemed to be stuck in my throat.

Part of me was standing in that hallway once more in front of the door, while the rest of me was lying in bed being pounded into by the doctor.

With every thrust I could see flashes of images with the door opening more and more. With some kind of dark mist spilling out onto the pristine white floor.

I could feel my heart race increase as it felt like it might burst from my chest. I could feel a cold chill run down my spine and stared into the darkness and it stared back at me.

'Ava' I could hear it, I could hear a distorted voice whispering my name as a shadow of a breath fanned across my neck.

"Ava!" Kerian grunted into my ear and I was instantly snapped back to reality as he thrust into me one last time, as hard and as deep as he could go.

A startled moan passed through my lips as spots danced across my vision and I bucked my hips forward as my climax hit me full force.

I could hardly register the fact that Kerian had moved to lay atop of me with both my legs now around his waist and his arms on either side of my head. He was leaned in close with his eyes squeezed shut and as my climax hit me I grabbed onto him and dug my nails into his backside, driving him over the edge as well.

"Ava..." he whispered my name again and laid atop of me, pressing his body to mine, as he relaxed. I could feel warmth pouring into me and it took a moment for me to relax as my own high fizzled away into bliss. Only then did my grip on him relinquish.

He was still partially holding himself up somewhat to keep from crushing me as we both lay there in a daze. Me more so than him. He pressed the side of his head up against mine before looking at my face but I was still in too much shock to register anything.

"you should get some sleep now..." he kissed my forehead before wrapping one of his arms around me and turning us both over onto our sides. Our legs were tangled together as he pulled me into his chest and let me lay my head across his other arm.

As much as I wanted to fight it at this moment I felt sleep taking over me and closed my eyes.

Kerians hand brushed over my head and I could faintly hear him whisper something to himself as my consciousness faded away.

Chapter 3

<hr>

Opening my eyes I could see myself standing in front of the black door once more.

Two numbers painted in black on the metal surface before me. 59.

I was standing in front of S-59's containment room again.

Wait. Again? How many times have i-

a strange distorted sound caught my attention, seemingly coming from inside of the vault and I froze. Feeling a chill run down my spine I looked down both ends of the hallway, seeing nothing but darkness.

"W-Who's there?" I called out but there was no reply. Looking back at the blast door I could see it was partially cracked open, just a few inches. Some kind of black mist was leaking from the gap and I could feel my heart rate starting to climb.

Something was inside. S-59. was inside that room. If there's a containment breach then everyone will be in danger. I-i have to pull the alarm and get the containment security here. I have to run-

"Ava," a distorted voice whispered in my ear. This time I could sense the presence standing behind me and all thoughts I had before, came to a screeching halt.

"Release me..."

—-

Gasping awake I sat up in a panic. A figure beside me grabbed my arm and shrieked before trying to push away. "Ava! It's me!"

I focused on Kerian's face realizing who he was then quickly glanced around the room seeing we were in my bed.

"it's okay you had a nightmare that's all. Relax, I'm right here... Nothing is going to hurt you." he pulled me into a hug while my heart raced in my chest and I slowly came back to reality.

After a moment I hugged kerian back and he pat my head trying his best to calm me down with small hushes and words or reassurance. After a few minutes I managed to calm my nerves and relaxed into his hold.

"What time is it?" I pulled away and kerian looked down at me.

"It's late, you didn't sleep very long and the night cycle is currently going outside."

"great, so coffee is out of the question..." I huffed. "Sorry if I woke you up..."

He patted my head and a small smile appeared on his lips. "don't worry I wasn't really getting much sleep either...want to talk about it?"

Pulling my legs up I rested my head on my knees. "no...it wasn't even that scary. I think it just startled me. Nothing really happened."

He watched me intently before pulling me against him into a hug and looking me in the eyes. "you don't have to be afraid of talking to me, I won't ever hold anything against you..."

This took me a bit by surprise, did kerian think I didn't want to talk because of him? Truthfully I just didn't see any reason to talk about the dream. I mean it was silly. Nothing happened to me, I was just...

I was just...

Reaching up I held my head and tried to think about what had happened. Why can't I remember it now? It was like a word that I knew on the tip of my tongue that I just couldn't conjure. Yet no matter how hard I tried I couldn't think of it.

"maybe you'd like to take something to help you get back to sleep?" I shook my head, still bothered by the lost dream. "Ava if your worried about another nightmare, I'll be right here-"

"N-no it's not that..."

He was silent before cupping my cheek and turning my head up so I would look him in the eyes. "if you insist that everything is fine then let us go back to sleep..." I looked deeply into his eyes once more and felt the tiredness from before seeping back into my body. I merely nodded as we laid back down and he held me close, kissing the top of my head while spooning me.

As much as I wanted to figure out why I just suddenly forgot the strange dream, I couldn't fight how drowsy I felt and let myself succumb to the darkness once more.

—--(next morning)-----

Sitting in the lab I continued to inspect the sample in front of me. "Whatcha doing?" jade spoke up, distracting me from my work.

"I'm working? Something I'm pretty sure you should be doing right now..." she pouted at that comment and crossed her arms.

"I'm just taking a break, no need to get on my ass for it..."

I rolled my eyes and wrote down some notes for the sample I was inspecting. "have you checked on subject 32 at all today?"

"well...he kinda got out of containment..." I stopped writing and looked over at her.

"again?"

She nodded her head and I sighed "and I'm guessing you didn't want to catch him..."

"to be fair he's completely harmless and no one minds having him run around!"

"That's besides the point jade, we could get in trouble if the higher ups see him freely roaming without supervision!" getting up from my desk I grabbed my key card and made my way out of the lab.

"hey where are you going?!" jade shouted.

"to go find 32 and put him back!" I responded.

Walking down the halls I passed by various lab doors where many other scientists were working on their own projects. Some involved experiments with chemicals and strange samples taken from certain subjects, others were simply doing research and paperwork jotting down things they've learned about some of the anomalous entities contained in the facility.

As I walked I had to pause seeing one of the lab rooms was occupied by scientists and guards. They were all gathered around a table with a clear containment box that held a strange glowing plant inside.

As one of the scientists brushed past the box. The strange glowing plant seemed to change color, turning red, and reeling back before banging against the glass with enough force to scratch the two inch thick glass box.

The guards on standby were on high alert keeping flamethrowers ready in case the thing did manage to break free. A small slot in the side of the box was opened as they stuck a large needle to take samples from the plant. It seemed to react violently and started thrashing around the heavy duty container until they finished and backed away.

Once the scientists had their samples, they loaded the container onto a metal cart and rolled it away back to the containment room it belonged In.

I moved on and headed for the area most frequented by subject 32. He has a knack for escaping. A lot. Despite how cautious we are around the containment rooms and how thorough we are when it comes to making sure all precautions are taken for each creature. But when you have something like subject 32 who can phase through things such as metal doors, it's kinda hard to keep containment 24/7.

Luckily for us subject 32 is passive and easy to please. If we keep it satisfied it tends not to wander off or escape as much. But being the kind of creature that it is, it doesn't always cooperate and gets bored easily within its chamber. I can't blame him. I would hate being locked in the same room 24/7 too. Especially alone. Specter creatures like him don't have much else to do their interactions with the living are about the only things that would keep them happy.

Subject 32 loves attention but with so much work having to be done around here it's hard to give him the constant affection he desires. no matter how cute he seems.

I looked around the empty hall searching for signs of s-32. He likes this area because of the bunker's generator room nearby. It produces quite a bit of heat much to s-32's delight. I looked all over the place, under chairs, behind desks, inside cabinets...

"Dammit where are you?" I moved to another room and looked under some of the furniture in the lounge trying to find the sneaky little escape artist. I groaned after about the seventh time of crouching down to look under furniture and got to my feet.

"If I were you, where would I..."

A distinct meow made me freeze and I slowly turned around to see a shadowy feline creature sitting in the middle of the hallway licking its paw with bright glowing green eyes.

After scratching itself it looked up at me curio,usly with another now merow and a sweet innocent face.

I sighed and shook my head with a smile before kneeling down and holding my hands out in invitation. "There you are, you rascal."

S-32 meowed again before happily striding over to rub up against my leg only for something unsightly to take most of my attention from s-32. A trail of bloody paw prints were left behind as s-32 walked to a, as to where I saw a bloodied body laying on the floor.

Standing up I stared at the mangled corpse a few feet away, in shock while s-32 happily continued to rub up against my leg.

How- who- s-32 is a passive creature who has never shown signs of aggression so I know he wasn't responsible for this he just happened to be passing by, but why is there a body here in the first place?! Who or what did this!? I covered my mouth holding back the bile rising in my throat and closed my eyes trying to get ahold of myself.

I need to call security, I need to figure out what did this I need to-

Snapping out of my thoughts I was startled by s-32 suddenly stopping between my feet and hissing angrily at something behind me before running off in a panic.

"ava!" I spun around to see none other than kerian walking towards me. "Are you alright? What are you doing down here?" he asked worriedly.

Our eyes met as I looked up at him and I blinked a few times still trying to overcome the shock I was in before realizing we might both be in danger. "kerian! Somethings wrong there's a body-" as I turned around to show him what I had found, it was gone.

There was no body, no blood, no trail left behind by s-32. The hallway was empty and spotless. 'what?! But it was just there, I just saw it!?'

"Ava?" Kerian walked up beside me seemingly confused. "You look pale..." he reached out to touch my cheek but I shook my head and blinked a few more times to make sure the body really wasn't there.

"I thought I saw something..." I mumbled quietly.

He looked down the hall following my gaze but quickly gave up on looking for whatever had my attention, more interested and worried about me. "What are you doing down here anyways?"

"I was looking for s-32 so I could take him back to containment. But I thought I saw something and panicked for a moment. He ran off... I think you spooked him."

I looked over to kerian who's mood seemed to sour slightly at the mention of s-32. "hmph that cat is a nuisance, don't worry about it for now we can deal with it later, for now let's focus on you, you looked really scared. Are you sure you're okay?"

"y-yeah like I said I thought I saw something but..." my voice trailed off as I looked at my hands. Did I imagine it?

Looking back up at Kerian I tried to change the subject to get my mind off it. "What are you doing down here? Shouldn't you be in the ward?"

He smiled before holding up some papers. "Just dropping these off, having some mechanical issues in the ward so needed the engineers to come take a look. "

"I see..." I watched him walk into one of the office rooms and place the papers on the desk.

"If you haven't eaten yet, why don't we go to the cafe?" he walked back over to me with a sweet smile and I did my best to return it.

"Sure, I could go for a coffee."

"Alright, I'll take the lead!" he started walking back the way he came from and I hesitated, looking back to the floor where I had seen the body. But there was still nothing there.

Sighing, I turned to follow Kerian, deciding to forget about what I had seen, Unaware of S-32 watching us from a dark corner, cautiously. He slowly crept out of his hiding spot as we left the area before going about his business and proceeding to clean the blood off his paws.

Chapter 4

Poking around at my food with a fork I sighed. My mind was continuously straying back to the encounter I had a few days ago with s-32 and what I had seen in that hallway.

Nothing about that situation made sense, and it's been keeping me awake at night.

One moment there was a bloodied body laying on the ground in a pool of blood, and the next it was gone. I Even watched S-32 walk right through the puddle, leaving a trail of bloody paw prints.

S-32 was also acting strange. He hissed and ran away when kerian walked up... I've never seen him turn aggressive like that before. Being a specter, he can't be harmed by much and he often likes all people so why did he suddenly flip like a switch?

Sighing again I grabbed my coffee and took a sip only to nearly spit it out because of the severe bitter taste. 'What the hell? I just dumped several packets of sugar in this and it's still undrinkable!'

"Ava!" a voice called out to me. Looking up I saw jade coming over to my table cheerfully, and watched as she sat down across from me.

"hey Ava did you find s-32 like you wanted?" I looked at jade unamused and set my coffee down.

"you mean after you neglected to have him placed back in containment and let him freely just roam around sector five?" Yes, I found him.

Jade winced before giving me a pleading look. "I didn't mean to, you know I don't like cats, they are scary... he purposely follows me around and rubs up against me like he knows too!"

I shook my head and crossed my arms. "Jade, he follows everyone and he just wants attention, I can assure you there's not a single hint of malice in that cat."

She proceeded to pout, laying her head on the table. "it's still scary... so did you get him back in containment?" she stared at me intently.

Why does it seem like she already knows the answer to that question?...

"n-no... I didn't get the chance."

"why? Did something happen?" Jade's playful mood seemed to disappear as she became more alert and was listening closely to what I had to say.

"i- was going to take him back to containment but something else had drawn my attention away from him. Then Kerian came up and s-32 got spooked and took off."

"what did you see?" jade asked in a serious tone, taking me by surprise.

She's more interested in what I saw then the fact s-32 got scared off by kerian? Shouldn't his strange behavior be more concerning? Jade is acting a bit strange. Should I even tell her?

I hesitated for a moment, looking at my coffee in deep thought. "i-...it was nothing, I thought the lights were flickering and it startled me a little. You know me, I'm not a huge fan of the dark..."

Hearing this surprised Jade a little but her serious tone was quickly replaced by her happy and cheerful one as she smiled. "See now you can't blame me cause you did it too! You didn't catch him because you were afraid of the dark, I didn't do it cause I'm afraid of cats! Therefore you can't scold me for not doing my job!"

"I guess you're right..." I admitted defeat to make her happy. As she went off on a rant talking about max, I couldn't help but zone out and turn my attention back to my cup. The dark liquid almost seemed black in color, and held no reflection, giving me an uneasy feeling.

Why do I feel so unnerved? Like there's a shadow looming over me?

"traitor" a subtle voice breathed in my ear. I nearly jumped out of my seat from fright as I looked back at the source of the voice but there was nothing. The hair on the back of my neck was standing on end and my heart rate had increased dramatically from the fright. What on earth was that?

Jade stopped talking and looked at me confused. "ava?"

"sorry W-what did you just say?" I snapped back to attention.

"I said Max had to do a 17 hour shift last night and keeps complaining about how his feet hurt but he refuses to get new shoes. He's too stubborn and doesn't want to listen."

I blinked a few times as jade continued on talking about max, but I was too shocked and confused to listen. I swear I heard a voice say something. And it made me feel strangely sick to my stomach. The voice was sickeningly familiar and made me extremely uncomfortable. It was distorted and raspy.

Shaking my head I stood up and grabbed my tray to leave the cafe. I can't sit here anymore.

"hey where are you going? I'm in the middle of a story!" jade called out.

I dumped my food and looked back at her. "ah I forgot I had something important to do back in the lab, I'll listen to your story later!"

I waved and quickly left the cafe. Why do I suddenly feel like this? Closing my eyes momentarily I tried to regain my composure to forget about it and move on. I should get back to work...

–(hours later)--

After a hot shower I plopped down on my bed with a groan. I have so much work to do it's not even funny. Not to mention tomorrow is sample day meaning we have to run twice the number of tests and gather samples from all our 'residents'. And of course I'm assigned to s-59's sampling.

Last month someone in the sample group was killed by S-59 and the entire sector had to go on lockdown. It was a bloody mess. I don't even wanna think about what might happen this time...

A knock on my door had me up on my feet once more as I walked over and opened it to see none other than kerian standing there awkwardly.

"I hope I didn't wake you." he smiled down at me before stepping inside.

"I just got out of the shower, what are you doing over here?" I shut the door behind me before leaning against it.

"just came to check up on you, jade said you were acting strange earlier and walked out on her in the middle of a conversation. Not that I can blame you, she'll talk your ears off if given the chance." He smiled back at me and I chuckled at his remark.

"That's definitely true. I'm fine now, I just didn't feel so great earlier...you don't have to come over here every time to check on me you know. I'm capable of taking care of myself, and if anything does happen I'll come straight to you."

He stepped back towards me and put his hand on my forehead as if checking for a fever. "I know, but what kind of boyfriend would I be if I didn't check in on you when I'm told you're not doing well?"

I rolled my eyes and pulled his hand away from my head. "I'm fine, Kerian. You don't have to worry about me, it was just my nerves getting the better of me..."

That seemed to really catch his interest and he arched a brow. "Why are you nervous?"

I pointed over to my calendar that showed the date and he followed my finger. "Tomorrow is sample day, and I've been assigned to S-59. Remember what happened last month? He killed someone in the sample group.

He? Why did I just call Subject 59 a he? I've never even seen it before.

Kerian grabbed my hand before bringing it up to his face to kiss my palm. "You're worrying over nothing. The security team will make sure nothing happens. You'll be perfectly safe I can assure you of that. And if anything does happen I'll come running over immediately."

"you'll be too busy helping the other sectors with any injuries the other team's get..."

"I could ask to be put on standby for your team?"

"Kerian!" I gave him a small glare. "You can't abuse your position or power to take care of me, you have a job to do."

He scratches the back of his head awkwardly while looking at me. "I'm just trying to help make it less stressful for you. If me being there would calm you down then I'll gladly do it. "

Sighing I shake my head. "You're more troublesome than half the subjects in this facility."

He smiled again before leaning in and pushing me up against the door. "maybe but at least I'm better company than anyone or anything else in this entire bunker. Don't you agree?" his lips crashed into mine and a small squeak escaped me, at the sudden move.

After a moment I melted into the kiss and closed my eyes as I returned his affection just as fervently.

Breaking the kiss to catch our breath we looked at each other and he smiled down at me so lovingly that I almost wanted to just collapse in his arms. His hand moved to cup my face, with his thumb brushing my cheek as his eyes darkened.

"you're so beautiful Ava. perhaps the most beautiful thing on this planet..."

"You only say that now because we are stuck in this bunker for the next few years. Once we go back to the outside world you'll see plenty of beautiful women." I pouted.

"No. I'd rather stay a prisoner here for the rest of my existence than leave your side." he said sternly.

I swooned a little at his words and smiled once more, leaning into his touch. I placed my hands over his as he held my face. "you're so dramatic..."

he leaned in for another kiss, it was slow, serene and short this time.

"I won't let anything happen to you. You know that right? No one will take you away from me..." he hid his face in the crook of my neck and I paused for a moment realizing what was going on. He was trying to comfort me while also reassuring himself.

I smiled and patted his head, making him glance up at me. "thank you kerian. I'm not so anxious anymore."

He smiled before leaning his head against mine and holding me close. "Want me to stay with you tonight? In case you can't sleep?"

I quickly pecked a kiss on his cheek.

"Sure"

—-

Opening my eyes I felt constrained and uncomfortable. Groaning, I sat up and found that kerian was sleeping beside me with one arm around my waist. Of course if wake up in the middle of the night.

Sighing I moved his arm and climbed out of bed, careful not to wake him. I moved to the bathroom and stretched my arms above my head. Flipping the light on I looked in the mirror while standing in front of the sink and sulked, just from seeing the dark circles under my eyes.

I can already tell i'm not going to be getting back to sleep anytime soon. And tomorrow is gonna suck.

Turning on the faucet I leaned over the sink and quickly dosed my face in water with my hands. The bathroom lights flickered off leaving me in the dark and I looked up at the ceiling confused by the sudden outage. Looking back at the mirror before me I paled, seeing a figure behind me, and I quickly spun around to face it.

A dark shadowy humanoid figure with hollow white glowing eyes stood there towering over and staring down at me.

My voice seemed to be stuck in my throat as I started back at the monster before me while my heart pounded against my chest.

The shadowy creature took a step forward and leaned in, pressing its forehead against my own. I stopped breathing and froze in place, absolutely terrified.

My mind was racing as fast as my heart as I tried to comprehend what was happening, what this thing was and where it came from.

It's clawed hand reached up to my face and I nearly whimpered, feeling it stroke my cheek. I squeezed my eyes shut hoping this was just some kind of nightmare, but my thoughts came to a screeching halt as a voice spoke up in the back of my mind. And my eyes shot open to look at the creature before me.

The voice said. "Ava."

Chapter 5

What is- what is this thing?! How did it get in here?! I stared in horrified shock at the shadowy figure before me as it stood there with its eyes closed, nuzzling my forehead.

It had a humanoid physique underneath all the wisps of dark smoke radiating off its body endlessly. Its hands were more like claws and its eyes were white. No iris or pupils that could be seen, just white.

Was this some kind of specter? But we don't have any other anomalous specters in this facility besides s-32 and he can't change forms like this!? Not to mention this thing doesn't feel like a specter... species leave a tingling sensation behind when they touch anything, and this thing clearly has a physical form not an interdimensional one. So what is it?

Why is it here? How did it get into my quarters?! No, focus ava, how and why aren't as important as what this thing really is and how to escape it. I don't recognize it at all but just from looking at it I feel a sense of danger from it. There's a few laws that most creatures follow with evolution and usually when something evolves with claws, they are used for either offense or defense.

Hunting or protection. I seriously hope it's the latter with this creature because as close as it is to me now, those claws could easily tear out my throat.

A subtle high pitched bellow escaped the creature's throat as it nuzzled the side of my head with its face. I could hear the blood rushing through my ears as my heart threatened to beat out of my chest.

I pressed myself further back against the ceramic sink behind me and watched the creature unsure how to react.

All anomalies are different; they all react differently to various things such as noise or movement. Move too fast and one might panic and run away. Stay still for too long one could pounce on you, some even get triggered by the simplest things like light or colors.

Precautions with strange anomalies usually aren't effective because of this randomized factor, more often than not, one must go based on their own judgment of the situation. That's how we were trained.But being this close to an unknown entity?

I could very well already be dead.

Shuddering I glanced over to the door that led back into my room, it was barely cracked open more than a few inches. As I saw it another thought came to mind that made my stomach sink.

Kerian. He's asleep in the other room.

If I try to run, cry for help or piss off this creature in any way I could very well be putting him in danger as well.

If he gets hurt or dies because of me I will never be able to forgive myself...

I have to get out of here, I have to get away from this entity but how-

"ava~" a hushed disoriented voice came from the creature before me as it pulled its head away and opened its eyes to look down at me.

How does it know my name?

Swallowing the lump in my throat I meekly glanced up at the creature seeing it was slightly slouched, with hooded eyes, almost making it seem like it was tired?

I stared at it for a moment and it stared back without saying anything, or doing anything. It was just there.

Regaining a bit of my composure I relaxed some just seeing it wasn't being immediately hostile and decided to speak up. "h-how do you know my name?"

The creature before me chitted before leaning in closer once more to look at me.

I almost whipmered as it's nose nearly touched mine. It had no mouth from what I could see so does it communicate telepathicly? It wouldn't be the strange thing I've experienced...

It watched me closely for a moment before leaning back to crouch down on the floor in front of me, pulling it's knees to it's chest. "because you are mine." it spoke up once more.

What? What does that even mean? Because im it's? Or his...this think looks like a he. Shaking my head I tried to refocus.

"i don't understand."

It looked at me sleepily before tilting it's head to the side and resting it's chin on it's knees. "mine." it spoke again calmly.

Ok that really doesn't help. I guess I should be grateful this entity seems to be call for the moment and isn't actively trying to hurt or eat me.

I relaxed a little, looking the creature over carefully. Through the black misty smoke I could see horns atop of it's head and a long tail laid out across the floor. The more I looked at it the more it sparked my curiosity. The more I wanted to research and learn about the creature.

"what are you?"

It lifted its head this time, sitting up straighter as it looked at me more intently. Silence ensued for a moment before it stood back up, practically towering over me. My anxiety spiked once more as I worried that the questions might be just ticked him off.

"I..." the shadowy figure spoke up before taking a step closer. I held my breath as it reached for my face with one clawed hand.

"I am anything you want me to be."

Squeezing my eyes shut I held my breath waiting for something to happen. Waiting for the entity to tear my face off, gouge out my eyes or maybe even take over my mind.

But as seconds ticked by, nothing happened. No tearing of flesh or invasion of the mind. In fact I couldn't even feel it touching me.

Cracking one eye open I was startled to see I was in a completely different room. The entity was gone, and I was dressed in my lab coat.

"what?" glancing around I realized I was in an observation room down in the labs. On one side was a large glass wall peering into a pitch black room with a single door to enter the room. On the other side were various consoles that controlled the door locks, and internals for the observation room. Some equipment was strewn about and on one wall, there was a closet filled with hazmat suits and oxygen tanks.

"Hello, anyone?" Confused, I called out to see if anyone was around but there was only silence. How did I get here?

Stepping over to one of the consoles I noticed a clipboard filled with pages and picked it up.

Immediately my eyes locked onto the case file name, and a chill crawled down my spine at the sight of it.

Subject 59.

That means- a loud bang against the glass wall had my head shooting up to look at the dark room but I could see nothing through the thick inky blackness.

Hesitantly I walked over to the glass wall and stared at the void before me. No. The room wasn't just simply dark. It was filled with a dark mist that seemed to block out all light. It was impossible to make out any details beyond the black smoke as it squirmed and writhed inside, hiding the entity within.

I'm not sure what is happening or how I got here but there is one thing I know for sure. Everything is connected to this...to subject-59.

"It hurts..." a voice spoke up from beyond the glass and I had to take a step back, in surprise. Did s-59 just...speak?

Shaking my head I reached out and put my hand to the cold glass trying to peer through the darkness for a glimpse of its real form. Another quiet whisper came from the other side, it sounded strained, weak even. "it hurts."

"hello?" I called out to it and the entire room seemed to react to the sound of my voice as the shadows shifted and moved.

I watched for a moment as the darkness swirled and writhed but didn't receed.

"are you-...are you okay?" I questioned, while looking into the room before me.

There was no response but I swear I could see movement in the darkness in front of me. Squinting I tried looking closer, trying to catch a glimpse of the creature inside.

A chill crawled down my spine the longer I looked, and I could feel it watching me. Growing a bit more anxious I pulled my hand away from the glass.

Instantly a clawed hand slammed against the glass where I was, making me scream and jump back in fright.

"Ava!" it called out my name. Shaking my head I fearfully backed away as a giant crack formed in the glass wall before me.

"AVA!"

I jolted awake with a gasp and my eyes flew open, seeing kerian hovering over me. "ava?" Are you okay?

He looked at me concerned while holding my face in his hands as I quickly glanced around at our surroundings, with my heart racing through my chest.

I...w-we are still in my room? In bed? But s-59, the lab, the entity! It felt so real! It had to be real!

"hey hey, come back to me ava please, look at me! Focus on me! Look me in the eye."

I faced kerian once more, seeing the work on his face, the concern and warmth in his eyes. I blinked a few times, taking deep breaths to calm myself and my beating heart. "It's okay, Ava, I'm here..." he gave a small smile while stroking my cheek with one hand.

I relaxed a bit more and carefully sat up as he leaned back. "You had a bad dream didn't you...what was it?"

I nodded before reaching up to hold my head with one hand. A splitting headache racked my brain as I tried to think about what happened as I tried to remember the dream. I winced and squeezed my eyes shut as only small bits and pieces came back to me. It's as if it was being pushed down hidden away from me. And the more I tried to see those memories the more it hurt.

"Ava, open your eyes, look at me." Kerian grabbed my hand and I looked up at him once again. "It's okay, it's all over now." he reassured with a smile.

The headache faded along with all thoughts of the dream I had before. It was gone. All of it was gone.

He pulled me against his chest in a hug and I stared blankly at his shirt, my mind feeling like a jumbled mess. "It's over now, nothing happened. None of that was real okay? You're still here with me." he stroked my hair while holding me doing his best to comfort me to help me move on from whatever nightmare I experienced.

But as I sat there with him all I could think about was this feeling in the back of my mind, that something was wrong, that I needed to remember what happened. That I shouldn't have been able to just forget like that.

That whatever happened wasn't a dream.

chapter 6

Once again the coffee this morning was bitter and practically un-drinkable no matter how much sugar or creamer I added to it. It left this sickening taste in my mouth that seemed to add to this nauseating feeling that something felt... off.

Sighing, I continued my walk to the observation labs, clipboard in hand. Today is s-59's sample day. The one day of the month that s-59 seems to dislike the most. Any other time it's usually pretty docile but when sample day comes along it turns hostile.

I'm not looking forward to it...

"Ava!" A feminine voice called out from behind. Stopping, I turned and looked back to she jade speed walking down the hall towards me. Once she finally caught up to me I continued my walk with her beside me. "Good morning ava! You look like you had a rough night! Did you and kerian have fun?~"

I rolled my eyes at jade and glanced at my watch to see what time it was. "No, I simply didn't sleep well last night and the coffee has been god awful the past few days..."

Jade snickered with a grin on her face. "Suuure..." as I picked up the pace worried about being late she did her best to speed up with me. "Where are you rushing off to anyways?" She questioned and I gave her a look of disapproval. She should know what today is.

"It's sample day, I've been assigned to s-59 this month and the director is supposed to be there. I'd rather not get in trouble for being late. shouldn't you be looking for s-32?"

She paused for a moment, falling behind slightly before running up beside me once again. "Wait, you didn't see the email?"

This time I paused and she followed suit. "What email?"

"The email that got sent out this morning! Sample day has been postponed, we are supposed to take the day off and resume normal working hours tomorrow."

Sample day, postponed? That's... impossible.

The direction would sooner have half the facility staff be hospitalized than let sample day be canceled! I rushed through the hall towards the observation room for s-59 and jade called after me. "Hey where are you going?!"

As I approached the door I felt uneasy, seeing no guards posted outside. Pulling out my keyboard I swiped it over the scanner and the door slid open showing the empty dark viewing room.

I stood in the doorway in shock seeing the lights were off and no one inside, no director, no scientists or guards...no one.

The blast doors for the window peering into the vault was also sealed shut and all the warning lights for the door were glowing bright green signifying that the room was vacant.

My mind reeled with questions as I stepped inside. This area should be bustling with scientists and armed guards prepping for sampling.

Something seriously big must have happened for the director to have suddenly postponed the entire event.

Jade came up Behind me, panting slightly as she tried to catch her breath. "Seriously ava, how do you keep yourself so fit?! Is it because you spend so much time at the pool?"

Ignoring jade I entered the room and sat down at one of the computer desks before logging in. I checked the working schedule and daily plans and sure enough it said sampling was postponed. Going to my email I opened it up to see one unread message.

Opening the email I read through it and sure enough it said sampling was postponed until further notice. That's it, no explanation, no expected delay time just that it's not happening today.

I should be relieved by the fact I don't have to worry about the sampling but the strangeness of it all has me anxious.

"Ava you okay?" I looked up to jade who was standing by the desk watching me curiously. Shaking my head I closed out of the email and leaned back in the chair. "Yeah, I'm just not sure what I'm going to do for the rest of the day..."

Jade hummed, looking towards the door before shrugging. "I'm probably going to go to the lobby and have a few drinks, everyone else is taking the time off to unwind and de-stress. You should do the same! With that jade left the room leaving me in my solitude.

Sighing I leaned my head back and stared at the ceiling. De-stress huh. After a few minutes of debating u got up and went back to my room to gather a few essentials. Leaving my room, towel, and spare clothes in hand, I made my way to the employee pool area.

Upon entering the showers I was pleasantly surprised to find no one inside. It was odd considering no one was working today but I didn't question it. Setting my stuff on a bench I entered the pool room seeing it was dark, the only light illuminating the room came from the pool itself, casting an eerie glow throughout the open space. Shutting the door and locking it behind me, I moved to the thermostat on the wall and cranked up the heat.

Bubbles from jets under the water formed as steam rose from the surface. Crouching by the edge of the water I dipped my fingers in, smiling at the warmth it gave off.

Stripping out of my clothes I took a few steps back before running to the edge and jumping in. Warmth enveloped me as my head went under. Pushing myself off the bottom of the pool I swam up and surfaced. I removed the wet hair from my face with one hand as I kept myself upright in the water.

Swimming to the other side I relished in the warmth and tried floating on my back letting all my worries fade away.

As I floated on my back staring up at the ceiling I heard a noise of some sort from the shower rooms. "Hello?" I called out, righting myself while watching the door.

There was no response and an unsettling feeling started gnawing at me. Slowly I made my way to the edge of the pool grabbing onto the ledge.

As soon as I got to the edge of the pool the lights completely went out and the jets that had been spewing bubbles completely shut off. I glanced around frantically as the temperature dropped and the pool suddenly felt cold.

Jade! Matt! If this is another one of your jokes it's not funny! I called out but once again there was no response, just dead silence. Pushing myself up and out of the pool I shivered and stood up looking back at the water. The only light remaining was the emergency ones near the shower rooms that emanated a red glow.

Even with the light provided I couldn't see anything past the surface of the water. Besides my own reflection it was as if I was staring down into a void. Taking a step back a foul odor wafted through the room along with the scent of stagnant water. I quickly covered my mouth and nose to block out the smell, feeling sick to my stomach.

"What is that smell?!"

Stepping over towards the bench with my stuff I grabbed my towel and wrapped it around my body.

"Ava."

Spinning around I faced the pool once more and I could see a dark figure standing on the opposite side. A chill ran down my spine at the sight and I could hardly make out the figure's feminine appearance. I opened my mouth to say something but the words just wouldn't come out.

"Ava... are you happy now?"

What? I squinted and took a few steps closer trying to get a better look at the person before me. "Jade?"

A sinister laugh echoed through the room as the figure turned to absently gaze at nothing in particular. "Such an idiot. I can't believe we kept you around for so long. Honestly it makes me wonder what the hell the director was thinking..."

The figure had the same voice as jade but the sweet tone she usually spoke with was gone, replaced by malice and anger. I've never heard jade speak in such a way and it bothered me, not simply because she was being mean but something about this just twisted my stomach into knots.

"Really though I'm not surprised with how things turned out, in the end I knew you would be the one to fuck everything up. We should have ended it as soon as it started. We should have locked you up and thrown away the key... then this all could have been avoided."

What is she talking about? The more my eyes adjusted to the darkness the more clearly I could see something was wrong with the woman standing before me. Her high heels she usually wore were missing and I could see dark marks all across her bare legs. Her pencil skirt was torn and I thought I could see dark red splotches all across her lab coat and shirt.

"Jade, what is going on?" I asked nervously. Slowly she turned her head to look at me and I swear I could see a smile on her lips.

"This is all your fault."

"What- I don't know what you're talking about!?"

Suddenly her eyes moved to the pool in front of me and I followed her gaze. "Why don't you ask HIM?"

not seeing anything different I stepped closer to the pool looking down into the inky abyss, my reflection clear in the still water. My eyebrows scrunched together as I saw movement in the water and suddenly a body rose to the surface revealing the pale face of Matt, with a large cut across his face, and his eyes missing.

Jumping back I screamed and fell back onto the wet floor, scraping my arm as I fell and covered my head.

The air around me suddenly changed and the warmth returned as I laid there curled up hiding my face in my arms. Peeking out at the pool I saw the lights and jets were back on and everything was back to normal. No jade standing on the other side of the pool, no corpse in the water.

Slowly I pulled my arms away from my face and looked around for any signs of what I saw but there was nothing. Had I somehow imagined it?

Shakily I got back to my feet and looked at my hands that were now trembling. What the hell was that...

"Having fun?" A voice jostled me and I quickly spun around in the water, to look towards the entrance.

Standing by the door stood kerian in his lab coat, arms crossed over his chest as he stared at me with a smile. How did he-

His smile fell as he saw my panicked state and bleeding arm. "Ava, what happened?!" He rushed forward reaching for me and I quickly latched into him hiding my face in his shirt.

"Hey, hey come on, you're okay!" He held me close and gently stoked the back of my head as I shook in his arms.

"Hey it's just a scratch, it'll go away in a day!" He tried to comfort me. He thought I was upset because I hurt myself?

I hugged him tighter and took a deep breath relaxing as his scent washed out the odor hanging in the room.

"Come on let's get you washed up and I'll bandage your arm okay?"

I didn't respond as he pulled away and took my hand taking me into the shower room. I glanced back at the pool once more feeling sick to my stomach before following him out.

chapter 7

A ll I could do was absently Stare ahead unsure what to do. Was there even anything to do? My head, ached slightly and I let out a soft groan as I closed my eyes and held my head with on hand.

"So are you gonna tell me what happened?" Kerian questioned, briefly glancing up at me.

Opening my eyes I watched as he cleaned the scrap on my right arm delicately with the softest touch, I admired and always fawned over how gentle Kerian was with me. It was one of the reasons I loved him.

When I didn't respond he looked up at me again, only this time much more expectantly as he paused in his work.

Blinking a few times I snapped out of my lovesick puppy daze and focused on him. "S-sorry what did you say? I zoned out."

"I can tell, I asked you if you were gonna tell me why I'm here bandaging you up and playing doctor on my day off."

"Oh..." My voice trailed off and I looked away thinking about what happened at the pool. How I saw Some kind of dark version of jade and Matt's body floating in the water with his eyes missing. It was all still very fresh in my mind and I felt goosebumps crawl across my skin as my stomach churned just at the thought of it.

"I um...I was just tired from lack of sleep and slipped."

Kerian stared at my bandaged arm with an unreadable expression. "Ava..."

I returned my attention to him and he looked back up at me with a somewhat hurt expression. "You may be clumsy At times but I know you're not that clumsy."

I bit the inside of my cheek feeling bad about lying to kerian, he's always been supportive but I don't really see how talking about what I saw would really help. That he could help.

"I just– I'm not sure exactly what I saw nor if you would even believe me." I admitted.

He smiled a bit andreached up with one hand to touch my cheek. "I've seen some crazy stuff working here. I doubt anything you say Is gonna surprise me. And nothing you say will change how I feel about You."

I smiled and leaned into his touch, feeling reassured by his words. "Just, don't go ratting me out to the director or telling everyone I'm crazy okay? You might think taking a few days off work would help but it really won't."

"Alright I won't." He assured me before working on my other injured arm.

Taking a deep breath I tried to recall everything that happened. Everything I heard, saw, felt and smelt. "It was all just so surreal, like I actually felt the watcher change from warm to ice cold in the matter of seconds. And jade– the way she spoke was unsettling, almost as much as seeing matt..."

The more detail I put into it the more kieran's attitude seemed to change. His eyes got darker and his gentle touch became stiffer.

"D-do you think I'm crazy?" I asked quietly.

This simple question Seemed to snap him out of whatever trance he was in as he looked back at me. "No! Of course not!" with a sigh he finished up working on my arm and seemed to silently contemplate to himself.

"Then what do you think?"

"I– well, from experience this just seems to be a case of delirium from stress and lack of sleep!" He suddenly said cheerfully. Why was he saying that like it's a good thing?

"You just need some rest and proper sleep is all ava ok? Don't think into it too much." He held my face with a smile practically making me look into his eyes.

I somehow managed to relax a bit and the whole thing just seemed to get thrown into the back of my mind. Like it didn't matter anymore.

"Are you sure? And you don't have to report me to the director or put me through another one of those damned mental health evaluations?" I questioned.

Kerian just laughed as he leaned forward pressing his forehead against my own with a smile on his face. "Yes, I'm sure. Should anything else happen or you see anything out of the ordinary then come to me, don't be afraid. I'll make sure to take care of you no matter what... ok?"

"sure... I'm sorry you had to come baby me and patch me up on your day off."

"don't worry about it ava. I'll do anything for you... Anything." his tone and expression seemed to turn a bit darker with that last phrase only to return to normal seconds later.

"Now I've gotta go take care of some things, are you gonna be okay by yourself?" he asked as he pulled away and grabbed his lab coat off my desk chair.

"Yeah…I'll be fine, gonna try to get some sleep."

"great!" He smiled back at me. "then I'm gonna get going. I'll check in on you in a few hours!"

"sure…"

With that kerian left my quarters, leaving me alone in the quiet dimly lit room with nothing but my thoughts. That was…strange? No it's probably just me imagining stuff Again. Whining I laid back on my bed and stared at the ceiling, feeling off about the whole situation.

Closing my eyes I tried to think about what happened at the pool but for some reason everything seemed fuzzy and I could no longer remember all the details, my mind felt muddled and warped. Even as I opened my eyes again I felt dizzy. God what is wrong with me? Maybe I really Do need to get some proper sleep.

giving up on trying to remember what happened at the pool, I flicked off the light and pulled my blanket over myself as I curled up in bed and closed my eyes.

Here's to hoping I get some sleep tonight…

—hours later—

Opening my eyes I was greeted by nothing but darkness. Blinking a few times I sat upright, rubbing my eyes. "Uhg what time is it?" looking over to my alarm clock, I found No numbers or lights lit up on the screen. Confused, I picked the device up, tapped it a few times and pressed the power button but there was still no response.

'shit is it broken?' my eyes followed the cord and I checked to make sure it was plugged in properly. Seeing it was. I glanced towards my desk and climbed out of bed, setting the non-functioning clock down.

"I better not have slept in and been late for work." pressing a few buttons on my laptop I was confused when nothing happened. Once again I tried the power button and it didn't work. 'What on earth is going on? I had this thing fully charged!'

Moving towards the front door I flicked on the light switch and once more, there was nothing. Was there some kind of power outage?

Looking around I couldn't help but also notice the calendar I had hanging on the wall was now on the floor.

Stepping over I picked it up, flipping it open to this month's page, but what I saw left me feeling unnerved. All the days were crossed out.

It's only the 15th of this month– flipping through I found the next two months were also completely crossed out. Opening up on the third month I saw a few days crossed out and then one day practically destroyed and covered in X marks and circles. I couldn't make out anything underneath the red ink that might hint As to why that day was so important but judging by the rest of the calendar I knew the date was Oct 25th.

Thinking back I tried to remember if there was anything special planned for that day but nothing came to mind.

Maybe this was some kind of prank? Setting the calendar down on my desk I Glanced towards the door.

Stepping over to it I opened it up and peeked out into the hallway. Everything was dark and only the emergency lights were on, illuminating everything in an Eerie light.

Hesitantly I left my room I'm my pajamas and made my way down the hall, noticing many of the rooms' doors were ajar. As much as I wanted to check inside each one to see if anyone was inside, something told me that no one was around. Some strange urge was pulling me forward down the hall, so I just kept walking.

Eventually I came to the end of the hallway and saw the elevator doors attempting to close but some kind of dark mass on the ground was blocking them from closing. They opened and attempted to close repeatedly and I felt myself dragging my feet as an unsettling feeling set in my stomach.

As I stepped closer I could make out the mass lying in the doorway of the elevator was the upper half of a soldier's body, his lower half was obscured by the darkness inside as he just laid there unmoving.

I stopped in my tracks feeling the hair on the back of my neck standing on end as I stood there frozen. Unable to move any closer.

I could only stare at the soldier's body as my mind struggled to comprehend What was happening. Before I could even begin To understand anything however I saw movement from within the elevator.

A vine-like tendril snaked Out of the darkness and coiled around the corpse, dragging Inside out of sight. I heard a sickening squelch as my feet finally started to move and I began backing away.

More of these vines started spreading out from The elevator slithering along the walls and floor As they came towards me like snakes seeking out prey. As I backed away my heel caught on something and I shrieked as I fell back landing harshly On the ground.

When my hand came in contact With something wet I lifted it up to see nothing but dark red all across my arm and palm. Refocusing my eyes I found that the thing that I had fallen on was another body.

my heart sounded against my ribcage as my breathing came out uneven and rapid.

As something coiled around my leg I returned my attention to what was before me and could see the vines were now right on top of me, with one gripping my ankle in a tight squeeze. Feeling panic take over I kicked at the vine helplessly, making it tighten its grip as more closed in.

A dozen Of the plant-like tendrils coiled around the body beside me, dragging it towards the elevator and another gripped onto my wrist before I felt myself being pulled along as well.

"No no! Stop!" I struggled to pull free and thrashed around desperately before screaming for help.

The second body disappeared Into the darkness of the elevator as I was dragged closer and closer with tears now streaming down my face. Rolling onto my stomach I clawed at the ground trying to keep myself from being dragged in but my struggles seemed futile as more Vines wrapped around on my body.

Squeezing my eyes shut I quietly begged for someone to help, for someone to save me.

Before I could be pulled into the dark the sound of some kind of animalistic snarl sounded before me as something rushed past directly into the pit of vines.

There was some very audible banging and what sounded like in-human hissing from within the elevator as the vines That once held me let go, recoiling back to the source.

No longer trapped I scrambled to get away and looked back at the elevator as the sound of a struggle ensued within. After what Seemed like seconds. The sounds completely stopped.

I stared at the darkness, unable to hear anything else from within, and unable to see anything.

Gulping I tried to get back up, using the wall as support, without looking away from The elevator.

A strangely familiar chittering sounded from the dark and I held my breath as the sight of glowing white eyes appeared in the darkness staring right back at me.

The fear I had seemed to wash away as I looked back into the eyes of whatever Creature was before me. My feet seemed to move on their own as I pushed myself off the wall and stepped closer. 'Why am I approaching it? Shouldn't I be running?'

I stopped less than a few feet From the elevator door staring up at the eyes that watched me. I could hardly make out the dark humanoid appearance of the creature before me, through the darkness.

My mouth seemed to move on its own as I said something, but nothing came out, like my voice was just, Gone.

The creature stepped closer and my body refused to move as its clawed hand reached for my face. Closing my Eyes I half expected it to hurt me. To tear out my throat or rip off my head, but another part of me knew it wouldn't.

I shuddered as it cupped my cheek ever so gently And I opened my eyes to look at it Once more. My eyes widened at the sight of him Now that he had stepped out of the dark. It's The same creature I saw in my room...

Another chattering sounded from the beast as it leaned in and nuzzled my forehead. I struggled to comprehend What was happening as that all too familiar voice spoke in my mind.

"You shouldn't be here."

CHARITY JAMES

"You shouldn't be here."

chapter 8

As soon as those words rang in my head, "you shouldn't be here", I jolted awake with a gasp.

Looking around frantically I found myself still within my room and my own bed, everything seemed normal, My alarm and computer both functioned as well as the lights meaning that was all just another dream. But just like before, it felt so real.

I grabbed my head trying to understand why I would dream of such a thing. It's common to have nightmares with this kind of job but to have two with that same creature? And such vivid ones at that, Is it really just a coincidence? I've never even met or seen such an anomaly...

Raising my head I looked towards the cabinet and quickly climbed out of bed. Opening the cabinet door I found numerous supplies inside but the one I needed most was a notebook I often used to take notes.

Finding the booklet I flipped to a blank page and started writing everything I remembered from the dream, even going as far as writing down everything I knew about it, from how it communicated, how it looked, and how it even sounded. Once I finished with the notes I flipped to another blank page and drew a picture of the creature. It's horns and hollow white eyes, the way it slouched slightly.

Once I was satisfied with the drawing I tore the page out and folded it up, placing it in my coat pocket. Even if I don't recognize the creature, perhaps someone else might. Just as I closed the notebook, my door opened and I spun around in my seat, Startled.

Kerian Stopped in his tracks looking a bit surprised. "Ava? Why are you still awake at this hour?"

I relaxed and put my hand to my chest. Why am I so jumpy? Did I think something else would come breaking into my room? "You should have knocked!"

Kerian Looked at me questioningly before stepping closer. As his eyes moved to the notebook in front of me he furrowed his brows. "Ava, don't tell me you've been up, working instead of sleeping-" as he reached for the notebook I quickly Snatched it up and stowed it in my desk drawer. I didn't want Kerian seeing it and getting worried.

"No, I just woke up and needed to write something down. What are you Doing here, kerian?"

"I came to check on you- is something Wrong ava?"

"No, I just can't sleep." I lied while avoiding his gaze.

Kerian didn't seem to believe me as he kneeled down in front of me and grabbed my hand. "ava if there is something the matter then-"

"Nothing's wrong kerian! Can't you just drop it?!" I snapped, almost instantly Regretting it.

Kerian looked at me surprised, saying nothing as we stared at each other. Why did i- looking away ashamed we were both silent, unable to say anything to one another. I didn't mean to snap at him, I just... Squeezing my eyes shut I leaned forward on my desk and grabbed my head.

"Dammit what is wrong with me." I whispered.

Hesitantly kerian reached out and placed his hand on my back comforting me despite the fact I lashed out at him.

Opening my eyes and lifting My head I looked back at him before hugging him. He Was quick to wrap his arms around me and hold me close. "I'm sorry." I mumbled into his shirt.

"It's alright." He replied, while running his hands through my hair.

"You're not upset?" I looked up to see him smiling at me.

"Of course not, it's not your fault, you're just tired is all, and besides how could I be angry with something as beautiful as you?" he chuckled.

Sulking I turned my head away with a pout. "I don't deserve you."

Bringing his hand to my cheek he turned my head to make me look at him once again. "nonsense. If anything it's I who doesn't deserve you..." his smile nearly turned to a frown before returning in the matter of seconds. "I'd like to stay here for the rest of the night, if that's okay?"

"sure." I agreed before hugging him once again. Kerian always knows how to make me feel wanted and safe. How could I possibly deny him anything? How could I be so heartless as to snap at him for worrying over me. 'I really am the worst.'

Clinging to him I hid my face in his shirt while he patted my head, wishing I could just forget all of this and go back to sleep.

As Kerian smiled, keeping me in his arms, I failed to notice his gaze stray towards the desk drawer and the dark look in his eyes before he returned his full attention to me.

We both lied Together in bed before drifting Off into oblivion once more.

Waking up I opened my eyes, finding myself in bed once again. This time however I wasn't waking up in a panic or rush. I was completely content in my spot on the bed.

Yawning, I sat up and stretched happily. finally feeling like I got some proper sleep. Looking around I noticed kerian was no longer around. I guess he already left for work. I kinda wished he was gonna be here when I woke up but I guess I can't be too greedy.

Climbing out of bed I got dressed and put my lab coat on before making my way towards the labs. As I stuck my hands in my pockets I felt a folded up piece of paper inside and stopped on my tracks.

Pulling the paper out of my pocket I slowly unfolded it feeling uneasy about the image on it. I nearly forgot about that dream I had last night. Staring at the image I felt some kind of de-ja-vu.

Maybe I can find information on this creature in the database at my work computer? With that idea in mind I folded the paper once more and made my way towards the labs.

Upon entering I was surprised to find jade wasn't in yet, although I don't think I mind, the idea of seeing her right now bug's me.

Shaking the thought from my head I sat down at my desk and opened up the central database files for A.C.O.R.N and tried searching up different keywords that matched the creature from my dreams, such as white eyes, dark complexion, telepathy, horns, tails, and so on…

Only about a handful of anomalies actually came up with my search but none of them matched the dream visitor. Maybe if I look through this facilities specified subjects? Forgetting about the keywords I pulled up the list of anomalies within bunker 34. As I scolded through the list I found nothing even remotely similar. At the bottom of the list there was one thing that did, however Catch my eye. The classified flies. One of which was Subject-59.

Just seeing that name made me feel strange, s-59 is hardly talked about, I'm not sure I've ever even heard anyone talk About how it looks.

I clicked on the file to open it up and a pop-up appeared on my screen saying I needed an admin password to look at said documents. 'Go figure…' I thought to myself. Leaning back in my chair I glared at the screen before moving my eyes to jade's desk.

'She's an admin, maybe I could…' looking around the lab I made sure no one was around before getting up and stepping over towards her desk. Looking everything over I opened a few drawers until I found a sticky note With a obvious password written on it.

'Nice one jade.' She never really was that great at remembering Her passwords. shaking my head with a sigh I returned to my computer and entered the password into the computer.

It started to load and I could only anticipate What I would see as the progress Bar filled up. Holding my breath as the loading bar hit 100% the file opened only for the screen to suddenly go black.

'What the hell?' Tapping the monitor and side of the computer I tried to get a response but nothing came up. I tried to turn it on and off but The device refused to respond any further, leaving me with no information at all. 'Great!' I huffed, Leaning back in my chair. 'Now what?'

Maybe I'm just overthrowing all of this. I mean it's not Like it's impossible to have two similar dreams? It may be uncommon but not impossible. Out of all the creatures within this facility and the database there's not been a single one like this, it's probably just something my brain came up with randomly.

I should be focusing on work, not some random junk my sleep deprived mind conjured. Maybe it's best I just forget about it.

Folding up the picture I stuffed it into my pocket and got up to leave. I won't be able to get much work done If I can't use my computer so now I have to hunt down the tech guy.

Leaving the lab I made my way to the engineer's quarters in hopes to find someone who could fix my computer but as I passed the lounge and pool Area I thought I heard a voice call out to me.

As I looked around, there was no one around, just me Standing in the middle of the hallway. I started to question if I had actually heard something or I had been imagining it but when the voice called out again I spun around in the direction it came from and saw a door closing behind me.

Dread seeped into me as I realized it was the door that led into the showers and pool rooms. I carefully made my way to the door and stood before it, hesitant to reach out and open it. Everything fiber of my Being wanted to just walk away and forget about it but my mind just wouldn't let me.

I reached out and grabbed the doorknob but couldn't bring myself to twist it open, it was like I was frozen in place. As I stood there I could suddenly smell the foul odor that I had smelled when swimming the day before, and it was clearly coming from this area.

I felt sick to my stomach and nearly let go of the doorknob only for a pale hand to move over-top of my own, keeping me in place. I stopped breathing as I felt a presence beside me and heard the familiar condescending tone of Jade's voice whispering in my ear.

"oh ava, don't tell me you're too scared? Are you afraid of what you might see? You should be used to it by now-"

The doorknob turned on its own and I jumped back startled as it opened. The presence of felt beside me instantly disappeared and the smell vanished as a man stepped out and gave me a confused look, he wore a mat maintenance suit and hat, and carried a toolbox under his arm.

"sorry mamm pool's are off limits for the time being, you can't go in there." He stepped out and shut the door behind him before locking it and plastering a paper on the door.

I blinked a few times relaxing and looked at the paper he posted, stating the pools and showers would be closed for the next few days due to maintenance issues.

"closed? B-but they were fine yesterday." I tried to compose myself as I looked to the man for answers.

"Sorry, don't know what to tell ya, I got a complaint that there was an issue. Until I can get it fixed no one's allowed in."

A complaint? It couldn't be...

"Just give me a few days and you can come back and go swimming as much as you'd like." With that the man walked off leaving me alone in the hall.

I looked at the door and had a nagging feeling kerian had something to do with this. But why? Why close down the pools? All I did was slip? The more I thought about last night the more uneasy I felt. Closing my eyes I could see flashes of what I had witnessed and heard. Before, the memory was so foggy But it was slowly becoming clearer and clearer.

Opening my eyes i Glanced at my bandaged arm. I don't understand what is happening to me...

A distinct meow caught my attention and I looked back to see s-32 sitting in the hallway watching me.

It waited momentarily before getting up and walking away, but after taking a few steps It stopped and glanced back at me to see if I was following.

Something Was telling me I might get some semblance of what was happening if I did so with one final glance At the door I followed after subject 32.

chapter 9

Following s-32 I grew increasingly aware of how empty the facility felt. We hadn't encountered anyone in the main halls on our way down. That alone was strange to me but as we neared the containment zone I felt uneasy.

"Where are we going?" S-32 paused to look back at me and meow, waiting for me to catch up before continuing forward. Reluctantly I continued to follow until we reached the observation room door. S-32 sat in front of the door looking at me expectantly as I approached.

Looking around I saw nothing out of the ordinary and looked at the transdementional cat confused. After a moment he got to his feet and passed through The door.

Grabbing my keyboard I scanned it and watched as the door opened into a dark room. Stepping inside I reached for the light switch and flicked it on only to pale at the sight before me. The large glass wall that operated the observation area from the containment area was cracked, and the room was in disarray.

"What happened here?" I looked around and even peered Into the empty containment room for any clues as to what might have caused this. But there wasn't really anything left behind. A small mew from s-32 had me turning my head to see him sitting atop a consol watching me.

"You know what happened here don't you?" I stepped closer to him and reached out to pet the feline as he purred. "Is this what you wanted to show me?" I kept petting s-32 until His eyes started glowing and he suddenly lashed out and bit me.

Startled I stumbled back and held my hand Shocked but when I looked up I found that the room was different and I was no longer alone.

"Miss ava!" A familiar voice snapped and I jumped a little looking over to see none other than the director standing need the glass wall with. Number of soldiers at his side. "Pay attention!" He glared at me holding and I coldly felt fearful.

He turned away to refocus his attention on the containment room. I took note of how the glass wall was now repaired and the room around me was back to normal. S-32 was nowhere in sight leaving me in this strange scenario by myself.

"Doctor, what's the creature's status..." the director spoke up. A figure off to my side dressed in a white lab coat approached him and I felt myself go rigid as I recognized him. Kerian.

"stable for now but it seems to be throwing another tantrum and has an elevated heart rate at the moment..." Kerian answered coldly.

Creature? Curious as to what they were talking about I stepped. Closer and peered through the glass wall into the containment room. Half the lights were out while the other half were flickering out of control. I could faintly make out a dark figure curled up in the corner of the room huddled up and attempting to hide itself in the dark. It looked...scared?

"this useless thing never cooperates..." the director spat.

"might I suggest a different solution?" Kerian said, while turning away to pace behind us.

"What kind of solution?" the director asked intrigued.

Kerian suddenly stopped and turned his attention to me, causing an unsettling feeling to churn in my stomach. He stepped over to me and as he stood before me I noticed something I had never seen before on kerians face that was...familiar? A large brutal scar across one of his eyes.

"It's simple really, if you want a disobedient dog to obey you need only train it, and what better way than to give it a bone? After all, a mutt wouldn't dare bite the hand that feeds it." Kerian smiled, grabbing my shoulders and I felt my heart race as something inside me told me to run, to get away.

Panicked, I pushed him away and stumbled back as everything dissipated into smoke. I watched as kerian, the director and everything dissolved right before my eyes leaving me in the shambles of the observation room.

Panting I tried to calm my steady heart. "What was that?" I looked over to see s-32 sitting there, simply watching me. "Did you-" the shadowy feline jumped down from The console and strides over to the broken glass wall before Turning to look at me.

Hesitantly I stepped over and kneeled down by s-32. "You're not gonna bite me again are you?" I asked as I reached Out towards the feline. He only meowed before rubbing up against my hand and disappearing right before my eyes.

I blinked and the room around me changed back to how it originally should have been, only this time there were no guards, no kerian and no director. Seeing no one in the room I looked back to the containment area and saw the black figure that had been hiding in a corner before was now laying on the ground curled up. The lights that had been flickering were now stable but the danged lights were still out leaving the room a bit dim.

"Hello?" I called out and I could see the creature in the room flinch. Moving closer to the glass wall I observed it curiously. I don't remember ever seeing such a- within seconds the beast had jumped to its feet and slammed itself against the glass Wall making me fall back in fright with a scream.

It snarled angrily glaring down at me with familiar white eyes. Only now did I realize this was the same monster from my dreams, only I've never seen him show such emotion before. He seemed angry.

Taking a moment to steady myself I stood back up as it eyed me with a glare and slunk back down to its haunches while it's tail flicked around behind it. With a huff it turned away and huffed before sitting with its back towards me. Was it trying to scare me off?

Stepping back over to the glass wall it seemed to sense my presence and look back at me growling. I've heard this creature speak before, so surely it can speak again? Maybe it could give me some answers... that has to be why s-32 brought me here!

Feeling determined, I sat in front of the glass wall. "What are you?"

The figure was silent as it eyed me suspiciously. "Leave me alone." A familiar voice rang in my head.

He didn't seem very happy to see me despite being somewhat...affectionate the last time I saw him. "Can you tell me your name?"

The creature growled seemingly to get even angrier. If it wasn't for the glass barrier separating us I might have just left it alone like it asked. "Are you okay?" the words suddenly came out of my mouth on their own accord and I shook my head confused.

Standing once more the creature turns and banged in the glass snarling down at me."Let me out!" I jumped a little but wasn't as startled by the violent outburst like the first time.

I couldn't muster any words as I looked at the monster before me. Its snarls died down as it looked me over and its gaze seemed to linger on my shoulder. Curious I looked down and my eyes widened in surprise at the bruises that had suddenly appeared. 'When did i-' "I can't, I'm sorry..."

The creature slid down into a crouching position this time staring back at me. It was still irritated based on the look on its face but not nearly as angry as before.

"It's okay the doctor and director won't be coming back anytime soon, and I won't hurt you. I'm just here to watch over you." I couldn't control the words coming from my mouth nor the strange flow of emotions that Didn't make sense. So much fear and sadness... Why is everything so familiar?

The creature huffed. Turning his gaze elsewhere but stayed Where he was crouched Down in front of the glass.

"If you don't want to talk then that's fine I just thought you might want some sort of company since you've been locked up and isolated for so long. Some of the other sentient subjects enjoy talking so I figured you might too." Where is this coming from? Why Am I saying this?

"Why are you doing this..." the voice spoke up in my head. Lifting My head I gazed at the creature curiously. "Why do you humans keep Me locked in here..."

I was silent for a moment before looking at my hands, strangely enough the bitemarl left behind by s-32 seemed to be glowing.

"This place Is meant to contain things, creatures or objects that don't belong in our world. Sometimes just To protect them and keep them safe, other times To give them a place to exist in peace... But more often than not it's to contain the dangerous anomalies that could hurt Someone. I don't know you Or what you did on the outside but they believe you're too dangerous to let go. I'm just one of many of the researchers here whose purpose is to observe and learn about creatures like you..."

"The humans here see me as dangerous...I am only dangerous because they seek to control me...to use me. I am not a tool." It Bellowed.

"I'm sorry... but I can assure you I'm not like them. I don't wish to use you in any way. I'm not in charge so I don't get to say who is allowed out of containment but perhaps if you showed them less hostility and convinced the others you're not as dangerous as they think...then you can get some freedom back."

The creature was silent as he stared off at nothing in particular. "I'm sorry that's probably not the answer you wanted to hear..."

Huffing again his gaze moved back to me. "why do you speak in such a way?" He questioned.

I looked at him confused as he huffed. "You say you have no control that you are not the one responsible for my capture nor my containment yet you apologize over and over for such things. Why do you blame yourself for something you had no control over?"

His words made my heart ache painfully and I clutched my chest feeling like I suddenly couldn't breathe. I started hyperventilating as everything blurred and my head spun. "ava?" the voice called out to me worriedly.

I was having a panic attack, I knew this yet I could stop myself from spiraling. Have I completely lost control of my body? Why does my heart ache so much?!

"ava!" kerians voice called out and I opened my eyes barely able to make out his face as he held Me Seeming scared. "Ava snap out of it, it's okay!" He held me against him and I clung to his shirt to use him like an anchor as I tried to calm down. It took a while but my vision cleared and I was able to calm my breathing as my head stopped spinning. The ache in my chest faded but left a lingering feeling that just didn't seem to let me forget.

"It's okay...shh." kerian said quietly while petting my head. After a moment he pulled back to look at me, cupping my face in his hands.

"Ava what happened?" concern was written all over his face and I couldn't conjure words as I sat there.

Looking over kerians shoulder I could see s-32 hiding away beneath a desk watching us. Within seconds he passed through the wall disappearing from sight.

"ava! Look at me! Please, you need to tell me what happened, why were you down here? Why were you on the floor?!"

Seeing kerian now, he seemed so different from the one from that vision. Not only was the scar across his face gone but he wasn't nearly as cold or intimidating. Yet something was nagging at me telling me I shouldn't trust him...

"i- nothing. I was just tired."

He seemed shocked, almost hurt by my answer and hesitated before grabbing me more firmly, reminding me of the kerian I had seen before.

"Ava, you need to tell me-"

"I told you it was nothing!" I pushed him away and shakily got back to my feet. I made my way to the door as kerian got back to his feet to chase after me.

"Ava!"

As soon as his hand reached for me I snapped. "don't touch me!" He immediately stopped, pulling away as if he had just nearly touched fire. "Just leave me alone, kerian! Give me some space and time to think!" I rushed out of the room refusing to look back at kerian as he stood in the doorway and watched me.

chapter 10

Slamming the door shut I locked it behind me and leaned against its surface. I felt like I was drowning In a tide of emotions, guilt, uncertainty, fear and confusion.

I know I shouldn't have snapped And lashed out at kerian the way I did but after what I saw in that...that vision, I didn't know what to think or what to do.

He seemed really worried about me, and It's easy to tell when he's genuinely concerned about someone but when I saw him in that hallucination or whatever it was. He was completely different. He was cold, and uncaring. It was kind of unnerving.

My mind wandered To the creature in the containment room. The same creature that I had seen in my dreams, it looked the same but different... groaning, I Grabbed at my head. Nothing makes sense! I don't understand any of this!

Looking down at my hand I could still clearly see s-32's bite mark, It was no longer glowing. All the strange visions, dreams, whatever they are must have Some kind of connection surely, I just have to figure out the meaning behind them and figure out what that creature has to do with all this.

Feeling a bit determined, I straightened myself and went over to my desk. I need to write down everything I saw so I don't forget and-

As soon as the drawer opened I paled. The notebook was gone. "No, no no! I left it right here! it has to be here!" I frantically Dug through all the drawers for it but the notebook was nowhere to be found. This can't be happening i know It was real I didn't just imagine it i-

Pulling the picture out of my pocket I looked at the drawing. I wouldn't have this if it wasn't real so where did it go? Who could have...

A knock on my door startled me from my thoughts. "Ava? It's Me... can we please talk?"

I stepped back away from the door as my mind came to only one conclusion. Kerian took the notebook. But why- what reason would he have to steal a notebook that only has notes from my dreams?!

"Ava come on please talk to me you've got me worried sick! Just tell me what happened and we can fix all of this I promise!"

What do I do in this situation? How do I know if I can even trust him?! Grabbing my head I backed away from the door. "Go away!"

"Ava please."

"Just go away kerian! Give me some time to think!" silence ensued afterwards and I could hear it in his voice when he spoke up again, just how hurt he felt.

"okay... I'll check back later, just don't hurt yourself." I listened for footsteps as he left and felt like I could finally breathe again with him gone, but it didn't make me feel any less guilty.

What if I'm wrong? What if I'm misjudging kerian, hurting him for no reason-

"Well ain't this a surprise." a familiar voice spoke up from across the room. Looking over I saw none other than jade standing in the darkest corner of my room, blood staining her shirt once more. Just like at the pool.

"to think you would have the gull to chase him off, you always were a selfish little bitch." jade remarked.

"stop-"

"aw is the little lab rat gonna cry and go running back to-"

"Why are you doing this!?" I snapped, making her go silent. "Why are you tormenting me!? I thought we were friends!?"

Jade's glaring gaze bore into me from the shadows. "friends?" She started laughing, at first it was small and subtle then it quickly became full on maniacal laughter.

"friends!? Why would I even be friends with a worthless nobody like you!? We were never friends!" The lights started flashing above us and I backed away as jade suddenly started approaching. "as to why? You already know the answer to that!" I backed up into my desk and looked around looking for a way out.

"You think you can get away with what you did to me? You thought you could continue loving as if none of this ever happened!"

"Jade please, stop!" I begged. As she stood in front of me.

"no matter how many times you try- you will never get rid of me."

Squeezing my eyes shut I covered my head trying to block her out as tears welled Up in my eyes. The flashing lights Seemed to stop and I no longer felt Jade's overbearing presence lingering over Me.

Opening my eyes I lifted my head to see she was gone and everything was back to normal. Glancing down I could see my hands were shaking.

Hugging myself I sat there on the ground still frightened by what I saw. Why did I keep seeing these things? Why do I keep having strange visions? What is wrong with me!?

Squeezing my eyes shut I stayed huddled on the ground as so many questions raced through my mind, until I couldn't keep my eyes open anymore.

--

Waking up I found myself slumped up against the side of my desk in the corner of my room. Did I fall asleep here?

Pushing myself To my feet I looked around and saw the picture I drew lying on the floor, and a flood of memories of what happened previously rushed To my head, overwhelming me and giving me a migraine.

Groaning, I grabbed my lab coat and made my way out of the room to go to the cafeteria. I needed some coffee. Once I get something to drink and help me wake up then I'll be able to deal with all this nonsense.

Upon entering the cafeteria I noticed jade and the others all sitting enjoying their breakfast. Upon seeing me they all went quiet and watched as I dragged myself towards the coffee machine to pour myself a cup.

The sound of a throat being cleared behind me made me pause and glance back. Jade was standing there looking me over worriedly but just seeing her face was enough to trigger the memory of her at the pool and in my room to come forth.

I quickly looked away from her to focus my attention on the coffee in front of me as my hands shook. "Ava, I think we need to talk." she spoke up.

Chewing on the inside of my cheek I tried to force the image of the bloodied version of jade out of my mind.

"not now jade."

"Ava this is serious. Kerian is worried sick about you-" she pushed.

"Please jade, give me some time to wake up..." I begged quietly.

"he found you passed out on the floor! And you just ran off without any explanation, locking yourself in your room!" she exclaimed. "you wouldn't even talk to him! That's not like you! You always tell him everything. " She pushed again.

I tried to block her out as I poured a heapload of sugar into my cup.

"If Something happened you need to talk to one of us! Kerian deserves to know!" She Spoke again, the sound of her voice making head hurt even worse than Before.

I took a large gulp of my coffee only to take nothing but bitterness and musk, I practically spit it out onto the counter in front of me exasperated by how bad it tasted. I put in so much sugar... How is this possible? What Is Happening?!

"Ava! Listen to me!" Jade snapped as she grabbed my shoulder.

At the same time I felt a presence behind me and a cold breath Against my ear as an all too familiar voice whispered to me. "Fucking traitor."

Immediately I shoved jade off of me and threw the coffee on the ground, making the cup shatter across the floor.

Jade stepped back looking at me shocked as everyone at the table watched On, staring at me in the same way.

Somehow it was like I could hear each of their thoughts as they looked at me, muttering to themselves.

"What is wrong with her?"

"Why can't she be fucking normal."

"She doesn't belong here."

"They should've gotten rid of that woman."

Jade looked to the shattered coffee mug on the floor then back up at me unsure what to say or do. Shaking my Head I ran out of the cafeteria as jade and the others called after me.

I didn't pay attention to where I was going nor did I care. I could still hear their voices I'm my mind as they belittled and berated Me.

"You should've just stayed obedient," one voice said.

"Why can't you do anything right?!" another voice snapped.

"you should be locked away like the monster you are!" the first voice continued.

"Why do they even keep her alive?!" another voice chimed in.

Slowing my run to a stumbling walk I grabbed at my head and squeezed my eyes shut trying to drown them out. "Stop it!" I cried out.

"You were never my friend. Your nothing more than a traitorous bitch who needs to be put down like the dog you are..." jade's voice chimed in. Soon enough all the voices were chiming in chanting and repeating the same word over and over.

Traitor.

Tears streamed down my face as I collapsed to my knees in the hallway. The lights around me seemed to flicker and everything changed as my surroundings became much darker. The hallway was destroyed with blood splattering the walls and floor. Papers and bullet casings littered the floor. Some of the ceiling lights were flickering and hanging by just a few wires.

But even with everything in complete disarray, there was only one thing my mind could focus on as the voices grew louder.

Right before me was S-59's vault door cracked open, the inside little more than a dark void of nothingness.

Hesitantly I got to my feet and approached the door reaching for the opening. The voices started screaming and begging for me to stop as my fingertips grazed the cold exterior of the door.

I was suddenly grabbed from behind and pulled into a warm chest with one of my arms pinned to my side. "Ava!" kierans voice broke through my mind and the voices went silent.

But I was so close. The door was right there! Just a little closer and I could see what's inside! I have to see what's inside!!

I squirmed as kerian held me and tried to calm me down, but I refused. "let go of me!" I shouted.

He seemed to hesitate his grip loosening momentarily before becoming firm once more. "Ava I'm sorry- i cant."

There was a sharp pricked in my shoulder and I looked over to see him injecting me with something.

Immediately I went into a full-blown panic and screamed demanding he let go of me as I struggled and pounded my Fist against him.

"I'm sorry, please, forgive Me for not obeying, just this once..." He pleaded and I felt the strength draining from my body as my eyes grew heavy.

"No!" I cried, looking towards The open door. I was so close...

My body slumped and kerians arms suddenly disappeared. Replaced by the dark figure from my dreams. He was holding me close, comfortingly as I lay in his arms weak.

"Please forgive me..." His voice spoke up within my head as my eyesight blurred and I failed to keep my eyes open any longer.

Closing my eyes I Drifted off into the abyss. Unknowing to what we did wrong.

(Note: I'm sorry I know this is confusing af am curious tho as to what theories you guys might have? Do you know what's happening? Is ava sick? Is what she seeing real or fake? Do tell me your thoughts!)

chapter 11

Opening my eyes I was nearly blinded by the bright lights above. My head throbbed in pain as I tried to block out the light on my face with my hand.

My body felt stiff and I couldn't remember where I was or how I got there. Blinking a few Times I let my vision clear and turned my head to look around at my surroundings.

This wasn't my room, it looked like...the medical bay? Why am I here? I would never fall asleep here so why– a crashing sound from a nearby room startled me.

Sitting upright I looked in the direction the sound came from and could see the open door to kerians office. Inside I watched as a figure paced back and forth.

"how many times must I tell you she's not ready!" kerian angrily spat.

His harsh tone made my skin crawl even without it being directed towards me. Kerian has never raised his voice in such away, he's never sounded so angry...

I couldn't see anyone else in the room from where I was but it was clear he was talking to someone.

"Why can't you understand that?! She can't be allowed to remember if she does then all of my work and all the effort I've put into this will be for nothing!" He harshly whispered.

Silence ensued for a moment before kerian spoke again.

"can't you see what it's doing to her? All of this is for her! I don't care if you think it's wrong, I don't care if you think she's ready. I refuse to start over. Last time you interfered she nearly died!"

My heart started to race as I listened and it felt like the walls were closing in on me. What is he saying? Who is he talking to?

What is Kerian hiding?

"you will cease any and all interference or else..." kerian almost growled out in a deep tone.

As I tried to get out of bed my head swam and I got dizzy, stumbling into a nearby metal cart.

Kerians form in the other room suddenly stopped as he heard me and I felt panic start to wash over me as he stepped out of his office.

As soon as his eyes locked onto me, that familiar caring and soft look washed over his face with a bit of relief.

"ava! You're awake!" He rushed over towards me as I leaned against the side of the hospital bed. "thank goodness, I was so worried– how do you feel?" as he reached for me in an attempt to help I flinched away.

He stopped looking at me confused and shocked by the fact I recoiled. He had never hurt me before. And Never had i looked at him with so much fear and uncertainty. I'm sure the sight of me refusing his aid and pulling away was something no one would've expected. We were always close, always reliant on each other. I had trusted kerian with everything I had, given him my body, My love my everything.

Yet now here I am afraid of him even touching me...I wasn't even completely Sure why. It seemed wrong. It was wrong, yet I can't get over what I had heard him say.

"Ava?..." He spoke in a quiet and questioning tone.

I couldn't muster any words and merely held my hands to my chest as I kept myself as far from him as possible. At least as far as the hospital bed let me.

"Ava what's wrong? Why are you looking at me like that?" He didn't approach and seemed genuinely hurt by my reaction.

He was hiding something from me. Something big. What would he do if he realized I found out? What would he say if I demanded an explanation. Would he tell me? I felt like I already knew the answer to that... I'm afraid of what he might do if he finds out I overheard him. I have to say something to keep him from realizing.

"y-you... drugged me." I stammered out. I could hardly keep it together. So many emotions were coursing through me so many questions swirled in my head.

Kerian looked at me surprised and seemingly regretful as he stepped closer. "Ava, I'm sorry, I didn't have a choice. You were hysterical, the others... they said you were screaming and throwing stuff. I had it put you under before you hurt someone or hurt yourself!"

He stepped closer but didn't touch me. "Please Ava, I didn't want to do it but... you had me worried sick. You lashing out when I found you, and then freaking out in the cafeteria. You have to tell me what is happening!" slowly. Up at kerian i could see how stressed and tired he was. my shoulders slumped as I relaxed a bit feeling guilty for making him worry so much.

He gently took my hands in his and kissed my fingers. "You know I would do anything you ask of me, anything. So just please... tell me what is happening tell me why you're acting so strange. So I can fix it... so I can fix you.

That last sentence sent a chill down my spine and I couldn't bring myself to look kerian in the eyes.

Fix...me?

Shaking my head I squeezed my eyes shut and pulled my hands away slowly. "I'm just tired." I lied. Again. "I just need some rest, I'll go back to my room and stay in there for a bit so I don't cause any problems."

He looked at me somewhat hurt and lowered his gaze to his empty hands. He was at a loss of words as we both stood there.

"Maybe we should spend some time away from each other while I try to figure things out and recover..."

"what...what did I do wrong? Where did I mess up?" He spoke quietly to himself.

" Kerian, I'm sorry for making you worry. You didn't do anything wrong, I just don't want to drag you down anymore is all, okay? And I just need some time alone to process my thoughts." My words seemed to fall on deaf ears as he continued to stare at his empty hands.

My heart hurt a little seeing him like this but I needed to get away from him. My eyes briefly glanced towards his office. 'At least until I figured things out.' "I'm going back to my room."

Turning away I walked towards the door but before I could leave a hand grabbed me by the wrist stopping me completely. Wait."

Looking back I found kerian standing there holding my arm in a firm grip with a serious look in his eyes. He suddenly tugged me closer and lifted my hand up closer to his face as he inspected the bite mark on my palm.

The sight of it seemed to make him seethe with rage. "Where did you get this?" his voice came out deep and was laced with untapped rage I had never heard or seen before.

My stomach dropped as I tried to pull away but he didn't budge in the slightest. "kerian!?"

"did He do this!? Is this why you've been acting like this?! Is this why you've been avoiding me!?" He started to raise his voice and my fear and panic grew tenfold.

"I don't know what you're talking about!"

"don't lie to me Ava! I'm trying to keep you safe! Tell Me where and when you got this!!" He snapped.

"let go of me kerian!" I shouted.

He hesitated, and as if by force. Loosened his grip letting me pull away. His anger seemed to sizzle down as he watched me back away towards the door.

"Ava, please..." he pleaded once more.

Without another word I shook my head and ran out of the med bay, to get as far away from kerian as possible.

I was at a loss of where to even go or what to do as my run slowed to a walk. Leaning against the wall in the hallway I squeezed my eyes shut and tried

To understand what was happening, tried to understand why... Nothing seems real anymore, nothing makes sense.

It felt like my mind was shattered and I couldn't put the pieces back together. Clutching My chest I slid to the floor, Unable to stay standing anymore.

I just wanted all of it to stop... For it to end and for things to go back to normal!

The silence was Deafening as I sat there leaning against the wall. What was I supposed to do now?

A small merow made me lift My gaze to see none other than s-32 sitting in the middle of the hallway before me, watching with curiosity. We both stared at each other as my mind swirled with questions.

Living my hand up I looked into the bite mark he had left behind. Somehow I knew it was connected to all those visions and dreams I was having. Somehow he was making me see those things, but I couldn't understand why.

Kerian said I wasn't ready that I was unstable and having me 'remember' could be dangerous. Were those dreams and visions memories? If they are, How did I lose them in the first place? What secrets are being kept from me?

I lifted my eyes back up to s-32 who was waiting patiently before me with his tail flicking back and forth.

If kerian won't tell me then the only way I'll get answers is if I remember. Once I do this though, I fear there will be no turning back...

Taking a deep breath I sat upright and stared the multidimensional cat down.

"show me. Please." I spoke quietly.

Seeming to understand my request he stood up and walked over to me, rubbing up against my leg. I hardly hesitated before placing my hand atop his head to pet him.

The mark started to glow and I squeezed my eyes shut as the room started to spin and everything around me changed.

———

Opening my eyes I was standing in the observation room. Surrounded by various scientists whose faces I could hardly make out.

Glancing around I could see kerian standing in the back of the room leaning against a Wall, watching on with interest.

"Ava." A cold voice snapped me out of my daze and I looked forward to see the director standing before me with a glare. Gulping I lowered my head, unable to meet his eyes.

"Yes sir?"

"you need to focus. And pay attention for this assignment, understand?" He questioned.

"y-yes sir."

"Then let's get started." He turned away to walk towards the glass wall of the observation room and I easily followed. To my confusion however, when I peered into the room on the other side of the glass, I noted it was completely empty.

"Get the airlock open, and make sure the camera systems are on, before we open the gate." the director said to guard beside him who nodded and proceeded to do as he was told. I stood by the director as he stood in front of the airlock leading into the other room where the entity was supposed to be.

What are we supposed to be doing? I glanced toward the director, confused. "sir? I thought you wanted me to speak with him again today?"

His eyes moved to me and I shrunk a little as he stepped closer and put his arm around my shoulder. "Yes initially that was the plan but the subject has been less than responsive in the past few sessions so we decided to take a different approach today."

The airlock opened and before I knew it. I was shoved inside and the door was closeted behind me. Dread filled my entire seeing as I looked back at the director and everyone on the other side of the glass.

No no this can't be happening! I slammed up against the door pounding on it desperately as the director merely smiled down at me. "Wait please! You can't do this! If you leave me in here he'll kill me!"

S-59 has always attacked guards and scientists on site when released from his vault. Being locked in the observation room with him was a death sentence for anyone unfortunate enough to end up in that situation.

Sure I had be the first person to properly communicate with the entity, but he hardly spoke after our first interaction when we were alone together. He always grew irritated and tried to scare me away by attacking the glass when I was forced to have a session with him and ask questions.

If they put me in the room with him then there would be nothing stopping him from tearing me apart.

"Apologies for not inquiring with you about the change in plans miss ava but oftentimes it takes sacrifice to progress science."

I shook my head, unable to believe what was happening. The second door opened up into the observation room and I was already hyperventilating, unwilling to step inside and leave the small bit of safety I had within the airlock.

"I suggest you cooperate with this experiment miss ava, I would hate to terminate you for insubordination." the director warned.

My body was shaking as I hesitantly dragged myself out of the airlock. As soon as the second door shut behind me. My stomach sank and I couldn't think anymore, all I could do was stare at the vault door in front of me that inevitably contained the creature that would end my life.

"open the vault." the director ordered from the other side of the glass.

Warning lights flashed as an alarm rang out warning anyone within the vicinity of the containment room opening. The loud creak of the heavy metal doors sliding open, couldn't be heard over the beat of my racing heart as I stared at the dark abyss within.

Tears stung my eyes as I heard a distinct snarling from within and black mist seeped through the opening, filing the room.

The bright white lights above Me flashed as white soulless .eyes peered at me from the darkness.

The cameras in the control room bugged out, going completely blank as S-59 stepped through the threshold of his containment chamber and into the observation room. The lights all went out, and black smoke surrounded me as tears stung my eyes.

I turned my head away and squeezed my eyes shut waiting for everything to come to an end as he approached me, I held back my sobs as his presence lingered over me and a deep growl rumbled from his chest.

The director watched on excitedly through the thick smoke clouding most of the onlookers' view of the room. Perhaps they didn't expect anything from this... it was all just an excuse to get rid of a useless intern and watch their prized subject slaughter another human.

They were more focused on trying to get a closer look at S-59 than getting him to communicate. I was just another mouse for them to put in a box with a snake to watch die. There was nothing scientific about it, there was no sacrifice on their end. It was all just for their own entertainment.

Opening my eyes, I could see S-59 stepping closer Through my blurred, teary vision. I didn't bother to run or try screaming for help, for someone to save me. All I could do was accept the end of my pitiful life, there was no fighting it, I knew that after witnessing him massacre numerous scientists and guards before me.

He hated us. And honestly I'm not sure I could blame him, he was treated like a monster in here, a lab rat. They only wanted to control him and keep him in a cage while he just wanted freedom.

A small laugh escaped me at the thought. I felt bad for him, I could hardly imagine how miserable such a existence could be. Living in a prison. Even if he was to kill me any second now I hoped he would eventually get the chance to be free once more. Be able to live however he wishes away from those who see him as nothing more than a monster.

As S-59 reached for me I closed my eyes for the last time. Praying for my end to be quick and painless. 'If only I could've lived a life of freedom as well...'

Everyone in the control room lost visual as I was suddenly pulled into the darkness, disappearing from sight. Swallowed by the abyss.

chapter 12

Everything was dark as I opened my eyes and I found myself surrounded by a thick fog of black smoke that made it hard to see more than two feet in front of me.

Groaning, I sat upright and rubbed my head, confused as to where I was.

"Why did you come here?" A voice rang in my mind.

Gasping, I turned around in search of its origin but it was hard to see anything through the fog. I faintly could make out the walls and broken ceiling lights above me but still had no clue where I was.

Seeing no one around I tried to remember what happened before I passed out but the only thing that came to mind was–

My stomach dropped and I paled as realization dawned on me. S-59.

"i am not a plaything for you humans to toy with." the voice said with a hiss, but this time it sounded like it was off to the side. Slowly I turned my head to peer through the fog. If I watched long enough I could make out the faint silhouette of someone standing there.

Questions raced through my mind As I tried to comprehend what was happening.

How am I even still alive?!

After a moment the figure moved, disappearing from sight and my heartbeat raced a bit more. I looked all around me, trying to catch some kind of glimpse of the creature but it seemed to be moving, never staying in one spot for more than a few seconds.

"You humans are afraid Of what you don't know, what you don't understand. Yet you continue to push and push." The voice echoed, sounding like it was coming from all directions.

Panicked I started scooting backwards until my back hit the wall and I found myself cornered.

"You mess with things beyond your understanding, unknowing to the consequences of such actions!"

The voice spoke with malice.

The figure reappeared Again before me, slowly stalking closer. It's soulless blank white eyes practically glowing against the dark fog.

my heart pounded In my chest as his massive stature all but Towered over me.

"You poke and prod with your needles and equipment calling it science. Expecting to learn all there is to know, uncaring of the damage you do, or loss you obtain."

I squeezed my eyes Shut as it came closer and I could practically feel it looming over me. "Tell me why." it demanded.

I could feel a hot breath fan across my face as I sat there fearfully. Unsure of how to respond. if it didn't like my answer, would it kill me?

Despite all that, as seconds ticked by I grew more and more curious about the creature before me. I couldn't understand it, and so many questions were racing through my mind As I tried to come up with an answer. Why is he asking me this? Why hasn't he killed me already?

Like a flick of a switch it suddenly dawned on me and my eyes flew open. "Curiosity." I replied excitedly. The creature before me flinched back surprised and I briefly saw a seam disappear across its face where its mouth should have been. S-59 looked very humanoid in appearance with its overall shape, especially its face. Besides the white eyes, black shadowy Skin, and lack of a mouth, it still showed expression, something few creatures other than humans are capable of.

"But Curiosity isn't just a human trait... nearly all living creatures have it." I spoke up. No doubt that was the reason I was still alive, S-59 was curious. "Even you are affected by it."

He watched me carefully before pulling back a comfortable distance to where it was still visible but not crowding my space.

"I would not risk my life over mere curiosity as you would." he Huffed.

Relaxing a bit I looked over S-59, taking in his in-human features up close. "Why did you enter here?" he questioned, narrowing his eyes. "I thought I made it clear in your previous attempts to communicate that I want nothing to do with you." He all but growled in my mind.

"it...it wasn't by choice." He seemed surprised by my answer.

"The director, the man in charge, forced me in here. I wasn't given a choice." I said solemnly.

"Despite them knowing all the others before you have died?" He questioned. "do They not care at all for your wellbeing?"

"Some humans are selfish beyond reason. You've seen it before, why does this surprise you?"

He turned his head away thinking to himself. "I had imagined that humans were more caring for their own kind, but I see I was wrong." His claws scratched the cement floor beneath Him and he grew frustrated over the new I formation.

"Well, not all humans are the same…" His gaze returned to me. "Some may be violent and uncaring but others are kind and peaceful. The latter may be harder to find in places like this but it's impossible to say all humans are the same."

"And which One are you?" He glared in my direction before moving closer once again. "A selfish and violent human or a kind and peaceful one?"

"I–" he was mere inches from my face as he stood on his haunches before me giving me little to no room, and no possibility to escape. "I can't answer that."

He narrowed his eyes even more. "all Of us are different so you can't categorize Us all by good or bad… I'm not violent and tend To be peaceful, but you may consider me selfish for something simple such as wanting company." I replied awkwardly.

"Why do you allow the violent ones to force you into doing things? Why do you not fight back?" He tilted his head to the side.

I turned my gaze away shamefully. "Because I'm powerless, to stop them…"

"Explain." He demanded while sitting on his haunches before me.

"There's a kind of hierarchy among humanity where those with money, knowledge and strength are capable of changing the lives or even control the lives of people beneath them. There's lots of ways people obtain this power but it's not always easy.

I myself have little to no power so In order to survive I must bend to the will of others...

S-59 scoffed. "You obey them to survive even though their demands may cost you your life?"

I stared at the floor in front of me. "If I don't they could easily kill me anyway so there's not much choice. If there's the slightest chance of surviving one dangerous task, then it's a risk that has to be made."

"Why do you not kill them and take their power? You continue to stay weak and they will continue to bully you." He growled.

"it doesn't work that way for us... and unlike you I'm not exactly strong. I can't simply kill another human if I wished to."

He gazed at me for a moment and suddenly leaned in closer. I pressed myself against the wall as one of his clawed hands grabbed my face and another grabbed my arm. My heart pounded In my chest and I squirmed to pull free Only to be pushed down onto the floor by the massive creature.

"Be still." He growled into my ear in warning. A small whine sounded in my throat as S-59 practically climbed over me, and I did as he commanded , staying as still as possible.

I could only watch as he lifted my hand to his Face to inspect it. He seemed interested in the fact My fingers were small and stubby, compared to his long clawed ones. Continuing his inspection of my body up My arm he narrowed his eyes and seemingly grew frustrated by the short-sleeved lab coat and shirt covering me.

His clawed hand grabbed my shirt and tore it open completely exposing my chest. I nearly yelped in surprise as a deep bellow rumbled from within his own body. His hand trailed across my stomach and up over my breast to my neck as he looked me over before stopping at my face.

He slowly turned my head side to side before forcing my mouth open. He pulled my top lip up to get a better look at my teeth. As he did this, one of his claws nicked my lip making me flinch and he stopped in his exploration staring at the small cut that was now bleeding.

finally releasing me he pulled away to return to sitting on his haunches.

I watched him a bit breathless and slowly sat up, unsure if it was safe for me to move again.

"I have never Had the chance to get close enough to look over a human's body before. You truly do Lack claws, fangs, or any kind of armor to protect yourselves...you are soft and feeble." He mused.

my eyes widened In surprise. 'He was examining me?'

"Most of the humans who enter here come with weapons. Why do you not have any kind of weapon to protect yourself? If you had the same weapons then you could obtain power couldn't you?" He asked.

Doing my best to cover myself with my coat I sat up To face him once more. "I am not allowed to have such weapons for that reason... Those in power tend to keep those below them defenseless to prevent rebellion."

S-59 growled. "You are no less a prisoner than I am."

"I'm sorry, It's just the way things are..." I replied quietly.

"Enough of that. You have made it clear you have no power, why must You apologize?!" He scolded.

I couldn't help but smile at his reaction before giggling a little. He practically froze in place and stared at me as I covered my mouth. "sorry– I mean, It's just– I can't help it. I don't mean to laugh!"

I quickly composed myself as I found s-59 watching me with keen interest. After a moment he turned his gaze away and stood up looking towards the dense fog.

"enough talking, it's time for you to leave." He stated before walking away.

"w-wait!" I jumped to my feet and he stopped, Glancing back at me over his shoulder.

"Can I come speak with you again?" I asked.

He was silent for a long Moment before turning away and replying with a deep 'No'. Within a few steps he completely disappeared from sight leaving me standing there alone in the fog.

Slowly the fog seemed to fade around me revealing the rest of the observation cell. It retreated into the containment room as the vault door started to shut and all I could do was stare at it, feeling a bit rejected.

Turning around towards the glass wall I found numerous eyes staring at me in shock. Kerian stepped towards the glass to stand by the director as they looked at me, surprised that I was even alive.

Gulping I felt unease keeping back up my spine once more. There was no telling what would happen next.

chapter 13

I blinked A few times as a light was shined In my eyes and my pupils tried to adjust. My gaze moved back and forth as it moved all around before finally being clicked off.

"Basic physical responses are normal..." kerian mused, turning away to look at a clipboard.

I sat by silently watching him pace for a moment before putting down the papers To retrieve a few items from the cabinet.

"answer me once more, you do not feel fatigued? Sore? Drowsy? Sick? Anything?" Kerian asked Before walking over and taking my arm to draw blood.

"No, I feel fine...he didn't do anything to me, as far as I can tell, we just...talked."

Kerian paused to glance up at me. "He?" He said questionably.

Turning my gaze away out of awkwardness I mumbled reply. "yeah. From the way S-59 sounds and looks up close I just kind of guessed he was male."

Kerian hummed as he looked at me then finished gathering a blood sample. Pulling the syringe away he inspected it before putting it away on a tray.

"and exactly what were you two 'talking' about? Did he say why he hasn't been responsive since your first interaction?"

Staring at the floor I couldn't help but feel like I shouldn't be telling Kerian or anyone about what happened with S-59.

"no…"

Kerian watched me for a moment before his gaze moved to my torn shirt. "Remove that. I will grab you another one to cover up with." He went over to a cabinet and grabbed a clean shirt for me as I removed my coat and the torn top. Instinctively I covered my bra and chest to the best of my abilities with my arms.

Walking back over, Kerian seemed to hesitate as he stared at me and then glanced at the shirt. "May I examine you for injuries?"

His request caught me off guard and I looked up at him surprised. He's never actually asked my permission for anything before, usually checkups are mundane and repetitive, he always does what he needs to and sends me off. Not once has he ever hesitated or asked me before proceeding.

I merely nodded and he stepped closer, setting the clean shirt off to the side. Slowly I lowered my arms and keiran looked over my front, keeping his gaze away from my breasts and his touching to a minimum.

"you said it didn't attack you… I see no injuries but it doesn't explain why your clothes were torn."

"He ripped my shirt but it wasn't to hurt me… he was just curious."

Kerian froze as he heard this and his eyes snapped up to mine briefly before he pulled away. "Curious how?" He handed me the shirt which I gladly put on to cover myself up in.

"I believe He was just trying to figure out how humans protect themselves."

Kerian watched me with an unreadable expression. "And did 'He' do this to you?" he asked, gently grabbing my chin to look over the nic on my lip.

His proximity and touch made my cheeks flush ever so slightly. After a moment he pulled away and turned his attention elsewhere. "You are free to leave now, you are to return to your quarters And rest until called upon again. if anything happens or you feel strange You are to come to me immediately. I will do another checkup in 12 hours."

Climbing off the examination table I made my way to the door. I hesitantly looked back at kerian before leaving, as he focused on the task at hand and I couldn't help but wonder as my fingers grazed my lip. 'What was that about?'

__ Days later__

Walking into the cafeteria, my ears were immediately greeted by the sound of laughter. Glancing over to the far right table I saw none other than jade, Matt, and Sarah sitting at a table conversing with one another.

My stomach immediately twisted at the sight of them and I turned my gaze away to b-line it for the coffee machine.

Things seemed to grow quiet as I passed them by And I could feel multiple eyes on me, making my anxiety worse.

Getting to the counter I poured myself a cup, added creamer and some sugar before blowing at the steam. A smile spread across my face as I gazed at the heavenly delight before me. I could never survive without my caffeine.

Before I could take a sip I was suddenly harshly shoved from behind. The scalding hot coffee spilled Across my hand and I yelped, dropping the cup onto the floor.

Looking up I saw none other than Matt walking by with Sarah at his side. "sorry! Didn't see you there!" They both snickered and laughed As they walked off.

Why do they find it so amusing to torment me? I moved to the sink to run my hand under some cold water, but as I reached for the cold handle another hand grabbed my arm in a tight grip and another turned on the hot water.

"Wha-" I tried pulling my arm away with little success and looked up to find none other than jade holding me.

"Tell me how you did it." She said in a threatening tone, holding my arm close to the spray of hot water that was now steaming.

What?! "What are you talking abou-" She forced my already burned hand under the hot spray and I cried out in pain trying to push away from the counter.

"Tell me what you did! no one has ever survived after being put in a room with that thing! What did you do to make it leave you alone?! Was it some kind of pheromone? Did you hide a weapon on yourself?! Tell me!" Jade shouted.

"I didn't do anything!" I managed to slip free from her grasp And push away from the counter only to fall back on the floor and couch my arm in pain.

The sound of Matt and Sarah laughing from across the room could be heard but my attention was solely on the woman standing over me, glaring down at me like I was little more than a stain on a brand new carpet.

Turning away she walked off like nothing happened and I watched as the others followed after her, snickering at me. Sitting uo I heard Matt call me a 'freak' before they all left the cafeteria, leaving me alone, sitting on the floor.

I couldn't understand why they hated me so much.

Standing to my feet I changed the sink water to a cooler temperature and placed my hand underneath, wincing in pain. Bumping into me, making me spill papers and coffee, That's not unusual but they've never done anything as cruel as this before.

Sighing I looked over to the spilled coffee then my painfully red hand. I could already tell it was decently burned.

Sulking I cleaned up my mess then went to kerians office.

Upon entering I found Kerian buried in his work. When he noticed my presence he lifted his gaze towards me confused. When his Eyes locked onto my injury He immediately dropped his papers on the desk and stood up.

"What happened?" Coming over to me he looked over my hand seemingly bothered by how red and inflamed it was.

"I Just spilled some coffee is all." I replied.

"you're not usually so clumsy..." kerian stated.

I didn't respond as he sighed and grabbed some ointment from a cabinet. "Here, it looks like it's a second degree burn. I'll apply ointment and a cold compress, just take some pain medication in the meantime." He quickly patched me up before standing back to look me over.

"Has Anything else happened since your exposure to Subject-59?"

"No, nothing to make note of..."

Kerian was quiet as he finished up bandaging my hand. "The director will Probably try to have you communicate with it again in a day or two, outside the containment room... if things don't work out he may force you back inside again."

"You need to do your best to get subject-59 to respond, even just a little, do that and you may avoid Another life threatening situation." His blue eyes met Mine momentarily. "Understand?"

I almost couldn't believe what I was hearing. 'Why would he tell me this? Information like this is classified Even if it revolves around me...is he worried about me?' I could only nod in response.

"Good now go rest and keep that injury cooled. Try not to get yourself hurt again. He turned away to go back to his desk and I made my way out of his office.

Placing my hand over my chest I felt my heart beating a bit faster. 'Am I imagining it?'

Glancing back at his office once more I shook my head and walked back to my room.

—-3 days later—-

"It refuses to cooperate!" The director's voice was distant but clear.

"Might I suggest an alternative?" kerian piped in as my head swam from my dizzy spell.

"Give a dog a bone and it will obey, a beast shall not bite the hand that feeds it." Kerian finished and I finally snapped back to reality, my heart racing as panic took over.

"n-no!!" I shoved him off me, backing away as I looked between the two men fearfully. He can't be serious!

Kerian stepped towards me, grabbing my arm to pull me away for a moment to speak. "let go!" I demanded.

Turning to look at me he grabbed me by the shoulders. "calm yourself miss ava! I am trying to help you!" He scolded.

Help me? Help me?! He just suggested the director use me as bait or a lure to gain S-59's trust.

"I-i don't believe you!" I tried to push away.

"he's going to kill you!" Kerian snapped quietly, making me freeze.

My mouth felt dry as I listened to kerian. His hand Suddenly moved a stray lock of hair behind my ear and I lifted my head to look at him surprised as my heart skipped a beat.

"On Sample day you stayed back to clean up this office after everyone had left, somehow you managed to converse with a creature whose only shown violence since the day it was captured. After days of failed attempts to do the same thing the director threw you in its cage believing you to be useless, he did That to dispose of you and instead you not Only survived, you commuted with the creature, interacted with it...that has kept them from trying to dispose of you again. If you do this...if you stay useful then you can prevent such from happening. This is the best chance you have at survival, I'm doing this to help you ava, get us something. Anything. Data, knowledge, samples, anything to satisfy the others. Let us use you... so that you may live."

I couldn't deny anything Kerian said and he sounded... sincere? Perhaps he really is just trying to help? No one here has ever done anything like this for me before–

Looking back towards the director I could see he was getting impatient. It had been nearly a week since I entered S-59's cell last time he told me he didn't wish to commune.

"What if it doesn't work? If he wants Nothing to do with me?" I asked quietly, afraid of the answer.

"It will work. Trust me."

Digging my nails into my own arm I took a shaky breath. I didn't have much choice, besides kerian has never lied to me before. He has always spoken the truth even if it's a harsh one. He's never done or said anything bad to me, he's always been quiet and minded his own business he's not like the rest of them...

"Okay... I'll do it."

Kerians lips curled up into a smile, something I've never seen him do before. "Good. Then let's get started."

(Note: thoughts?)

chapter 14

Staring ahead at the glass window before me as the dark fog moved around against the glass obscuring the view of most of the room, I could help but feel like this was a bad idea.

Glancing back at kerian he only nodded as one of the guards came up beside me ready to enter the room as well.

He was fully geared up with bulletproof padding and tactical gear, to protect him, and a big gun. I on the other hand was given nothing but the clothes on my back.

The airlock door opened and we both stepped inside. When the door behind us closed the one leaching into the containment room Opened and the dark fog creeped in, across the floor.

The soldier at my side raised his gun towards the dark mist before us and we slowly stepped out of the airlock. Through a bit of fog we were able to see back into the observation room through the glass where everyone was watching.

Kerians words repeated in my head as I turned to face the darkness. 'Just ask a few questions, get some kind of response from it and then we will pull you out.' That's all I have to do... but if he refuses to interact with me through the glass, how is entering the cage any better?

taking a deep breath I looked around hoping to see some semblance as to where S-59 was, but there was nothing.

"H-hello?" I called out. No response.

"S-59, can we talk?" I asked. Again no response.

"I know you told me I couldn't come back to communicate with you but–" my voice trailed off. Even if I told him my life was on the line, he had no reason to care, he co sidereal humans a nuisance. If he doesn't want to communicate or interact then he won't.

"Please, come out, or say something. Anything."

The guard beside me was slowly scanning the room with his rifle, ready to shoot anything that moves towards us.

Silence continued to be the only response I was getting and I could see the director growing frustrated.

Walking over towards a console he grabbed an earpiece and connected it to the speakers within the room we were in.

"push harder. Order it to come out of hiding or else!" He demanded.

I looked back at the glass wall and panicked a bit. Kerian seemed unphased with little to no concern upon his face and it made my chest tighten.

"I-i can't just make him do as I ask– if he refuses to speak that's not something I can control!"

"You will make it communicate again, just as you did before." The director stated coldly.

I shook my head in disbelief. "But I didn't do anything before! He was the one who approached me! He said he didn't wish to speak with me again–

"Hmph... I see. Guard, Return to the observation room with Miss ava. This was a waste of time..."

My blood ran cold at the director's words and Kerian shook his head in disappointment before turning to walk away.

'If the director thinks you are useless he will simply throw you in the cell of another monster that won't hesitate to kill you.' Kerians words replayed in my mind.

"Let's go." The guard demanded. Grabbing my injured hand. I cried out and struggled to pull away from him.

"No wait!" I shouted in an attempt to stop what was to come. If I left this room I'll be as good as dead.

The guard didn't relent on his hold and even tightened his grip making me whimper in pain. "Stop, please! You're hurting me!"

"Enough of this!" He reached forward grabbing me by the hair and I yelped as he tugged me towards the airlock. Tears stung the corners of my eyes as My heart raced and I tried to figure out how to get out of this situation. Looking towards the dark fog I knew S-59's cooperation was my only hope.

Pulling myself free from the Guards hold I blindly ran into the fog as the soldier shouted at me to come back. I didn't get far before running into something solid, forcing me to stop. As I looked up to see what I had run unto, I found familiar soulless white eyes staring down at me.

he was unmoving, standing just out of sight of the people behind the glass wall. I was still fairly visible to them so my sudden stop caught the attention of a few in the room.

The guard came after me only to stop a few feet away when he noticed S-59's appearance. Immediately he raised his gun at the creature and ordered be back to the airlock.

My heart was racing as I stood there before him. Taking a single step back I didn't break eye contact with the creature as he gazed at me with an unreadable expression and didn't move.

"please." I whispered quietly as tears welled in my eyes. His eyes narrowed and he still didn't move.

"I said get back!" The guard came up behind me keeping his gun trained on S-59 as he grabbed me and pulled me back away from him to take me to the airlock. I Struggled to breakfast from his grasp but it was pointless. He was stronger than me, and if I continued to resist he would just shoot me.

Suddenly, the arm gripping me let go and there was a thud sound of something hitting the ground. Looking over to the guard my eyes widened as I saw his arm completely missing with blood dripping from his shoulder as he stumbled back.

Looking down I saw the arm that he had once been holding onto me with, was now lying on the ground, completely severed from his body.

He dropped his gun to grab at his missing arms as he started wailing in agony. I could feel a presence standing right behind me and ended up freezing on the spot.

Now we had everyone in the observation room's attention as S-59 loomed over me and the guard collapsed back against the glass, blood spilling everywhere. The fog became thicker As s-59 stepped around me and approached the man flexing his claws as his tail whipped around behind him.

I reached out wanting this to stop, not wanting him to kill the man who had just been following orders. But my voice was gone. I could do nothing but watch as S-59 tore the man apart, painting the glass red.

I couldn't breath and my head felt light and dizzy as I watched everything unfold. The fog around me grew thicker and thicker and I felt S-59's tail coil around me right before I collapsed into the darkness.

————

"trust me" kerians voice called out.

gasping awake I found myself in a familiar predicament. Lying on the ground in a dark room surrounded by fog.

"You are safe." a deep voice rang through my head. Sitting up I looked back to find S-59 sitting behind me, staring ahead. Following his gaze I could faintly make out the glass wall far on the other side of the room, though all the fog.

I fainted, and he dragged me back here far out of their sight...

Turning his head slightly to look at me he waited for me to compose myself. "Why did you lose consciousness after I saved you? I assumed it was a defense mechanism the first time it happened. You were scared of me so it came as no surprise... but this time it happened after the threat had been disposed of. Why?"

My body trembled slightly at the memory and he turned his head even more. "i-i couldn't handle seeing you do...'that'."

He fully turned his attention toward me now, seeming interested in what I had said.

"Is that not what you wanted from me? I saved you from that wordless bag of flesh, he was hurting you, so I tore him apart as a warning to all the others. Is that not what you wanted?"

"N-no! I didn't want anyone to die! I didn't want any blood shed! I-i just..." tears priced the corners of my eyes as S-59's tail suddenly lifted my head. As I looked at him he tilted his head observing me.

"I just wanted to live..."

He was silent as he looked at me. The tip of his tail gently wiped away a tear just under my eye as I sat there on my hands and knees.

"What is this?" He questioned. Looking at the residue on his tail.

Wiping my eyes with the back of my hand I sniffed. "they are tears... When humans are sad or miserable they usually start crying and shed tears." I responded quietly.

"So you truly are displeased with my actions..." his eyes narrowed and he turned away, facing his back towards me.

I was finding it hard to understand the creature before me. He seemed to have wanted nothing to do with me before so why did he help me?

Standing up I moved over to S-59's side as he glared out towards the fog. "Why did you try to help me?" I asked.

The creature beside me growled, refusing to look my way. I kneeled down beside him, hugging my knees.

"You pleaded for my help and I complied. Yet you still aren't satisfied." His claws dug into the concrete floor, and I could practically feel the anger radiating off of him.

"I thought you hated me..." I mused.

His Head suddenly snapped to the side to look at me and before I could react he was grabbing me by the neck, and pinning me to the ground.

I yelped in surprise as S-59 hovered over me growling. "If I hated you I would have already ripped the flesh from your bones."

I grabbed at his arm fearfully While looking up at himaking. 'He's angry with me now? But why–' realization fell over me.

"I-im sorry." He narrowed his eyes even further. Letting go of his arm I moved my hands to his. "I do appreciate you helping me... you did save me just as I wanted. I was so panicked and afraid at the time I couldn't think straight... I should have told you not to hurt the man. That's my fault." I admitted.

His anger seemed to lessen as he released my neck. "Why do you dislike the idea of the people who hurt you, dying?" He questioned.

"Because some of them don't have a choice... like I told you before. Many of us are just pawns to those with power..."

his tense posture melted away as he returned to his sitting position and stared at the fog in deep thought. "That is why you also came back when I denied you before..." he practically stated instead of asking.

Sitting up I merely nodded. "my being able to interact with you is the only thing keeping them from killing me." I told him honestly.

He glared ahead at nothing in particular. "You are...a peaceful Human, something rare from my understanding and yet they wish to eliminate you. You aren't strong enough to protect yourself."

I stayed silent as he mused beside me. "It is infuriating to watch...I do not understand your reasoning for wishing to keep those worthless humans alive." He growled.

"If we killed them then we would be No better than they are." I replied.

S-59 scoffed in response.

"We have a saying for such…it's considered the natural order of all living things." I whispered.

His head turned slightly in acknowledgment. "The strong live and the weak die. Survival of the fittest."

He was silent once more as he gazed at me before turning his attention back to the fog.

He growled once more in response. "I reject those ideals." His tail then encircled Me on the ground, lying over the tops of my feet.

"If you are too weak to protect yourself then I shall do it for you…"

chapter 15

"He agreed to cooperate to some extent..."

Kerian listened, intrigued by this information. "How did you manage to convince it? S-59 showed zero signs of interest before..."

I anxiously sat before Kerian on the examination table, staring at the floor. "I didnt do anything he just... chose to. I dont believe i did anything particularly special for him to agree, i told him the truth and that's it."

Kerian leaned back in his chair after finishing his examination of me for any injuries or changes. "When it killed the guard in the room with you we were almost sure that it was going to kill you as well, but once again the creature left you unharmed and has agreed to 'cooperate'." he wrote some notes down on his clipboard before setting it off to the side.

"Either way Ava, you succeeded in keeping the director's attention, you dont need to worry about him trying to get rid of you for a while. He is obsessed with subject-59, getting close to that creature is your best bet for staying on his good side and staying alive, perhaps even escaping."

I could only sulk more at kerians words. "I never signed up for this." I mumbled.

"On the contrary this is exactly what you signed up for... we all did. We were all given the chance at escaping poverty and munade lives, through our set skills and offered a chance of a lifetime to study and learn about things that could change the world. but some of us however, weren't lucky enough to see the trap laid out in front of us, disguised in leaf litter and debris." He glanced back at me and I balled my fists, frustrated over my current situation. None of this was fair.

"But that does not mean everything is hopeless." Kerian stood up in front of me and I raised my head to meet his gaze. "Some of us are able to rise above with a little help from an outstretched hand. Even if things aren't as we hoped, with a little help it's still possible to steer ourselves back on track so we don't fall deeper into the pit and become lost forever..."

I looked at kerian a bit surprised as he held out his hand for me to take. 'is he- offering to help me? but why...'

"you will only continue to struggle if you don't learn to adapt. even the smallest and weakest creatures can learn to survive under the harshest circumstances. if given the proper conditions."

'Kerian...he's offering me a way out, a way to escape this hell. He's the only person to ever offer me his hand and help. He's the only one who cares...' swallowing the lump in my throat, I took his hand and stepped off the examination table.

"If it means getting out of here, I'll do anything." I said confidently.

kerians usually stoic face turned up with a small smile as he gazed at me before placing his other hand on my shoulder. "good. just like before, all you need to do is trust me."

___Days later___

as the pressure of a door closing behind me created a hiss, I glanced back towards the glass wall behind me, seeing kerian and numerous others watching me as I stepped into the containment room.

he gave the slightest nod and I turned my attention back to the dark misty room around me. taking a deep breath I focused on what he had told me to do. talk to S-59, ask him a specific set of questions and attempt to learn more about him.

my stomach twisted in nervousness as I stared at the darkness before me. 'That is all easier said than done.' squeezing my eyes shut I shook my head. 'No, I can do this, I need to trust Kerian. S-59 hasn't hurt me before, and we've engaged in conversation at least 3 different times. He agreed to cooperate with me, I have nothing to be afraid of...' I reassured myself.

staring at the black smoke before me I felt unsure. 'but what if he was lying? what if I make him angry again and he snaps?' knowing there was no turning back i hesitantly took a few steps into the dark mist.

I couldn't help but notice how it moved around me, clearing away as I stepped further into the room, only to envelop me from behind as if to block out the view of those who were watching. I had only taken a few steps and already it was hard to see the observation room from where I was.

'kerian wanted me to bring him out into the open, so they could observe our interactions. but something tells me subject-59 isn't going to show himself that easily.'

facing the darkness I looked for any signs of him but saw none.

"hello? Are you there?" I called out into the darkness. Just like before, no response. I chewed the inside of my cheek before walking further into the room. Glancing about i tried to keep an eye out for any movement or signs of s-59, but it was hard to see anything through the dense fog.

Soon enough i came in contact with the wall all the back of the room. Placing my hand against its surface i walked along the wall until i reached an opening—the vault door to s-59's containment chamber. Looking inside i found that it was even darker than the room i was currently in. It was as if i was staring into a void of nothingness, a portal into another dimension. It was unsettling to even look at, I've never been afraid of the dark before but for some reason, it felt like if i were to step into that room, i would be lost forever.

"Closer..." a familiar voice called out to me from the darkness.

I didnt move from my spot in the doorway, i couldn't move. My feet were glued in place as i stood there peering into the void. "Closer." the voice spoke again, much clearer than before and much more demanding.

"I-I can't," i murmured quietly.

It was quiet once more, and i worried that my refusal to enter might've upset S-59, but after a moment i saw his eyes glowing in the dark as he approached the doorway. Taking a few steps back i held my breath as he passed through the doorway, towering over me as his tail swayed side to side. "Why?"

"Well, it's really dark in there— darker than it is in this room, I would be walking in completely blind, I could hurt myself..."

he circled around me slowly, looking me over before stopping a mere few feet in front of me once again. He then crouched down to be more level with me. "Why would you hurt yourself?" He asked.

I found his actions strange but relaxed once he sat back on his haunches before me. "humans can't navigate in the dark very well so I might trip and fall...do you prefer the dark?"

he quietly glanced back to his chamber seemingly in deep thought. "It is comfortable. The light bothers me, I only come out of the vault to stretch my limbs, being locked in such a small space isn't ideal."

"the light bothers you?" glancing up towards the ceiling of the observational room I saw that some of the overhead lights were destroyed others simply were just not working, leaving the room dim and hard to see in.

"Why is the cloth on your body always different? what is the purpose for it?" He then suddenly questioned.

"You mean my clothes? it's sorta a form of protection, we cover ourselves to protect our bodies from our environment such as the temperature or other things."

S-59 all but scoffed as he looked at me and reached out. "This cloth does not protect anything, I could tear through it with ease–" he tried to grab my shirt but I quickly stepped back out of his reach, making him narrow his eyes in turn.

"It's not that kind of protection! clothes keep us warm, and can keep some things from harming us, not all. They also help maintain our comfort while around others. much like how this mist maintains your privacy while you are in this room."

his eyes widened as he looked around momentarily. "Why do humans need to maintain their comfort around their own kind?" He asked curiously. I couldn't help but find his Innocence charming. this creature knew so little about us, so far all his experiences with humans have been hostile...

S-59 doesn't seem inherently hostile at all times, perhaps his violence has only ever been a means to protect himself? He hasn't had any friendly humans to commune with and lacks trust for our kind. being so intelligent I wonder if it would ever be possible for him to exist among us naturally?

smiling I stepped over and crouched down in front of him. "Humans are complicated as I told you before, we are all different.

clothes represent many things for our kind and can help us do many things. as for basic comfort? Well, our bodies are vulnerable to the elements and each other... sometimes a few layers are all we need to keep ourselves safe."

"These clothes do not protect you from those outside the glass wall from what I've seen." He mused.

"Not in the way you think, no. But humans are easily swayed by emotions... if people started to just walk around naked, others could potentially harm them physically and mentally."

he seemed displeased by this information as he listened. "others would hurt you simply from not being covered?" I nodded in response. "why...how?"

feeling a bit uncomfortable I squirmed in place. "People tend to let their urges take hold– it goes both ways but a man may easily assault a woman if she does not have clothes to protect her more intimate parts..."

realization practically washed over his features as he sat up straighter. "Has another human male done this to you?"

I stayed silent, unwilling to talk or even think about the ways I've been harassed by the people in this facility. S-59 seemed to take my silence for an answer as a growl rumbled in his chest and his tail slammed on the ground.

Suddenly he stood up from his spot and started pacing the room around me, angrily glaring at nothing in particular. the dark mist around us swirled as he moved through it growling as he paced.

"Why are you upset?" I asked curiously.

he turned to look at me with narrowed eyes while his tail swayed behind him. "It is nothing..."

I stared at him as he stood off to the side practically fuming. "Uh besides that... clothes are mainly used to keep us clean since humans could easily get sick if they are dirty!" I stated in an attempt to change the direction of the subject.

The tension seemed to slowly leave him as he came back to crouch in front of me. "Does your kind not bathe?" he asked.

"Of course we do! we have showers and the pools for that– but it's not really convenient for us to be cleaning ourselves constantly. This job is really messy sometimes..." As I said such, my eyes moved to S-59's claws.

Last time I was in here he slaughtered a guard and his arms were covered in blood, but right now I see zero traces of said incident on his body. The cleaning staff only takes care of the messes he makes in this room while he's locked in the vault, so how does he clean himself?

he hummed and tilted his head slightly as I stared at his hands. "Why do you stare?" He questioned, snapping me out of my daze.

"ah- I was just wondering how you wash the blood off your hands without a shower or bathroom." I admitted with an awkward chuckle.

huffing he leaned his head against his palm while gazing at me. "just as any other creature would... I groom myself. I'm actually not fond of such messes and dislike the feeling of things sticking to my skin."

my eyes widened a bit hearing him talk about himself. "groom? how do you groom yourself?"

he narrowed his eyes at me like i had just asked a foolish question. "with my tongue."

'tongue?! but he doesn't even have a mouth!' Before he could even react or I even realized what I was doing I stood up and reached for his face. He flinched back initially before freezing as I cupped his cheeks and ran my thumbs over the flat space where a mouth would be. "You don't have a mouth though...do you?"

He stared at me for a long Moment with an unreadable expression before grabbing one of my wrists gently with his claws.

Slowly, a horizontal seam appeared across his face underneath my thumb and I tried to jerk back out of reflex but his grip on my wrist kept one hand close as the another seam opened up. this one was vertical and went down this chin, stopping close to where his neck started.

as the seams opened up, separating from one another my eyes widened at the sight of the large maw filled with teeth. and a long tongue that unfurled and licked my outstretched hand.

I couldn't fathom what I was seeing nor feeling as his long wet tongue slipped between my fingers and nearly coiled all the way up my forearm.

"I do have a mouth, I just prefer not to show it..." his voice rang in my mind with a purr, without a single movement from his mouth or throat. I could feel a warm breath against my palm as his tongue gently glided across my skin and the rows of teeth carefully avoided my hand.

his tongue then snaked back, slipping free from my arm to curl around my fingers briefly then slip back to his mouth as it closed back up and the seams completely disappeared.

I could feel heat rising in my cheeks as my heart raced and my mind ran wild with excitement over the discovery as I stared at S-59.

He watched me carefully, still keeping his hold on my wrist as he stood up to tower over me. "You allowed me to see and touch parts of your body in one of our previous encounters so now I have returned the favor... despite my distaste for your kind I am still curious and wish to know more. Perhaps next time you come to visit me we can learn more about each other? I'm sure there's still many things I've yet to learn about humans and you have plenty of questions."

I nodded a bit Dumbfounded by what I just experienced. Leaning down until his face was mere inches from mine. "good, I will be looking forward to it."

chapter 16

_days later__

"We are sending in another scientist in your stead today."

sitting up straighter I looked at kerian concerned. "what? w-why?!"

Flipping a page on his chipboard he finished reading the notes and looked towards me. "samples. We need samples from S-59."

"but– we've already gotten so much information about him the past few days from my visits isn't that enough?!"

kerian sighed before standing up to step over to me. "Ava I understand it's not easy going in there to speak with that thing each day but you've hardly scratched off half the questions on the list I've given you. The director wants results, information. not the musings a monster–

I had turned my gaze away feeling upset over the conversation. Kerian seemed to hesitate when seeing this and waited a moment before suddenly grabbing my face gently.

The action surprised me and I looked up into his eyes confused. "You've done well, but the director is an impatient man... with the knowledge you've shared, we now have a better chance at learning about the creature.

Today we will gather samples from it, and if all goes well then tomorrow you will go back to speaking with the creature. understand? just take the day off to relax and unwind."

I relaxed a bit but still felt like this was a bad idea. "What if he doesn't let you gather samples?"

Kerian was silent for a moment before his hands fell away from my face to return to his pockets. "don't worry, we know what it is capable of now to some extent, we've taken precautions to avoid casualties."

'So they really planned this whole thing out. by precautions kerian must mean they have an evacuation plan to avoid any deaths, I just home S-59 isn't in a bad mood when I go in tomorrow.'

sighing I nodded in understanding. "Okay then I'll see you in the observation control room tomorrow."

Kerian smiled. "then go on and get some rest."

He led me out of his office and I made my way down the hall back to my quarters as I thought about how S-59 might react to another scientist.

'would he tell them off and refuse to cooperate? maybe... but I don't think it's because it won't be me in there, even if I was the one to carry out the sampling, I doubted he would be very happy about it.'

slapping my cheeks I tried to distract myself. thinking about it would only end up making me stressed out, I'll just have to wait until tomorrow to see how things go.

__the next day__

Upon entering the observation control room I was greeted by the sight of the glass walls blast doors closed, blocking out all visuals of the other side.

Many of the scientists in the room looked visibly upset and Kerian was standing by the glass wall, seeming unusually frustrated.

As soon as I entered the room some people went quiet and their gazes turned towards me making me feel nervous. 'What is happening?'

kerian seemed to notice the silence and turned to see me, his frustration seemed to melt away at the sight of me as he quickly walked over. "Ava!" He said my name excitedly.

I couldn't help but look around at the many eyes watching me, and noticed the director wasn't in the room for once.

"what happened?" I asked looking up to kerian. his face fell as he avoided my gaze before taking my hand and slowly walking me to the airlock. "things didn't go as they were supposed to. S-59 turned violent suddenly and a few people were killed, so there's been a change of plans today."

'He turned violent and people were killed?! but he had been so tame the past week! Is that why everyone is looking at me strangely?'

"kerian, I don't understand–"

"Just listen to me Ava," he grabbed my shoulders to make me face him and look up. "You won't be speaking with it today, when you go inside you are to find the sample box that got left behind yesterday, grab it and get out. Do you understand?"

He then pulled out a Ear bud and placed it in my ear. "We have to keep the blast doors closed for now so we won't be able to see what's happening in there, this will help us communicate without using the speakers and upsetting S-59."

my head was spinning with questions as kerian set me up to go inside. "kerian I dont– what happened?!"

"I'll explain later for now just grab the samples and get out as quickly as possible. " He urged me into the airlock and stepped back as the door closed behind me. Turning I looked at him confused and worried as the airlock sprayed me with decom before opening up into the observation room.

"in and out Ava." Kerian spoke through the earpiece.

looking ahead towards the dark mist, it seemed thicker than usual. walking out of the airlock I looked towards the glass wall and immediately my stomach churned and nearly emptied itself.

The remains of at least four guards were strewn about on the floor in front of the wall, blood was smeared across the glass surface and a large crack had formed within the reinforced glass.

"Ava! Please hurry, get the samples and get out before it notices you!" kerian spoke up again.

my heart was now racing and my breathing unsteady as I forced myself to look away from the massacre and towards the dark mist. I hadn't been afraid of S-59 since the first time I entered this room with him. somehow I knew he wouldn't hurt me all those times before but right now? right now I wasn't sure if he would be the same person I had been talking with or if he had become something else entirely.

steeling myself I hesitantly stepped into the dark mist, much more cautious. attempting to be quieter than usual.

I would occasionally see blood splattered on the floor or even a severed limb and bullet casings as I searched for the case but I tried not to focus on them too much.

Eventually I caught sight of the black sample case lying on the floor next to the body of another scientist that was missing their head. almost as if it had been bitten off.

as I took a step towards them It felt as if something moved behind me and I quickly spun around to face it only to be met with the thick dark mist.

I waited a moment, glancing around for any sight of S-59 but found nothing but dark smoke. the hair on the back of my neck stood on end as I felt like I was being watched.

Turning back, I quickly went to the sample box, gathering any of the un-broken, spilled vials strewn about and placed them inside. I paused seeing a good number of the vials filled with a dark viscous liquid resembling blood. only it was gray in color.

a deep growling echoed throughout the room and I looked around for its source seeing nothing. "hello?"

Silence was my only response. "Ava have you found the samples?!" kerian asked.

bringing my hand to my ear to press the button, I responded. "y-yeah i just got them…"

"good. now get out of there quickly before that thing finds you!" some-thing stirred the mist up behind me and I gasped quickly turning to face it only to watch the mist settle back to its original placement.

slowly I stood up and looked around. somehow I could yell he was there, I could tell he was watching, circling.

hesitantly I pressed the button again to respond to kerian. "He already has…I'm going to try talking to him."

"what?! Ava no! get the samples and get out of there!" Kerian snapped but I didn't listen.

staring ahead at the dark mist I could almost make out S-59's hunched over form, staring me down with a snarl.

gulping I gave a gentle smile and reached out one hand for him. "it's okay it's just me, Ava–"

In an instant he lunged forward and I felt myself falling back as claws slashed across my chest. as I hit the ground my ear piece fell out and I heard S-59 screech angrily.

something warm and wet was starting to soak the front of my clothed and I shakily brought my hand to my abdomen to touch it before looking at my hand.

blood covered my palm as my arm trembled and my mind slowly started to register the pain after being sliced open.

four deep claw marks across my front bled heavily as I lay there on my back in shock. a deep growl made me turn my head to see S-59 on all fours circling me with a glare. as he approached I could see dozens of bleeding injuries across his body. He was hurt.

I opened my mouth to speak but was quickly silenced as his clawed hand grabbed me by the neck and squeezed. a choked gasp was all I could get out as I feebly scratched at his hand with my fingers.

I could feel his claws digging into my flesh as he hovered over me growling. I could only stare in horror as the seams of his mouth appeared and opened up to reveal his Maw as he brought me closer.

a strained whimper escaped me as I could faintly make out kerian shouting my name from the ear piece. S-59 practically hissed as he brought my face closer to his mouth and his tongue writhed angrily and trailed across the side of my face. time seemed to slow down as thoughts began racing through my mind. so many emotions washed over me as my life slowly came to its end. anger, regret, sorrow.

I squeezed my eyes shut as tears stung my eyes and I stopped struggling. there was no point. He was going to kill me, and I could do nothing to stop him.

I hated this... I hated being so weak and useless I hated that I never got the chance to make friends and find where I belonged. I hated that I couldn't find someone and fall in love with them.

Even as his breath fanned across my face as S-59 prepared to devour me, I couldn't bring myself to hate him. After all, we were both just prisoners down here. lab rats to be poked, prodded and used however those with power wanted. a choked laugh escaped my lips before I felt the claws around my neck grow tighter, sinking deeper into my flesh.

it's ironic really...opening my eyes i stared at the creature before me sadly. Even though he's about to end my life, I can't help but feel so much sorrow for him. He's suffered so much already and I knew there was more pain and suffering to come. I doubted he would ever be free of this hell he's trapped in...

if things had been different. If I wasn't so weak, would we have been friends? would our lives be less miserable? I wish we could start over. I wish we had more time together, maybe then we both wouldn't have been so lonely.

reaching up I touched the side of S-59's face and smiled as tears rolled down my cheeks... "I'm sorry."

his tongue slid across my cheek, tasting my tears as he suddenly froze and his eyes widened slightly.

my chest hurt and I felt myself losing so much blood, to the point it was pooling on the floor beneath me. my vision started blurring as I watched S-59 pull away from me. his tongue receded as his mouth closed and slowly disappeared. his eyes were wide as he looked at me and his hand around my neck relinquished its hold for him to pull back and look at his bloodied claws.

he seemed stunned by his own actions as he looked at his claws then back to me. "Ava?" his voice was distorted as he spoke in my mind. I can't help but wonder if it's due to my fading consciousness or because of the mix of emotions clouding his own self.

I smiled sadly at him as he trailed his gaze down. "you're back– I'm glad..."

his eyes snapped back up to mine and he hesitated before leaning in to cup the side of my head. "Ava?" He called out, sounding distant as my eyes grew heavy.

"Ava!"

as darkness took over my vision I couldn't help but notice just how comforting it actually felt...

chapter 17

Waking up in my bed felt...wrong.

I knew I was no longer dreaming– no...remembering whatever happened but this reality, if I could even call it that, felt unreal.

lifting my hand up I looked over my fingers that were once covered in my own blood. in that memory I felt myself slipping. felt my life fading away as I lay there on the ground.

all of that was real, it had to be, so how is it that I'm here now? why is it that I didn't remember any of that before?!

I covered my face feeling overwhelmed and confused by the flood of information. why– how am I still alive? What happened to me? What is happening to me!?

How are there suddenly so many gaps in my memory? I can't remember anything before a few weeks ago, it's all so vague like everything is blurred out. Climbing out of bed I stumbled over to my bathroom to look at myself in the mirror.

pulling up my shirt I looked over my chest that should've had four deep jagged marks across it but there was nothing.

hot tears started reaming down my face as I sobbed and laughed at my predicament. Am I losing my mind? maybe none of this is real, it's all just some kind of hellish nightmare? Am I even awake right now?

"Ava" a familiar voice spoke up in my head making me freeze and go silent. I could see mist seeping through the doorway from my sleeping quarters.

hesitantly I moved into the doorway to look into the room. sitting on my bed was none other than S-59.

I was speechless seeing him once more only this time it wasn't some dream or memory... at least i think?

looking over his form I couldn't help but notice just how tired he seemed. "y-you..." I breathed.

"You are...confused," He said quietly.

His response took me by surprise and I stepped closer to him. "Are you...real?" reaching out to touch him he flinched away from me and didn't respond.

I wasn't sure what to say and could only stare at the being before me in uncertainty. moments ago I had witnessed him nearly kill me. 'What if– what if he did? am I even alive right now?'

"ha– haha!" I laughed, taking the creature by surprise as I backed up into the wall before sliding down to the floor. "this is all so fucked...my brain is just one giant shattered mirror right now with so many missing pieces."

S-59 just stared at me, not saying a word.

I grabbed at my hair, everything felt like it was falling apart. no, everything was falling apart, there was no question. about it now.

"I can't even yell at you or be angry because I have no clue as to what is happening to me. hell I don't even know if I'm hallucinating again or if I'm even alive! for all I know this is just some sick twisted afterlife! After all, how can I even be alive right now? you attacked me!" my voice was laced with so much frustration and I could see S-59 lower his gaze in shame.

"So you know about that..." he said quietly to himself. He seemed upset, almost as upset as I was over the whole situation. but more than anything, he seemed exhausted, if I didn't know any better I'd say he was the one being tormented by strange visions, nightmares, and insomnia.

We both sat there on opposing sides of the room. me staring at the creature before me, him looking to the ground, slumped over.

"I shouldn't be here, I should be around you like this. but I don't know what else to do..." he murmured quietly. I watched S-59 closely confused by what he meant.

"I don't understand you... I don't understand anything." I replied.

he sulked even more, his tail practically limp as it lay sprawled on the ground beside him. "I'm sorry."

he's sorry? Thinking back, I distinctly remember s-59's words to me back when we first spoke. He was angry when I apologized for something I had no control over... if he's apologizing now does that mean he's responsible for all this?

pushing myself up to my feet I moved to stand in front of the creature. "if you really are sorry, if you're responsible for all of this..." he lifted his head to gaze at me. "they help me understand! put an end to all of this!"

his claws gripped the side of my mattress tightly. tight enough that they tore into the fabric, shredding the cloth.

"I cant."

Balling my fists I grit my teeth and shoved him back. He didn't resist at all or retaliate and merely watched me. "why!? why can't you! why are you tormenting me like this!" fresh tears burned in the corners of my eyes as I sat there with my hands on his chest straddling him as he leaned back against the wall.

clawed hands came up pulling me against his body as one cradled the back of my head and one spanned across my lower back. "I do not wish to torment you. I do not want you to hurt… but I do not know what I am to do. I am as lost as you are." He whined.

I relaxed into his hold, unable to stay angry with him no matter how much I wanted to.

"if you will allow me I can make this all stop and make everything return to normal–"

pushing away to sit upright I looked into those saddened white eyes before me. "You mean make me forget all of this? make me forget about you and everything that has happened…"

He was quiet once more and I took that as his answer.

"I don't want to forget. I'm tired of being in the dark, I want to remember. everything."

"if you remember everything. nothing will change…" He sulked, turning his gaze downward. touching the side of his face with my hand I made him look up at me. "You don't know that. Staying like this is worse than trying to continue on like all of this is normal... this is all wrong, it's all messed up and twisted and I need to know why!"

"Is this truly what you want?" S-59 asked.

steeling myself I nodded confidently. "yes."

He looked at me for a long Moment before narrowing his eyes. suddenly he flipped us over so that I was now pinned to the bed with him hovering over me. his large Frame hardly fit on the small twin bed making him seem all the more larger.

"I'm sorry. but I will have no part in it."

'wait what?!' My eyes widened as the seams of his mouth appeared as his tongue snaked out to run across my neck and the side of my face.

"I must continue down this path, continue to push through this maze alone until it's time. I won't let history repeat itself..."

I tried to push s-59 off to no avail as he was so much bigger than me and he refused to relinquish his grip.

"What are you talking about?! what are you doing?!"

suddenly his tail snaked up my shirt before tearing the fabric clean off making me squeal. "Please do not tell me to stop, do not resist. I know I am undeserving of this, that I should be more patient but I can hardly control myself sometimes–"

his tongue slipped down between the valley of my breasts before curling underneath one and coiling around it. "I crave to taste you, to feel you...I want us to become one again."

my face was flushed red and I felt a strange heat pooling in my belly as he continued to lick and tease my breasts with his tongue. a deep chitter escaped his throat as one of his hands moved to grab the other, his palm far larger than the small mound on my chest.

"w-why are you doing this?" I managed to ask with a breathless sigh.

"because. I need you...do not worry, you will not remember any of this by the morning." He responded as I felt his tail brush between my legs. "I fix everything...make you forget everything."

my eyes widened and I squirmed to break free and get him off me. "no, no! you can't–!" I was suddenly silenced as his tail suddenly wrapped around my mouth silencing me and he narrowed his eyes.

"this is for your own good."

A familiar hiss drew our attention and looking over we both saw none other than S-32 standing on my desk puffed up with a glare as he growled and hissed at S-59.

a deep angry bellow sounded from S-59 as his tongue retreated and his mouth closed up. He loosened his grip on me, narrowing his eyes towards the dimensional cat.

"YOU." he practically snarled at the cat.

taking the momentary distraction. I pulled his tail away from my mouth and shoved at him with my free hand. "get off!"

The bite mark on my hand suddenly glowed and S-59's eyes widened before a sudden flash of light appeared from my palm as he was suddenly thrown back, violently hitting the wall.

I flinched back in shock seeing such a large creature like him go flying and looked down at my hand in bewilderment.

With a groan he sat upright getting back to his hands and knees as S-32 jumped on my bed standing between us. He was no longer hissing or growling but still continued to glare at the much larger creature before him.

"Ava..." he said my name as he stood up to his full height.

"Stay away from me, subject-59." he seemed to visibly recoil hearing me say that and just stared at me.

"I mean it. If you're not going to help me remember then I want you to keep your distance and do not touch me or else!"

he didn't say a word or move from his spot, he simply watched me. slowly his body seemed to droop and I watched as even more dark mist filled the small space surrounding S-59 until all I could see was his glowing white eyes. slowly they closed, disappearing from sight before the mist vanished taking him with it.

with him gone I felt the tension in my body drain away and my determination turned to confusion and guilt. I looked to my hand then back up to s-32 who turned his head to face Me before giving a small innocent 'mew' like he hadn't just practically scared off a giant monster.

I felt guilty, I didn't want to hurt s-59 and I didn't think he wanted to hurt me either. He seemed just as lost and afraid as I am, but he's refusing to help me, and I can't fix this if he won't cooperate! I grabbed at my head feeling a headache coming on. "Am I even doing the right thing? Am I making things worse?!"

a gentle headbutt on my arm and distorted meow was enough to pull my attention away from those thoughts as I looked up.

S-32 purred happily as he stood before me. "you helped me again...you're the only one who's willing and able to help me remember aren't you?" He stepped closer before crawling into my lap and bumping his head against my hand, urging me to pet him.

I stroked the strange cat's head and closed my eyes before laying back in my bed feeling a war of emotions flooding my brain. everything that just happened, had led me to one conclusion. I need to recover my memories if I want to fix everything. all of them.

lifting the cat up over me i opened my eyes and looked into its glowing orbs. "please, one more time. show me why everything is like this, show me what happened. show me so neither of us have to suffer anymore."

with a deep breath I closed my eyes letting the familiar feeling of darkness take over.

I need to know the truth.

(note: absolutely loving the theories guys!!! keep em coming! so fun to see what you guys are thinking! I love you!)

chapter 18

"M iss, Ava?"

gasping I opened my eyes to find myself lying in a hospital bed with kerian at my side. "You're awake. I'm relieved." He sighed before leaning back.

I could only stare at the ceiling and blink, confused. looking around I realized I was in the medical ward of the bunker. Two nurses were busy cleaning up across the room as Kerian sat In a chair next to my bedside watching me.

as one of them brought over a clipboard for him he looked it over before waving them off. Both nurses were quick to leave the room leaving us alone together.

I couldn't help but stare, unable to form any words or even comprehend what was happening.

"You seem confused. I assure you, that you are not the only one experiencing that feeling. Can you tell me what happened? you were sent into the observation room a few days ago to retrieve some samples, do you remember that?" He questioned.

I tried. I tried to think back to what happened, tried to remember anything past me entering the containment cell but my head started throbbing and everything was too blurry. I grabbed my head whining when the pain seemed to only get worse the harder I tried to remember.

He looked over his clipboard and flipped to the next page reading some of the notes and data on the sheet with great interest. "After losing contact with you we had to wait three days for s-59 to calm down and return to its vault. when the room was cleared of the dark mist we found you lying on the floor sleeping peacefully.

dragging you out of there you were quarantined and we ran tests to determine what might have happened. you seemed to have suffered from blood loss despite the lack of injuries." kerians blue eyes moved back to me as I slowly lowered my hands from my face and inevitably clutched my chest.

"you don't remember any of it do you?" I looked at him confused as he stared at me, intrigued by the way I kept my hand on my chest. He then started pacing back and forth muttering to himself.

"you can't conjure up the memories of what took place in there but sub-consciously you still have those memories locked up somewhere deep in the back of your mind." He leaned in, Brushing my cheek with my fingers as he looked at me and smiled. "fascinating."

shaking my head and blinking I tried to understand what kerian was saying but none of it made sense.

"i-i don't understand...what is happening?" I asked exasperated.

he looked me over, seeming to think about how he could explain the current situation. After a moment he sat on the edge of my bed. "we believe you're suffering a concussion. possibly due to s-59 lashing out. you might have fallen and hit your head while attempting to retrieve the samples the other day, hence why you can't seem to remember anything."

something felt off about kerians explanation but it was the only thing that even remotely made sense.

"For now you are to spend the rest of the day here to recover until we are sure there's no changes or sudden declines in your health. If you remember anything at all or start to feel strange, tell the nurses to summon me immediately. I do not wish to lose you to some head trauma while under my care..."

hearing that last bit made my heart skip a beat. Does Kerian really care for me that much? his hand brushed the side of my cheek briefly, before he got up, returning to his usually callous self. "I'll check in on you tomorrow and we will decide what to do then. I feel sorry for sending you in there while the creature was unstable, I should have waited but I was desperate to get those samples under the director's orders. I hope you will forgive me...for now just rest, Ava."

With that kerian turned to walk out of the ward leaving me alone in my hospital bed.

I feel uneasy and overall uncomfortable being here by myself. it's also clear that I'm missing something but what is it? Why can't I remember what happened? Did I really just hit my head and black out—but kerian mentions me being in there for three days... How is that even possible?

glancing around I saw no one in the room besides me. Climbing out of bed I decided to slip on some cheap sandals that were often given to patients, and made my way into the hall. looking both ways I didn't see anyone around who would try to stop me so I made my way to the observation room.

Once I got there I was disappointed to find the door locked, and I had no clue where my badge or belongings even were.

Cursing under my breath I realized it was pointless to even be here. s-59 was probably locked away in his vault so I wouldn't get to see him. my eyes moved to the vault door beside the observation room. that was connected directly to the hallway.

stepping over to it I gazed at the massive vault door with the number 59 painted on its surface.

he may have lashed out but I don't think he would have purposely tried to hurt me...right?

Thinking back to all my interactions with s-59 he may have been moody at times and perhaps a bit aggressive when we first interacted but he never truly hurt me. He was always so gentle.

closing my eyes I remembered a few days ago when I was in the observation room with him, how we talked about things we wanted. He was intrigued by my glasses at the time, finding it odd how I needed them to see properly...

~~~~

"This flimsy trinket is what enables you to see? then are you blind without them?" He lifted them off my face with her tail while sitting before me and I quickly tried to grab them back only for him to lift it higher above my head.

"no! I can still see, I just can't see that well! my vision is bad so I can't see things at a distance very well, it's all blurry. These make it so I don't have to squint or have whatever I'm reading directly in my face!" I reached for my glasses helplessly as he held them high above my head.

After a moment he moved closer to where his face was inches from mine before narrowing his eyes and tilting his head. "Can you see me like this?"
~~~~

smiling awkwardly I put my hand on his face and gently tried to push him back. "yes I can but I'd prefer not having you in my face!" I laughed and relaxed as he finally handed back my glasses.

"human bodies are strange, your eyes are forever damaged then? What if you lose that trinket?" He questioned.

"Then I'll need to get a new pair." I cleaned off the lenses with my shirt. "Trust me I wish I didn't have to have glasses, they can be a hassle to deal with sometimes but it's just part of life like many other unfortunate things."

he eyed me curiously as I placed my glasses back over my face. "What else do you wish you didn't need to deal with?"

shrugging I sat back down beside S'59 against the wall. "I wish my co-workers were nicer. They are like high-school bullies and often make my life miserable any way they can."

S-59 was quiet as he looked ahead at the mist before us in thought. "You know with all the stuff I've had to go through down here. there's been times I wish I could just leave and forget about all of it.

This seemed to catch his attention as he looked towards me. "You wish to forget everything?" His voice almost seemed saddened as he spoke up and I looked up to see him watching me intently.

"n-no! not everything! I mean...there's a lot of stuff that's happened that I wish never did, things that I regret doing most the memories I have here are not ones a person would hold dear, I think the only memories I would keep if I had the choice would be the ones of all our previous conversations. it's actually quite nice to be able to talk to someone, I've grown to consider you my friend."

"friend? I've heard this term but never fully understood it... Can you explain it to me? What are 'friends' ? What do they do?"

"A friend is someone who you enjoy spending time with, they usually make you laugh and smile and would never try to hurt you purposefully. friends are people you can confide in so you're less lonely."

"So we are friends." he mused quietly.

~~~

"yeah. we are...aren't we?" I looked at the vault door before me, receiving nothing but silence for my answer.

s-59 isn't like jade or the others, he wouldn't hurt me purposely. I trust him. kerian has to be mistaken about what happened I mean no one else saw it right? The only one who was there was s-59. He's the only one who knows what really happened.

—2 days later–

"that close to the airlock if you can and stay on high alert if anything seems off with the creature you should exit immediately. I will be standing near the door waiting." kerian said.

I nodded in response and glanced at the newly repaired glass wall. I think I briefly remembered it being cracked before but the memory was still so fuzzy.

I looked past the glass into the lit up observation room. slowly the vault door creaked opened and the red lights outside

flashed in warning as the gap widened.

me as well as everyone else in the control center waited for the mist to pour into the sterile room, for the lights to go out and for all visuals to become
~~~

distorted but as seconds ticked by neither the mist nor S-59 appeared from the vault.

"he's not coming out?" I asked quietly to myself, concern taking over my emotions. taking over. Usually as the vault door opened the entire room would flood with mist but it seemed to only barely trickle out of the doorway.

kerian scanned his keyecard unlocking the airlock for me. passing through the airlock I kept my eyes glued to the open doorway of S-59's vault, only briefly glancing back at kerian as he watched on.

seeing how S-59 wasn't emerging I decided to approach the doorway. It was strange being in the open room with the lights on and everything I felt exposed almost.

"hello?" I called out to the darkness but got no response, surely he knows I'm here, why is he hiding?

"S-59?" I asked questioningly.

"leave." was the only response I got from the darkness. 'He wanted me to leave?'

"why do you want me to leave? Can you come out? Can we talk?" I asked a bit confused. as I stood in the doorway I couldn't help but fidget feeling numerous eyes on my back. It was quite uncomfortable standing in the open for all the scientists to gawk at.

"No! leave!! go away!" He angrily snapped and despite not being able to see him I took a step back. There was a small ache in my chest from him snapping at me but I was more confused than anything.

'Was he angry at me? Why would he be though? Did I do something wrong?'

I was at a loss for words as I stood there staring into the darkness. "Ava, come out for now. we can try again later." kerians voice came in over the speakers. I looked between the glass wall and the vault a few times unsure before deciding to give s-59 some space. I left the room with my head down in disappointment.

'Maybe he's just in a bad mood... I'll give him some time to go back to normal.'

Kerian seemed curious about the strange behavior as well but we didn't speak of it, he just gave me instructions to wait. we could try again tomorrow and he would have someone keep an eye on the room over night to see if s-59 will come out.

somehow I had a feeling he wasn't going to...

—3 days later—

I exited the observation room once again. feeling dejected. glancing back through the glass wall, the room was still devoid of s-59's presence. This was the fifth attempt to try and get him to come out or even speak. and the fifth failure.

Even with no one around and the vault door wide open he has refused to come out or interact. He's been more isolated than he ever has before and I feel like I'm to blame. even when I attempted to enter the vault at one point he pushed me out and got angry.

kerian elected that I don't try entering his space and risk getting attacked so any and all progress with research has been halted.

I've been more stressed out and worried about s-59 than getting on the director's bad side. kerian has been mostly quiet about the situation but I could tell he's also bothered by it. I can only imagine how much pressure he's under to get things back in order, but what could we do? S-59 has refused to say anything more than "leave" or "go away".

sighing I looked towards kerian who was staring at the vault door quietly. he briefly glanced towards me and the rest of the staff in the room.

"everyone is dismissed for the day... I shall call upon you should there be any changes and we shall arrange a schedule for 24/7 observation.

I watched as everyone packed up and left the room but kerian stayed to peer into the room.

as if sensing my eyes on him kerian spoke up. "Miss Ava, go get some rest for the time being. I shall alert you of any change."

I hesitated before nodding and leaving the control room. glancing back at the glass wall one last time I could only wonder why things turned out this way.

stepping into the hall my mind came up. with various theories as to what might have happened or how I could have upset him but nothing made sense. 'maybe I should let it be for now? and give him the space he needs. That's all I can do anyway.

passing by various people in the hallways I made my way back to my quarters. My room was dark and cold, making me all the more achingly aware of how lonely I felt, not being able to talk to anyone. kerian was nice he cared for me but he was also a very busy man and I didn't want to be a burden.

glancing down the hallway I decided not to linger too much on my worries, stressing out wouldn't help anyone, I needed to destress and take some time to think everything over thoroughly. Maybe I've missed something.

I've just been too distracted and overwhelmed with recent events to remember it. Taking a swim always helps me to unwind and clear my mind, so why not use this time to have some fun?

grabbing some clothes I made my way to the pool area in hopes of finding some sense of tranquility. unaware that a set of eyes were watching me.

<h1 style="text-align:right">chapter 19</h1>

Stepping into the locker room I was pleasantly surprised it was empty, meaning one of the pool rooms might be empty as well. It's always nice to have the pool to yourself so you can swim laps and just relax.

grabbing a towel I made my way to the other rooms and found a vacant one. changing the sign to occupied I went in and closed the door behind me.

stripping out of my coat and uniform I turned up the heating dial on the wall and bungled into the water.

The muffle of the pool blocking out any other sounds filled my ears as the water encased me making me feel not only comforted as it surrounded me but also Clean.

as if my worries were being washed away, rinsed from my skin like specks of dirt. I stayed under, swimming across the room to the other end of the pool before surfacing as gasping for air. grabbing the ledge I leaned against it before angling myself to push away and float on my back back towards the other end.

closing my eyes I thought back to all the times I attempted to speak with s-59 in the past few days. 'I can't understand him, why hasn't he come out? Is he purposely avoiding me? or perhaps it's because of the sampling?'

When I asked kerian what happened before I came in to retrieve the samples he merely said s-59 got angry and ended up killing the guards and scientist present in the room. 'I didn't think he would simply lash out at anyone for no reason so why did he snap? He's been so gentle and calm with me! he's not one to attack without reason– right'

I could only stare at the ceiling while floating on my back in the pool. 'Is he just angry? even so he's never isolated himself to the point of refusing to leave his vault...' they even tried forcing him out by sending his food in through the observation room instead of the feeding chute connected to his containment chamber.

I felt bad seeing the kind of mush they were feeding him was little more than animal remains. they didn't even bother to process the food in any way. they left the bones, fur and all. but I suppose that's how they feed all the carnivorous creatures here.

it's not ideal to have to get food shipped to us constantly to feed the anomalies or even ourselves. Most of the food in supply is stuff that has to be frozen or is a staple that can last an extended period of time. I miss being able to have fresh meals, I'm sure he does too.

Now that I think about it, I hardly know that much about him or his past. He rarely talks about himself and has never made mention of any others like him or where he's from. I heard a rumor about him being discovered in a long lost cave that was sealed but how could he have survived down there without a food supply?

"Well, well, so this is what you were up to while we've been working our asses off," a familiar voice spoke up. gasping I spun around to see Matt leaning against the doorway with a smirk on his face.

"w-what are you doing here?!" I quickly moved over to the edge of the pool to climb out.

"oh I just happened to see you in the hall and was curious where you were rushing off to. should've known that while jade and

Sarah have been stuck taking care of your workload. You were off playing house with the doctor and taking a dip in the pool!" He mocked.

"You followed me? a-and I didn't ask to be put into the s-59's testing group, or to have them do my workload, these are all choices made by the director!" I replied. Climbing out of theMatt. I moved to the bench beside the door to quickly grab a towel to cover up in. Even if I still had my undergarments on, I don't feel comfortable being so exposed in front of matt.

he hummed watching me with a gleam in his eyes. "Now that I think about it, I'm pretty sure I have a good idea as to why the monster is so interested in you…" he said, pushing away from the door he moved closer to me and i started backing away.

"What do you mean?" I asked nervously.

"First off, what if I told you I could get Jade and the others to leave you alone? we will stop bothering you completely and start acting like normal co-workers."

my eyes widened as I looked at Matt, surprised. "y-you would do that?"

"yes!, but not for free of course. jade really has it out for you, convincing her is gonna be a drag and take a few days but I can assure you she'll back off after a few days if I tell her too. with her off your back I'm sure not only your life but your job will be hell of a lot easier to do and manage down here." He waved his hand around.

I almost couldn't believe what Matt was offering. a chance for the harassment to stop and for me to lead a somewhat normal existence in the bunker? That's something I've wanted since their bullying started...

but even so, I knew better than to simply take his word for it, he wouldn't just offer me salvation so easily. "What exactly do you want in return?"

looking down at me that same glint in his eyes returned as he grinned and stepped even closer.

"I want you to strip. completely."

The blood immediately drained from my face and I backed up into the wall.

"what?! no!--"

Suddenly lunging forward Matt grabbed my wrists pinning my arms against the wall, making me release the towel. "what? Am I not good enough for ya?" He laughed as he practically pressed his body against mine pinning me to the wall completely as I tried to push him off.

"I heard the other guards talk about how they dragged you out of that monster's cell with your clothes practically torn off! That's probably why it hasn't killed you yet! your just a play thing to it–"

"stop it, get off me!" I struggled desperately as mat leaned in and tried to latch on to the side of my neck with his mouth. feeling a shot of disgust course through my entire body I twisted in his hold and pushed him back as he bit at my skin leaving a mark.

"Come on this is why the doc's so obsessed with you too isn't it! he's probably already seen it all!" As I managed to slip one of my hands free he grabbed the front of my bra and pulled. it snapped, exposing my chest and I immediately shrieked before covering myself with my free arm.

"stop being so stubborn!" He said, sounding a bit frustrated as he grabbed my wrist trying to pull my arm away. was about to scream for help only to suddenly get knocked down as matt's fist collided with the side of my face.

as I hit the ground I felt the burn of the floor scraping against my arms and knee but it was nothing compared to the throbbing pain across the side of my face as my vision swam from the sudden hit.

"You are really going to make me work for this aren't you!--"

"enough!" another voice snapped from the doorway and Matt instantly froze before turning to face the new figure. glancing up I saw kerian standing there with a look of annoyance as he stared Matt down.

"Leave before I have you reprimanded. " He warned.

Matt scoffed at me before making his way out leaving me on the floor as kerian stood in the doorway.

slowly I pushed myself up, covering myself with one arm as tears burned my eyes. Kerian stepped into the pool room grabbing my discarded towel before handing it to me.

I quickly took it to cover my body as I trembled and tears streamed down my face. He stared at me for a long Moment not saying anything before offering his hand to help me to my feet. I took it, getting to my feet as he stepped back and put his hands back in his pockets.

"Try to dress yourself the best you can and come with me." he ordered before turning around and walking out the door. I felt frozen as my mind reeled over what just transpired. as if on autopilot I put on my uniform before dragging myself out of the pool rooms to the showers where kerian was waiting.

He led me back to the observation lab and neither of us said a word to one another along the way. using his keycard he opened the door and I stepped inside. walking over to one of the consoles he pulled out a chair for me. "sit so I can look at your arms and face."

shuffling over I sat down in the chair with my head down. kerian crouched down before me and lifted my chin, turning my head to look over my aching cheek before gently turning over my arms to look at the bloodied scrapes left behind from my fall.

"You shouldn't let this happen again, you're lucky I was passing by when I saw that guard follow you into the pools. I was hesitant to check on you at first... seems like it was a good thing I did or else you might have suffered more than just a few scrapes and bruises."

instinctively my arms moved over my chest and I squeezed my legs shut as kerians words made me shake in fear over what might have happened. if he had never come in to stop Matt. if he had never seen us—

fresh tears spilled from my eyes as he watched me for a moment, quietly.

someone stepped into the lab carrying a clipboard and called for kerian.

"Sorry to bother sir but there's an urgent matter that needs your attention on floor two!" the person said.

Kerian sighed as he stood up and looked in their direction. "I'll be right there." With a nod the person left, shutting the door and the doctor glanced back down at me. "Stay here, I'll be back in a few minutes to patch you up."

when I didn't respond he seemed to hesitate and looked up towards the glass wall across from us.

"I'll be back shortly." turning away he left the room leaving me alone in the lab.

looking up I saw kerians ID card lying in the console before me, and looking past it I peered through the glass wall to see S-59's open vault door.

unsure as to what I was even doing I grabbed the card and walked over the airlock. using kerians ID I opened the door and stepped inside. the tiny decam room hisses and I sniffed. wiping my untouched cheek with the back of my hand as I waited for the second door to open.

a swirl of emotions were raging through my mind As it finally did open and I walked in, headed straight for his vault. anger, disgust, hurt and betrayal. all those feeling twisted in my gut nearly making me stumble as I finally came up to the open vault.

"s-59?" I asked meekly. "c-can we talk?"

no response.

I hesitated, staring at the darkness before me as my tears blurred my vision. "why– Why won't you say anything?" I asked quietly. "why won't you speak to me or even show yourself?"

silence filled the room as the dark mist swirled before me and I felt my chest constrict further. "Why me? if you were just going to push me away eventually then why choose me!?!" I shouted, taking off my shoe to throw it into the void. "Why would you interact with me and let us grow close!? why would you let me think we're friends, just to shut me out and abandon me!?" I screamed as a sob escaped me and I slumped to the floor. "Why did you lie to me by saying you'd protect me?"

pulling my knees to my chest I sobbed and hid my face in my arms as my body trembled and I cried.

The dark mist suddenly seeped into the room around me gliding across the floor. it was nowhere near as thick as usual and hardly obscured the view of the opposing room, but that didn't matter since no one was around.

s-59 silently stepped out of the vault as the lights.in the room blinked before shutting off completely. noticing the change in lighting I lifted my head to see him standing before me solemnly.

After a moment he crouched down on his haunches In front of me and reached out to pat my head. "I am sorry Ava. I am not your friend..." he moved his gaze away, seeming saddened by his own words.

wiping some tears from my eyes, I looked up at him confused. "why? why aren't we– why can't we be friends?"

s-59 shuddered, pulling his hand away from me and I watched in surprise as he pulled back and glanced at his claws. "I hurt you Ava. This is why I wanted you to stay away. I am undeserving of your friendship..."

looking to the floor I thought back to everything kerian said when I woke up, about S-59 attacking me and lashing out but I thought it was strange how I awoke with no injuries. even my head didn't hurt like it should've had I actually hit it.

"Why can't I remember you hurting me then? Why were there no in-juries?"

s-59 was silent for a long Moment as he gazed at his hands. "I hid any evidence of what I had done."

"hid?" What does he mean he hid the evidence? turning his gaze back to me he seemed to practically lower himself even closer to the floor.

"I was ashamed of what I did. scared even too. it's the only reason I wanted you to stay away. I didn't wish to hurt you again, this is why I did not wish to interact with you further."

"but I'm fine now, I'm not in pain because of you or anything like that, so why do you have to push me away–"

s-59's growled suddenly before pushing me back onto the ground and hovering over me. The seam of his mouth appeared but he did not open it as his chest heaved and he dug his claws into the ground.

he gently reached out his claws barely Brushing against my neck as his entire body shuddered and seemed to recoil slightly.

"because Ava, I nearly ended your life. I am not your friend, I am a monster."

chapter 20

"It's not safe for you to be around me. That's why I've pushed you away. why I've refused to show myself... when I saw what I had done to you. while you lay there dying right before my very eyes, my entire being twisted, my heart ached and I was overcome by such a disgusting feeling unlike anything I had ever felt before."

s-59 lifted his hand to his face clawing at the seams of his mouth. "It was worse than any pain I had ever experienced. it reached so deep it was as if my very being was getting torn apart. the anguish the guilt...it was all too much for me. I felt weak and useless!"

he whined painfully as he pulled his hand away from his face to then place it over my chest. "Even when I fixed you, kept you from dying, it still hurt, like I had been mortally wounded. it lessened over time but each moment I thought of how you would react when you awoke, each moment I thought that you would come to despise or fear me, that ache grew worse.

I made the choice to make you forget about the experience because I didn't want to feel that pain anymore. I hurt you, and then I manipulated your memories all for the sake of making myself feel better...yet even now I still feel it, like a phantom pain, forever haunting me, reminding me of my mistake! I am undeserving of your friendship Ava."

he finally pulled away to sit back on his haunches as he grabbed at his head. "I am a monster." a pained sound came from his mouth as the seams disappeared and he kept his eyes on the floor.

sitting upright I stared at the creature before me in bewilderment. After a moment I got to my feet and he hesitantly lifted his head only to be shocked when I hugged him, wrapping my arms around his neck. "You are wrong. you feel pain, remorse, fear, guilt and shame. you make mistakes— you care! That's what separates you from a wild beast!" He sat there frozen as I hugged him tighter and tears welled in my eyes.

"You are more human than half the people in this forsaken bunker! you are a far better friend than anyone could ever hope for..." his tense posture seemed to relax as his tail curled around my feet and he closed his eyes.

We stayed like that for a long while before I eventually pulled away, feeling exhausted. S-59 opened his eyes to stare at me as I lowered myself back down to my knees. "feeling better?" I asked with a half smile.

"the pain has lessened... Your words and touch have lifted the weight upon my body." tilting his head at me he then reached up towards my aching face and ever so slightly grazed his claws over my skin making me flinch away and grab my arm.

his eyes widened at my reaction and moved between my arm and cheek. "Your skin is changing color, and your arm is bleeding? did i–" his entire body seemed to flinch back as he recoiled, fearing he was the one responsible for my injuries.

"n-no! it wasn't you! I was– I got hurt before I even came in here..." my voice trailed off and instinctively my arms wrapped around my body as I lowered my head. 'I shouldn't have come in here like this, I shouldn't have shouted at him and gotten angry when he had nothing to do with this.'

"Ava...how– who did this to you?" He moved closer, seeming reluctant to touch me while also wishing to get a better look.

"It's fine, it's not a big deal! it was an accident!" I tried to reassure him. He had enough to deal with, the last thing I wanted was to burden him with my own problems. "I can hardly feel it so please don't worry about me."

I clasped s-59's giant claw with my own hands and he seemed to squirm slightly as his tail whipped around, seemingly bothered by the fact I was hurt. it made me smile knowing that such a creature could care about someone like me but it also made my chest ache in guilt for making him worry.

"I do not like your dishonesty, you are in pain yet you try to hide it."

"I know, I'm sorry. It's just what humans do, it's...a defense mechanism I suppose."

"I shall not hurt you again Ava! I don't want to make that same mistake again– no. I won't make it again. you need not try to Shield yourself from me." He stumbled over his own words.

It was so strange seeing s-59 who once seemed so closed off and angry, desperately trying to help me. "I'm not shutting you out and I believe you wouldn't hurt me. this is just something neither of us have control over, and I don't want you to stress over such. I'd rather just forget about it all and move on."

he was silent as he sat back and contemplated something. "Will you at least tell me why it happened? Why you were hurt."

I looked at S-59 sadly. 'Does he blame himself and think it was because he wouldn't talk? This is precisely why I don't want him to worry about it but I suppose there really isn't any way around it. Avoiding the subject completely isn't an option.'

"It wasn't anything to do with you– one of the Guards that tends to...'bother' me sometimes ended up walking in on me in the pool room."

"and? He did this to you? Why, though, why attack you? you are harmless."

turning away feeling my gut twist in disgust I took a shaky breath. "He was trying to get a look at me without my clothes...I told you how clothes protect us to some extent. He was attempting to force me to remove my second layer, even when I told him to stop..."

S-59's entire body went stiff as he heard my explanation and he just stared. "It had nothing to do with you, I promise so please don't blame yourself thinking that I got hurt because you were being quiet."

he seemed to think to himself before reaching out to gently take one of my arms and examine my injuries. "What is a promise?"

relaxing some I watched as he inspected my arm. "a promise? well the best way I can describe it is something you can't break, it means you will do right by what you say and if you don't... well bad things could happen. breaking a promise means breaking someone's trust of you and lying. it's not good so you have to take promises seriously."

he narrowed his eyes before leaning down, closer to me, bringing his face closer to my arm. his eyes narrowed and the seam of his mouth appeared, opened just barely enough for his long tongue to slip out.

as he tried to lick my arm I pulled away out of reflex. "w-what are you doing?!" I asked, a bit shocked.

"helping, healing." He pulled my arm back, holding it much more firmly in his grasp as he dragged his tongue across the injury and I whined in turn from the burning sensation it left behind.

"I don't think you should–"

"watch." he cut me off as he repeated the process and pulled away. Looking at the cut across my forearm, I watched as the reddened skin around the injury turned to normal and the scrape started to heal right before my very eyes.

eyes widening I looked up to his face and he seemed pleased and I think maybe even mimicked some kind of smile as he looked at me. "h-how?"

"I regenerate faster than humans...I've noticed that one time when I injured one, they took weeks if not months to come back and they still weren't completely healed. When I am hurt badly by your weapons it takes a few days if not hours to heal and I usually lick my wounds to speed up the process. I did not know I could speed up a humans regeneration until..." his voice trailed off and he grew quiet. but I already knew the answer.

"until you hurt me..." I finished for him as he started to mope once again.

"yes..."

As we waited, the scrap on my arm completely healed without even leaving a scar and I hesitantly touched the area and smiled when I felt no pain. "amazing." I breathed.

"Ava, can I make a promise to you?"

looked up curiously I found him staring at me still with a somewhat saddened expression. "What promise?"

he paused, thinking of what to say as his tongue retreated but he kept his mouth slightly parted. "a promise to do anything you ask of me. to keep you happy, safe, and never hurt you. I make this promise to you and will forever keep it!" He finished a bit enthusiastically.

"if that's what you want then go ahead..." smiling I rubbed my eyes and chuckled a bit, feeling tears forming again. "You are so strange."

he tilted his head watching me as I tried to compose myself and keep from crying again. "I am?"

"yes! Yes you are! it's almost hard to believe any of this is real, that you are real!" I laughed.

"Why is that? I am here, am I not? you can see me and feel me, does that not show that I am real?"

laughing again I shook my head. "yeah that all helps me to know that you are but what I find unbelievable is just how sweet you actually are! if someone had told me four weeks ago that I would be sitting in here with you, laughing and having a chat with you like it's just another Saturday afternoon, I would've called them crazy!"

S-59 chittered in response as he sat before me with his tail curled around behind me. "I understand what you mean, I would not have been very...nice. four weeks ago."

"I guess this just goes to show how much our relationship has improved!" I beamed happily"

"indeed." He responded before taking my other arm and extending his tongue to lick at the other scrape.

"you don't have to do that– these injuries aren't that bad."

a huff escaped his mouth as he continued. "I do not like seeing you hurt, and the scent of your blood is also displeasing."

smiling I let him continue. "alright."

Once my arm healed he moved on to my leg which I had to pull up my pants for before he tore them. it was strange having a giant creature licking you but I wasn't going to stop him now, beside after the day I had I was too exhausted to argue.

as I waited for the injuries to completely mend and s-59 checked over me for more I yawned, feeling my eyes growing heavy.

leaning over he licked my bruised cheek and I closed my eyes whining a bit, as I felt myself becoming more and more sluggish by the minute. "can I just...stay here for a bit? I don't feel comfortable leaving the lab."

"I do not mind..." he responded as his tongue retreated and his mouth hid away.

I moved to lay on my side beside him on the floor and He tilted his head watching over me as I curled up and started drifting off, uncaring of anything other than feeling safe.

S-59 watched quietly before looking towards the glass wall across the room. through the thin haze of mist he could see the doctor watching them from the doorway that led out of the control room.

a growl rumbled in S-59's chest as the doctor simply walked away with a smile.

chapter 21

Snarling and shouting startled me awake as I opened my eyes to find myself lying on the floor.

"get back or we'll shoot!" a man shouted.

"back away from her now!!" another followed only to get an angry screech in turn. I had to cover my ears from the sound and look around to get an idea as to what on earth was happening, but I was hardly prepared to see what was unfolding right in front of me.

S-59 was standing over me in a defensive posture with his tail whining around violently behind him as four arms guards surrounded us with their weapons aimed at him.

"move away freak!" another shouted only for S-59 to open up his mouth and hiss in warning making the man jump back a little.

w-what is going on?! What's happening?! looking around confused I noticed kerian and a few other soldiers on the other side of the glass wall, watching everything unfold.

Once kerian noticed I was awake and alert he rushed over to a console to activate the overhead speaker. "hold your fire!! ava! get away from subject-59!" He sounded and looked worried as the speakers stuttered no doubt from S-59s dark mist that was slowly growing thicker by the second.

"what? what's happening?!"

snarling, at another guard who got too close I heard S-59 speak to me in my mind. "These humans suddenly entered the room with weapons and began threatening me!" He hissed out that last part opening Maw before lashing out and knocking two of the guards away with his tail and tackling one, screeching in his face.

the fourth man shot off a warning, passing him off even more and redirecting his attention to him. The man pinned beneath S-59's claws couldn't move his arm or gun and started screaming as his grip tightened and claws dug into his skin.

"permission to shoot!!" the last standing guard shouted while aiming at the monstrous creature before him.

eyes widening I got to my feet and jumped between them. "no!! don't shoot! please someone just tell me what is happening!" I pleaded, looking towards kerian.

leaning down to speak into the microphone again, his voice filtered in through the speakers. "afternoon leaving you alone in the control room I came back to find you in the observation area unconscious with S-59 standing over you, I'm not sure how you got in there but I immediately called security to get you out and the subject became aggressive."

so this is all just a misunderstanding they think he hurt me! "Please lower your weapons so he won't hurt anyone!" I looked towards the other two Guarda as they got back up and aimed towards s-59 who in turn looked their way and snarled.

turning around to face him I got in his line of sight. "don't attack! and let him go!" I pointed towards the pinned soldier.

turning hisnhead down to look at me he growled. "they showed aggression first–"

"you promised!"

his eyes widened as he looked at me for a long moment. "Please I don't want anyone to get hurt." slowly the tension in his form. faded and he released the pinned guard enabling one of the others to pull him back as they kept their guns trained on him.

S-59 seemed less than pleased with the guards as he glanced at them then refocused his attention on me. the seams of his mouth disappeared as he stepped back, retreating into the mist.

"stand down, and fall back." Kerian ordered.

"Thank you." I smiled at S-59 as he attempted to make himself less noticeable by those watching. Turning back towards the glass wall I saw Kerian waiting with an expression I had never seen before. He must've been worried sick, seeing me in here with S-59.

turning to walk towards the airlock, s-59 moved around to trail after me. "Ava–"

I stopped to look at him as he stood off to the side. "It's okay they aren't going to hurt me and you. I'm going to go talk to them so just stay back for now. and please no more killing people."

He seemed hesitant to let me leave and followed behind on all fours until I got to the airlock and stepped through. glancing back to see him watching he soon disappeared into the mist as it took Over the room.

Upon stepping out of the airlock I was greeted by kerian who immediately stepped forward and grabbed my shoulders to look me over. "Are you hurt? Did it do anything to you?" He questioned.

"no, no! I'm fine! he wouldn't hurt me!" I waved my hands.

"how did you get in there– why were you in there?" kerian asked sternly.

I quickly turned my gaze away in shame. "Well, you kinda forgot your ID card..." I pulled out his badge from my pocket and he took it back.

After a moment of silence kerian suddenly pulled me into a hug, shocking me to my core. "Ava please tell me you didn't enter that room in an attempt to hurt yourself or take your own life." He whispered quietly and my eyes widened.

'Was that why he seemed so panicked? That's why he summoned the guards!? because he thought I was hurt– that I tried to kill myself!?'

bringing my hands up I hesitantly hugged kerian back feeling guilty for making him worry. "no! it was nothing like that, I just– I was so confused and scared..."

"I understand, I knew I shouldn't have left you alone, but I wasn't sure what to say or do...I only brought you in here because I figured this was the best option. After what happened I guessed that you wouldn't have wanted others in the medical ward to gawk or stare. so when I came back and saw you in there"

I relaxed a bit in his hold, understanding him a bit more. 'Kerian is often cold and stern, I thought he just didn't like me.but perhaps he just struggles to express himself and his feelings...' hearing him explain himself I felt closer to kerian than I had before, he's just another human that makes mistakes sometimes and stumbles at times.

"I promise that wasn't my intention when I entered the cell." I reassured.

"good," kerian sighed before looking towards the glass wall where a pair of glowing eyes were carefully watching from the other side. "I'm not sure what I would've done had something actually happened to you…"

__1 week later__

"okay I get that the mist is like a part of you but where exactly does it come from? I don't get how you're able to just magically conjure more up at will, it doesn't follow the laws of science–" I looked up at S-59 to find him staring ahead, through the smoke seemingly watching the other humans working on the other side of the glass wall.

following his gaze I looked between him and those in the other room, lowering the notepad in my hands. "something wrong?"

he suddenly flinched before looking back at me. "you've been awfully distracted today. I know these questions are probably boring but it could be beneficial for us to learn as much as we can about you."

"I apologize I did not mean to get distracted. I've merely been thinking."

"thinking? about what?" i asked curiously.

S-59 merely hummed in response as his eyes narrowed. "That human with the mark on their face…who is he."

Glazing towards the glass wall i could see Kerian speaking with another scientist while looking at some notes, and S-59 was watching him closely, actually, now that i think about it, any time kerians in the lab lately, S-59 seems tense and more preoccupied watching them than interacting with me. "Kerian? Is that who you're talking about?"

He was silent for a moment, thinking to himself. "Has he hurt you before?"

I was a bit surprised by the question and decided to put my notepad off to the side. "No! Not at all! Kerian is probably the only human being here whos treated me well."

S-59 huffed before returning his full attention to me as the mist grew a bit thicker. "He lingers around you too much, i do not like it."

'Ah thats why hes so interested in kerian.' i felt a small blush heating my cheeks. "Well thats because..." my voice trailed off awkwardly, 'how am i supposed to explain this to him? S-59 probably has no idea what love or any of those kinds of feelings are like, heck i dont even know if he knows anything about romance. Im not even a hundred percent sure if kerians feeling for me are as deep as my own! Its all so complicated!'

"Because?..." he pushed, moving closer to look at my face.

"because kerian and I are really, really close. like our relationship and all that is a bit more complicated. He's a bit more than a friend."

"more than a friend?" He asked Skeptically.

'gods am I glad no one from the other room can hear this.' "Yes, sometimes when two people form a strong bond together after spending lots of time with one another, and if they both feel the same for each other they can become more than friends. This means they can spend even more time to- gether, and often seek each other's company when they make one another really happy." He listened intently as I tried to explain it some more.

"They are usually comfortable with each other and don't have to feel so protective around one another unlike how they do with others. Being a couple means keeping each other safe and happy..." I smiled just thinking about it.

'sure me and kerian haven't expressed our feeling but I know he cares about me he's made that clear. the only reason I haven't talked to him is because of work, I don't want either of us to get into trouble after all he's technically my boss.'

S-59 chittered and ended up bumping his head against my forehead lightly. "Does that mean we are more than friends?"

my head snapped up to S-59's face as he gazed at me thoughtfully. "huh?"

"all those things you said about feeling safe, wanting to be around each other and caring for one another– it is describing us is it not?"

my eyes widened and my cheeks turned ever redder as I thought about it. me and him?...more Than, friends?

"your face is changing hue's does this mean something?" He purred as his tail flicked around behind him.

We were abruptly interrupted as the staticy overhead speakers turned on and kerians voice called out to me. "Ava that's enough for today, please proceed to exit the chamber for debriefing."

S-59 all but snarled as he stood up and looked towards the speaker on the ceiling. forgetting about our previous conversation I gathered my notepad and such then got to my feet.

"Sorry, I'll be back again tomorrow and we can finish going through the rest of the questions, there's only a few left so if we finish quickly then we can talk about whatever you'd like afterwards!"

"..." he followed me as I walked to the airlock across the room but before I could step out of the thick mist, S-59 blocked my path getting up in my face. "Ava, I wish for more than friendship..."

I blinked A few times both surprised and confused. "I– uh...what?"

the speakers came up again with kerian speaking up. "Ava please proceed to the exit..."

"I have to go–"

S-59 practically whined before pacing momentarily. "then you must come back, tonight"

"I can't do that, I don't have access, I'm not supposed to be in here or even in the control room. I'll be back tomorrow then we can–"

"That's not enough! please Ava, I need more time with you."

I looked between S-59 and the door unsure what to say or do. no one outside could hear us talking about this so I wasn't going to get in trouble for speaking with him about such but I wasn't sure if what he was asking was possible. guards would be posted outside the control room and I don't have access. not to mention kerian might get worried or upset if I do something like this.

squeezing my notepad I chewed on my lip before lifting my head to face him. "I'll try to come back later tonight but I can't guarantee anything."

S-59 chittered happily before moving out of the way on all fours, giving me access to the exit. "I shall be waiting for you." His shoulder brushed against mine and I glanced back at him once more as he sat and waited almost excitedly.

returning my attention forward I stepped inside the airlock and sighed. 'why do I have a bad feeling about this?...'

chapter 22

'I must be out of my mind. I mean, what was I thinking? promising to go back and see him after the night cycle starts?! I'm just asking for trouble! What would kerian think if he found me sneaking in to talk with him?'

groaning I buried my face into my pillow As I lay in bed sulking over my predicament. ever since I finished my debriefing with kerian and came back to my room I haven't been able to stop thinking about everything S-59 said to me earlier.

He was such a strange being and hard to understand at times. Usually he's composed and keeps to himself wanting little more than to be left alone. He's been documented as a very solitary creature and he's proven that with the way he often tries to hide from everyone. He has no choice but to deal with me since it's either I constantly come back or they will send other strangers to.

strongly though as of late he's become more open with me, and quite curious. Today being a perfect example. He seems to be just as interested in me as I am with him. when I talked about myself and my relationship with kerian he perked up quite a bit and listened intently, I was shocked when he asked to be 'more than friends' as well... I'm not so sure he quite understood what I meant when I was explaining everything.

I think I almost freaked out when he asked for such, it had me seeing him in a whole new light. S-59 was kind to me and gentle, he seemed to genuinely care and looked forward to spending time with me, going completely against everything we know about him and his solitary nature.

it made me realize there was more to him than just some scary creature with violent tendencies. He has a heart and soul and feels pain and grief just like anyone else.

people would probably think I'm insane for caring about such a being..but is it wrong of me to think he could also feel something like love and affection?

a small mew sounded from across the room and my eyes shot open as I slowly lifted my head and looked towards my door to see a spectral looking cat with glowing eyes standing there watching me. it mowed again and ever so slightly tilted its head to the side as we gazed at one another.

"subject-32?" I asked questioningly and the nearly transparent cat sat down, curling its tail over its feet as it stared at me.

this was...odd? sitting up, I faced the strange specter before me. subject-32 had a tendency to break free from its vault and roam around the bunker so seeing him walking down halls and such was never that surprising and considering its nature he was never perceived as a danger so I have no reason to be afraid, but I was confused as to why he had come into my room when he had never shown any interest In me before.

holding out my hand I let him sniff my fingers as one might do with any other cat and he happily obliged before nuzzling my palm and getting closer, rubbing up against my leg. I smiled and petted him as he purred, pleased with the affection.

"could you not find anyone else to give you pets?" I chuckled as he mewed.

protocol for 32 usually included ignoring the creature and notifying the capture team of his escape so they could return him to his vault, but that hardly works when he just walks right back out of his cell to find someone willing to cuddle him.

He was such a docile being so most of the time people just let him be. He came to this facility years before me but supposedly he wasn't always a cat. He held a different form before, that of a deer. He only seemed to change forms when one of the lab assistants' cat passed away.

Most researchers speculate he changed forms as a way to help the lab assistant to overcome the grief of their loss, that was years ago...he still holds the form of a cat even though that person is gone now.

"such an odd creature..."

The audible cue for the night cycle went off and the lights in my room dimmed signaling its start. by now, most of those within the bunker would be asleep in their quarters.

"Guess that's my cue to go...you should head back as well, the director doesn't like having you roam around no matter how harmless you are." I got up from my bed and grabbed my lab coat, slipping it on before walking towards the door. waving bye to s-32 I closed the door behind me as I stepped into the hall and headed for s-59's containment.

as I approached the observation control room I saw the two night shift guards standing out front and tried my best not to seem suspicious. walking up to them they looked at me questioningly and I cleared my throat. "I've been assigned to check in on the subject tonight. I shouldn't be in there for more than an hour." I lied.

Both guards glanced at each other and didn't budge in the slightest. "It was a request made by kerian, he's making me do it since I'm the only one, subject-59 will show himself to." at the mention of the doctor they moved aside letting me scan my badge on the door and enter.

'Sorry kerian!' I mentally whined as the door automatically shut behind me. I felt bad using him as an excuse and I really hoped I wasn't gonna get him in trouble, but it was the only thing I could come up with.

Upon entering the control rooms my eyes wandered towards the glass wall where the blast shield was closed for the nightly lock down. Stepping over to the control console I disengaged the lock down and the blast doors opened up for the observation room giving me a full visual of the room.

stepping over towards the glass wall all I could see on the other side was dark mist filling the room. "Ava, you came." an all too pleased 59 spoke up inside my head.

"Yeah I did but I can't stay too long." I put my hand to the glass as he appeared from the mist and sat right in front of me.

"You cannot enter either, can you?" He asked, sounding a bit disheartened.

"Unfortunately no, I don't have access to the doors." I sat down in front of the glass and watched his shoulders sag a bit, but after a moment he perked right back up.

"no matter, I am merely glad to speak with you without watchers present." 'watchers? he must mean the other scientists...'

"Why did you want me to come here after dark anyways?" I asked curiously.

"I wanted to speak more with you. and speak freely with one another, having you come into my containment chamber simply to ask those useless questions the watchers give you is less than appealing but now...we can speak more about things we both want to speak about."

"Well, what do you want to talk about first?"

S-59 stared at me for a long moment before turning his gaze away. "I'm unsure."

covering my mouth with my hand I held back my laughter to the best of my ability but a few giggles slipped through, and 59 just watched. "I'm sorry! I don't mean to laugh!" After a moment I managed to calm down. and compose myself. "Okay, how about we start with something simple such as where you came from?"

Subject-59 was silent for a moment as he thought over the question. "will you be telling the other watchers what I tell you here?"

"no, for now I'm not here as a scientist, I'm just here as a friend, I'm only going to ask about things that I want to know that I am curious about. you should do the same! if there's anything we don't feel comfortable talking about then we can just skip it...okay?"

he seemed to visibly relax as his eyes closed before he looked up towards the ceiling.

"my earliest memories are that of looking up and seeing the stars... I found myself doing this quite often. I don't remember where I came from or how I came to be. I spent the days sleeping within caves and the nights roaming, exploring or hunting. humans back then often were afraid of our kind and did not bother me as much as they do now."

"your kind?" I asked questionably, and he then turned his attention back to me.

"yes. creatures and beings like me that are– abnormal... in human terms. I never cared to interact with humans much and merely watched from afar but others would seek them out for numerous reasons."

"but they said you were found in a cave sealed off for hundreds of years! if that was true that means you were around people of ancient times! how is that even possible?"

"There used to be many creatures like me roaming the world before, before I slept The last thing I remember was feeling this need to find somewhere dark and isolated...it was this deep urge to burrow and hide away so that I may sleep like the creatures that hibernate only it was such a strong instinctual need that it felt as though i was in a trance. I was not the only one to feel this however, many others felt the same, even those that lacked wit. so I went as deep as I could go, curled up within a small corner and closed my eyes. when I awoke, your people found me and I was dragged here into this prison. In the past few years I've seen how much humans have developed but much of it is still hard to understand."

'He hardly knows much more than the scientists who found him... what could've caused him to go into such a deep sleep for so long? Was it some kind of evolutionary preservation? were they sensing some kind of change in the world that could've been harmful to them?'

thinking it over I still couldn't wrap my mind around it. 'He says there's others like him. Does that mean all the creature's captured by the acorn foundation are somehow connected? but that's impossible right? none of the documented anomalies have any sort of resemblance! some of them aren't even animals, they are plants.'

shaking my head I returned my attention to s-59. "Can you tell me more about 'Your' kind? perhaps how they interacted with humans?"

humming to himself S-59's tail flicked absently. "some hunted humans. others seemed to be in their company. I once saw a creature like myself tie their life to a human before. I never understood why they did so although I was curious, I never got the chance to ask."

"What do you mean by tying their life to a human?"

S-59 grabbed at their head, seeming a bit frustrated and confused by the question. "it is hard to explain in words. The best way for me to explain is that they gave part of themselves to the humans so that they could stay with each other. it was like they had bonded their very essence, in all my years of existence i had never seen anything like it. Even now I still do not completely understand it."

"bonded essence?... you were around for hundreds of years so what stopped you from asking?"

turning his head to look at me his expression quickly turned grim. "because after they bonded, one of our own kind hunted them down and devoured them..."

- -

chapter 23

‘They were hunted down? but why...’

"i- don't understand why they were hunted down, and how this bonding thing works. How do you give a price of yourself away? what does it do?"

59 merely looked across the room thinking to himself. "I believe it has something to do with our cores..." he finally responded after a while.

"cores?" I questioned.

"yes... each and every one of us monster's have cores, it's what separates us from you humans and other animals. we cannot die unless our cores are severely damaged or destroyed. Our cores are what separates us and ties us together. There are two types of cores, one from plants and one from us creatures. They are the source of our abilities. I suspect the creature who bonded to a human somehow gave part of his core to them."

my eyes widened as I listened to 59's explanation. 'How have we never discovered this yet?!'

"You're telling me these cores are in every single creature? but that doesn't make sense. Why haven't we ever discovered them before?" S-59 stared at me for a long moment.

"you humans already have."

'what?...'

He lowered his head as his eyes narrowed. "this is something that I've observed in the time I've been trapped here. Each creature's core is different and often lies somewhere in their body that is hard to reach or where you would not expect this is to prevent others of our kind from killing us as easily." S-59 explained.

"I believe the watchers have been attempting to find my core, each time they come with their equipment they poke and prod at me, taking blood and other parts from my body as if they are searching for it. just like that day– when you got hurt."

"Why would someone want your core?" I asked, a bit worried.

"we monster's will often devour one another's core in order to grow stronger, as for humans, there's a number of reasons they might want a demon's core. my vegetative abilities aren't very common, you could imagine what they might do with something like that..."

"thats– I don't know what to say..."

"if they were to destroy my core or take it I will not survive the process..."

my hands fisted my lab coat as guilt tightly gripped my heart. 'How long would it take for them to find it? would they really kill him by removing his core? Was that their plan all along? Kerian wouldn't do that right?'

he must've seen the concern on my face as I struggled with my inner thoughts. "Do not worry too much Ava, it will not be so easy for them to find my core."

turning my head back to him I looked at S-59. "It is safe for now." I nodded, trusting his words.

"But that means you can't stay here forever, eventually they will figure it out and I fear the director will use that to his advantage."

We were both silent after that statement knowing that it was inevitable. should his secret be discovered he would be put in danger. I felt so stupid and blind thinking he was just some wild creature that suddenly appeared out of nowhere. him and all the others roamed this earth before us, they were part of its ecosystem. they didn't just appear out of thin air they had always been here. and yet here we are treating them as aberrations.

a meow from behind me caught my attention and I lifted my head before turning around to see subject-32 phasing through the wall.

suddenly s-59 got onto all fours and the seams of his mouth appeared as he glared at the smaller creature. "Why is that thing here!?" He sounded almost panicked.

"whoa whoa it's okay!" getting to my feet I walked over to 32 and picked him up in my arms. the cat happily purred as I pet its head and looked back to 59.

he just snarled in turn stepping away from the glass wall. "hey, it's okay! he's harmless!" I tried to persuade but he didn't look convinced.

"harmless to humans not to the rest of us..." He continued to growl as 32 just simply stayed in my arms purring and enjoying the moment.

I looked at the spectral cat confused as to how he could be harmful to other creatures, he's always been so docile.

"isn't he like you? another creature with a core?"

S-59 huffed and settled back on his haunches keeping a close eye on 32. "It is, however it does not die like the rest of us. its ability to phase through things makes it nearly impossible to kill and extremely dangerous. should that thing choose to, it could pass through another's body and take their core with ease.

eyes widening I held out the cat in front of me and stared at it as it just happily meowed and stared back like it wasn't a monster killing entity. "who would've thought…" pulling him back against my chest he continued to purr as I pet his head and scratch his chin.

"but he seems so innocent and cute!"

"They only seem that way because they love human affection and they feed off of it." I stopped mid-stroke on the cat's head.

"What do you mean feed off of it!?" turning his gaze away, S-59 seemed to sulk a bit, seeing me give the cat head pats.

"Those creatures take the form of lost loved ones of both monsters, humans and animals alike. It used to be their way of luring in prey to consume but their time with humans made them more docile. Now they do it as a way to comfort humans and animals while they grieve, like a doe that's lost its fawn. They take the form of the child and stay with the unfortunate parent and act like the missing animal to gain their affections until the animal moves on. Most animals will eventually realize that creature is not one of their own and leave it behind, that is why it likes humans most. Because humans understand what it is and therefore they do not shun it. Some used to pray to the creature's as if they were some kind of spirit." S-59 scoffed.

I looked back at 32 who rested happily in my arms. 'He takes the form of those people cared about, helping them overcome their grief so he doesn't have to be alone?'

"that's actually kind of sweet…"I smiled and rubbed the cat's chin before settling back down and sitting before the glass wall. "You just want someone to care for you like they care for their own, don't you?"

Subject-32 curled up in my lap closing its eyes to sleep as I continued to stroke its fur. "I suppose that's why you don't leave the facility either? because you get to be around so many people."

Subject-59 watched us carefully before turning his eyes to the floor in deep thought. "If I escaped… I wouldn't be able to see you again, would i?"

I stopped putting 32, letting 59's words sink in. seeing his reaction it was clear he wasn't too keen on the idea of not seeing me again. my eyes moved around the room as I wondered what either of us would do once he was gone.

"Probably not…the world has changed since you last saw it. things aren't as –green– as they used to be, humans practically took over and have been destroying everything. But in the past few years, more and more of your kind has started to emerge, so you shouldn't be too alone out there!"

I smiled at him trying to give him something to look forward to. returning his attention to me he seemed surprised by this information. "more of my kind has emerged?"

"Yeah, I mean more creatures with cores, I've not really heard of any that look like you but there've been numerous reports of such creatures coming out of hiding or being discovered in the past 5 years, they've caused quite a bit of panic and havoc on the surface because before then we never knew you all existed. That's why these facilities were built, to capture and contain them so we could study and better understand your purpose.

S-59 sat up straighter and his eyes widened as he looked towards the ceiling as if realizing something. "I see...so that's our purpose." He mumbled quietly.

looking at my watch i noticed nearly two hours had passed since i came here and i silently cursed. "I gotta go." picking up 32 I got to my feet, pulling S-59's attention back towards me.

"I'm sorry we can't talk more but if I get caught doing this I might get in trouble." walking over to the console, I noticed 59 watching me intently as I prepared to close the blast doors. "I won't tell anyone about what you told me, okay? and I'll be back soon." I gave a small reassuring smile to him but he didn't seem too enthusiastic.

"Ava, do not leave this place without me."

guilt clawed at my heart as my smile fell. He worries I'll leave him behind to rot. Why did things have to be so complicated? Why did he have to be locked up like some wild animal in this facility? taking a deep breath I tried to put on another smile. "I won't, I promise." He visibly relaxed before nodding and stepping away from the glass wall.

closing the blast doors I watched as his form disappeared into the mist. once the doors were sealed. I set subject-32 down on the ground and crouched, hugging my knees as tears welled in my eyes.

32 meowed questioningly, and rubbed up against my leg as I held myself back from crying. sniffling i took in a shaky breath and reached out to petW32's head. "What am I going to do?."

____3 days later____

stepping into kerians office I set down the notes I took on his desk and sat down with a sigh, closing my eyes.

moments later kerian came in and looked me over curiously. "You seem tired, have you been sleeping properly?" He asked as he moved to his desk and sat down, grabbing the notes I brought in.

"kind of? Some nights I do, others I don't."

kerian hummed as he listened then reached for a clipboard to look through it. "You only started having trouble sleeping after the sample incident, interesting... any strange dreams?"

"no, nothing like that." I replied quietly while staring at my hands.

I couldn't stop thinking about s-59's situation. it kept me up at night and continuously swam in my mind throughout the day. He didn't deserve being locked up and experimented on. He wasn't a threat that needed to be contained; he hasn't done anything to warrant such treatment!

"ava." kerians voice snapped me out of my thoughts and I looked up at him as he stared at me. "Is something wrong?" He set down the notes and clipboard, giving me his full attention. What should I say? should I tell kerian what 59 told me? Would he understand? If Kerian learned of all this then maybe we could work together and eventually convince the corporation that S-59 wasn't a threat and that we shouldn't keep him locked up. There's plenty of other creatures that are dangerous and unruly that they can test on but he doesn't deserve this!

I was silent as I thought about how to tell kerian and what to say.

"what if everything A.c.o.r.n. is doing is wrong? I could understand that we need to know more about these creatures to keep people safe but not all of them are dangerous– they should all be treated like they are monster's."

Kerian listened closely and leaned back in his chair.

"take subject-32 for example! He's harmless! what if we've been misjudging them and treating them horribly for no reason! I mean, there's evidence showing they've been here far longer than us so that means at some point humans had to have lived with these creatures in peace! If that's true then maybe we can do it again! we could learn so much more from them if we can gain their cooperation–"

"Ava." Kerian cut me off and I looked at him surprised to see the stern look he was giving me.

"I understand you don't completely agree with Acorn's methods, but we could never live in peace with these monster's. they are far too dangerous..."

"But–"

"Our entire purpose revolves around containing and learning about these creatures because they pose a threat to the human race!"

"What if you're wrong!?"

"Their entire purpose is to destroy us!" Kerian snapped back and I looked at him shocked.

with a long exhausted sigh kerian ran his hand over his face. "fuck, I shouldn't be saying any of this to you..." he paused for a moment before looking back at me.

"Ava, these creatures do not care for humans, do not let yourself be swayed by anything they say or do. Your job is to learn as much as you possibly can from them, that is all."

I balled my fists as I glared at kerian from over his desk. "Why? why can't you accept that we might be wrong about them?"

Kerian stood up from his desk with a dark look in his eyes as he stared me down with an unreadable expression. "because I know their true purpose.

and I refuse to sit by playing house with these creatures when they could snap at any moment. I will not wait for them to make their move, because if we do, then it will be too late..."

(note, I have requested a commission for subject 59 so hopefully we will get a visual of our shadow man soon!)

chapter 24

- -

Lying in bed all I could do was stare mindlessly at the ceiling. sleep was nearly impossible for me at the moment with my insomnia and my mind was filled with the constant worry that S-59's life was in danger.

Kerian was of no help either, he wouldn't listen to reason or look at the situation any other way, to him these beings were dangerous. He's fighting a war that hasn't even started, and 59 is suffering for it.

he's been experimenting on, for the sake of finding weaknesses and a weapon. I thought kerian would've at least listened to me but he completely disregarded everything I said. it hurt being pushed away by him, like with all the others. any other time we are together kerian makes sure I'm well taken care of and seems to genuinely care but today?... He was colder than usual.

maybe he's right? Maybe I'm mistaken about all of this? S-59 awoke from his slumber violently. He had killed and attacked dozens if not hundreds of scientists and guards up until we met. He is dangerous.

just because he's friendly with me doesn't change the fact he's a danger to others... he's an intelligent being as well, so what were the chances he was doing this pond purpose? it's not impossible, he could easily be lying and trying to deceive me. It's happened before with other subjects.

maybe it's just me, maybe I'm just the biggest fool in the world! I covered my face with my arm, feeling so utterly useless and distraught.

I'm torn between Kerian and Subject-59.

moments passed as the clock in my room ticked and I silently moped about the situation.

a subtle meow caught my attention and slowly I moved my arm and sat upright. sat on my bed next to me was Subject-32 with a feathered toy in his mouth.

standing up he stepped over and dropped it onto my lap before nudging my hand for pets. "Did you just bring me a toy from your vault?"

he meowed happily as I stroked his fur and scratched his chin. "I never knew you could phase through walls with objects. I guess I'm learning something new every day." I chuckled.

looking at 32 I couldn't help but think about everything I knew about him. He used to prey on other creatures as well, no doubt that included humans at some point. He was once dangerous, just like 59.

my hand stopped stroking his fur and s-32 turned to look at me before meowing questioningly. Even though he is merely a monster disguised as a cat to fool humans– I can't bring myself to hate him, not like kerian.

32 has never done anything wrong, he merely wants someone to keep him company. How could anyone justify treating him as a monster? grabbing s-32 I pulled him closer holding him against my chest and he snuggled up against me purring happily.

He changed. He became docile and learned to live among humans! So why can't the others? Who's to say 59 can't change as well?

I relaxed while holding S-32 in my arms and smiled down at him, petting his head once again. "Thank you." 32 merely tilted his head to the side and I quickly stood up, setting him back down on my bed.

looking to the wall I could see my Calendar hanging there. It's October 3rd, the next interaction I'll have with S-59 isn't for another two days. 'It's not soon enough.'

looking back to 32 who was patiently waiting, I gave him a small smile. "wanna play?"

———

Outside of the observation control room the two guards on duty stood vigilant while keeping watch, and stared straight ahead at the wall across from them.

hearing a meow down the hall they both turned their heads to see none other than subject-32 striding towards them with something in his mouth. glancing at each other both guards focused on the spectral cat as it strode past them without a care in the world carrying one of their keycards.

"hey, isn't that–" both guards looked at eachother again before quickly rushing after S-32 trying to stop him. "Come back!" they shouted as he phased through a wall into another room.

peeking around the corner I watched as the guards ran off after s-32 and smiled. calmly I walked towards the observation control room and let myself inside. The blast doors for the glass wall were closed meaning s-59 wasn't locked in his vault. 'perfect!'

as s-32 poked his head through the wall beside me I crouched down and gave him some pats on the head as he handed off the security card. "just keep them preoccupied for a bit, okay?" he purred happily before disappearing through the wall again.

looking at the card in my hand I took a deep breath and stepped towards the airlock. The security team that keeps guard here has access to the observation room but not the vault. for once I'm glad kerian leaves s-59 in the observation chamber to watch sometimes overnight.

stepping into the airlock I waited for it to do its thing before stepping into the dark misty observation room. I glanced around before stepping further inside.

After a moment I sensed his presence behind me before he even spoke up in the back of my mind. "ava?"

turning around I smiled at the confused dark creature before me as he stood there with his head tilted and his eyes half closed. "Sorry, did I wake you?"

he crouched down moving closer before circling around me on all fours. "It is fine, but I did not expect to see you here– why are you here?"

"I needed to come talk to you, to see you." He briefly stopped in his stride before continuing all the way around until he was sitting in front of me.

"Is something wrong? Are you hurt?" he asked.

smiling, I reached out both hands towards him. "no nothing like that, come here for a moment."

S-59 hardly hesitated before approaching on all fours and stopping less than a foot away. cupping his face I ran my thumbs over his cheeks before moving one hand up to pet his head. his eyes closed as he relished In the feel and I could help the grin that spread across my face.

'Kerian is wrong about him and I'm going to prove it. I'm going to prove it to everyone.'

"59?" He hummed in response, enjoying my touch as I ran my fingers through his hair and over his horns. "Do you trust me?"

his eyes opened once more to gaze at Me as he leaned into my touch. "yes."

"good... I want to help you get out of here, it's going to take some time and will probably be uncomfortable for you at first but I believe we can do it if you truly trust me."

S-59 was silent as he gazed at me, more alert than before. "I am listening" was his only response.

nodding I took a subtle deep breath. "I need you to show me your core."

his eyes widened as he suddenly flinched back and stared at me like I had just slapped him. "Why." He responded in a dark tone.

"It's okay! I know what you're thinking! I know your core is delicate and isn't something to be toyed with! I'm not going to do anything with it, especially right now. this is why I need you to trust me..."

S-59 was silent as he observed me. "I would never hurt you just as you wouldn't hurt me." I stepped forward to touch his face again as he seemed to think over it.

"I want to get you out of here, but the only way we can do that is if we can convince everyone you aren't dangerous!"

"Ava..."

"I know it sounds crazy but look at 32! He's able to freely roam because he isn't a threat. if we can at least get you out of here then–"

"Ava." He cut me off, narrowing his eyes and my smile fell. his large clawed hand came up to grab my wrist as he gave a sigh. "You are wrong about me ava... I am dangerous. I Did hurt you. The Humans are right not to trust me."

he lowered his head and I felt guilt pull at my heart. "No. I'm not, I'm not wrong about this, about you. I know I'm not..." cupping his face again I leaned in pressing my forehead against his. "You never meant to hurt me. I know you didn't, and I trust you! So please, trust me. believe in me, I don't want you to rot away in this prison for the rest of your life. you deserve so much more."

"You are too pure for this world..." he mumbled quietly.

he closed his eyes leaning into me as his hand cupped my face as well. After a few moments he pulled back and proceeded to stand up, towering over me. "I will show you my core, and allow you to touch it but first there is something you must do for me in return."

I was momentarily surprised but quickly shoved that feeling away and replaced it with determination before nodding. "I'll do it, I'll do anything."

S-59 chitted as he leaned in, cupping my face as he loomed over me. I had to tilt my head back just to look at him as he brought his face close to mine and stared deeply into my eyes.

the seams of his mouth just barely cracked open as his tongue slipped out and gently teased my lips, startling me slightly. a rumble sounded from 59's chest as his tail curled around us.

"Do you trust in me ava?"

swallowing the lump in my throat I replied. "yes." his tail then suddenly coiled tightly around my body, but not tight enough to hurt me.

as he leaned in nuzzling my shoulder I could only stare up at the ceiling. his tongue extended further and glided across my neck sending shudders all throughout my body.

"If I show you my core, I want to be able to see all of you. if I let you touch it, then I want to touch all of you. If you trust me then I shall trust you." He pulled back, letting his tongue retract as he cupped my face in his clawed hands once again and looked down at me.

my heart was racing as I stared back at him in bewilderment as heat flooded my cheeks. "You give me your everything Ava, and I shall give you mine... are you prepared to do that for a monster like me?"

he brought his mouth close to mine once more. the tip of his tongue slipped through the seams once more and licked across my lips before slipping into my mouth and practically coiling around my own tongue.

heat pooled in my stomach and I closed my eyes as a small moan escaped me.

s-59 bellowed as more of his tongue glided into my mouth and his tail held me firmly in place. "allow this monster everything and I shall give you anything you desire." his voice rang in my head as I started to feel dizzy.

slowly he retracted his snake-like tongue from my mouth, and I gasped, opening my eyes just in time to see the seams of his mouth disappear as he pulled away. his tail released me and he stepped back a few paces as I stood there trying to collect myself.

I clutched at my chest as my heart raced faster than ever before and a blush adorned my cheeks. S-59 watched on, crouched in the mist as it slowly surrounded him.

realizing he was starting to disappear I stepped forward and reached out to him. "w-wait!"

he disappeared into the dark mist leaving me disoriented as I looked around for him.

"I will be waiting for you...Ava." his voice faded in the back of my mind and I watched as the mist started to clear, allowing me to see the rest of the dimly lit room. The only darkness left was that of s-59's vault door. the pitch black void stared back at me as I stood there struggling to comprehend what I just experienced.

backing away I hesitantly left the room. I needed to prepare for what needed to be done. I had already made up my mind about getting subject-59 out of here, I held no doubt in my mind that it needed to be done.

kerian is wrong about him, I know he is. and if I must go behind his back to prove it then I will.

Subject-59 will be free.

chapter 25

(note for the meme above: so I saw this post where it said "when the cat
is more diabolical than The BBEG" And Immediately thought about
subject-32! had to share!)

__2 days later__

opening my eyes my eyes were greeted by the sight of my feet and the drain
cover on the floor. I watched mindlessly as water sprayed down all around
me and funneled down the drain as I stood underneath it.

I absently brought my fingertips to my lips as I stood in the shower letting
the water soak me.

I could still taste him.

it's strange how sweet he actually is...

never would I have expected for things to turn out like this, never did I
think I would be so enamored by something that isn't even human. Part of
me thinks this is wrong, but it feels, right?

closing my eyes I leaned my head against the wall. I was so set on this plan before but now I'm feeling nervous. Is it because I'm afraid of being caught or because I'm so conflicted with how I feel over the whole situation?

if I do this I'll be turning my back on kerian completely, I still care for him but we just can't seem to reach each other. Up until now all my efforts almost seem one-sided. He's shown that he cares for my wellbeing and I've tried to give him time, give him space to open up to me yet in the past two months I've gotten nothing.

on the other hand S-59 has completely opened up to me. He's nowhere near as reserved as kerian and has proven his affection and shown his feelings. hell he even kissed me! We are so different from one another yet he's made me feel cared for, safe, and wanted.

I hadn't noticed it at first because I thought kerian was the one standing in my sights but slowly I've come to realize just how different they both treat me. I can't wait for kerian to open up to me, I'm tired of it.

we can't see eye to eye and I can't go along with their plans to hurt the subjects, especially 59. not after all that he's done for me...

I've already told myself I was going to see this plan through to the end. If exposing myself to 59 is what it takes to change things around here then that's just what I'll do. I'm not afraid of him, I know he won't hurt me, I trust him! Now I just need to prove to him that he can trust me back.

I care for him far more than anyone could imagine, he's been so gentle and kind. He truly cares for me, so won't let him continue to suffer.

taking a deep breath I turned the knot for the shower off and wrung out my hair before stepping out and drying off with a towel. walking into my room I patted my hair dry and grabbed some clothes from my dresser.

slipping on my undergarments first I Proceeded to dry my hair then finished dressing myself. Once I was ready. I headed for the observation lab. immediately upon entering infound kerian and the other onlookers standing by the glass wall.

Everyone seemed to be fussing and trying to figure out why S-59 had refused to leave his vault. From what I could tell he had been in there since that night we made our deal. I had a feeling that had something to do with it but I kept my mouth shut and simply walked over to stand beside kerian.

he was irritated by Subject-59's current behavior and hardly spared me a glance, further driving me to pull away from him. "Why is it doing this now?! the last time it isolated itself was after the last sampling day, nothing happened during our last test so what changed?"

"Perhaps he needs a break. you've hardly given him a moment's privacy so he most likely wants some time to rest." I stated plainly.

Kerian huffed in turn before looking at me. "go in and try to coax it out-"

"I'm not his keeper, he doesn't just obey my commands like a dog, he cooperated with me because he wants to, not because he has to. if he doesn't want to come out then it's pointless being here." I stated calmly then turned to leave and Keiran watched after me seemingly surprised at the fact I talked back to him in such a manner..

After a moment of hesitancy he grabbed my wrist and pulled me aside away from everyone else. "Is something the matter with you? Is there something I need to know?"

looking up at kerian I could hardly meet his gaze before turning my head down. "nothing is wrong, I was just stating the facts. "And what business is it of yours if something happens to me?"

"you are important to our mission ava." he seemed to tense as I started to glare back at kerian. 'I'm important to their mission? That's all he cares about isn't it? Has it always been like this? have I been blinded by a dumb crush this entire time?...'

"the mission? I'm important when it comes to your testing but nothing else?" His eyes widened a bit and he looked as if he wanted to say something but was struggling to come up with an excuse.

He then attempted to grab my hand. "if you don't attempt communication you could risk upsetting the director and getting hur-"

"kerian." I cut him off. "You and I both know that nothing is going to change if I go in there, he doesn't want to come out right now. there's no need for either of us to waste our time attempting to bring him out."

Kerian stared at me in silence. "I'm going back to my room to rest. you may call me if he comes out but you're probably better off closing the vault." with that I pulled away from him and left the observation room.

Kerian stood there frozen as he watched me leave, and his hand balled into a fist. he then gave the order for the vault to be closed before leaving as well.

I'm actually quite relieved that I won't have to face 59 in front of a bunch of people again after what occurred.

it hurt a bit knowing that kerian wasn't the person I made him out to be. He doesn't care about me, he's merely doing the director's bidding. He's not hiding how he feels he is just a cold hearted man. He said he wanted to help me but the moment I asked for him to see things my way he refused.

entering my room I learned against the door and quietly scoffed at myself. How could I be such a lovesick fool? closing my eyes I thought back to the differences, the ways both kerian and 59 treated me.

kerian hardly batted an eye when i was nearly assaulted yet I looked to him like he was my savior, and 59 he- he tried to comfort me. he took care of me while I was hurting even though he was also suffering.

'God's I'm such an idiot!' I grabbed at my hair sliding down to the floor as tears welled up in my eyes.

hugging my knees to my chest I closed my eyes and drifted off, waiting for nightfall.

————

"Ava..." a whisper of a voice called out quietly in the back of my mind. jumping a little I woke up on the floor of my room. The lights were dimmed and looking around there was no one in sight. rubbing my eyes tiredly i was confused as to what woke me until I heard it again.

like a whisper in my ear, ever so faint, I could hear it again. I could hear subject-59 calling out to me. it was so quiet I almost missed it. "59?" i called out, but there was no response.

normally I would've thought it to be my imagination but as a strange tingle crawled down the back of my neck I knew it was real.

Looking back at the door I imstinctively knew what to do. pulling myself to my feet I left my room and made my way down the hall. Everything went by in a blur and it was as if my body was on autopilot until I arrived outside Kerians lab.

hesitantly I peeked inside to see the room vacant. The door leading into the adjacent office was open and I could make out Kerians voice from within as he was going over some data and making a recording.

within the lab room near the counters was his chair and lab coat. sticking from one of the coats pockets was his security card, and my key to S-59's vault.

sneaking inside I stepped towards the chair keeoing most of my attention on kerians office in case he appeared. snatching the keycard from his coat pocket i slit it into my own pocket and turned to leave.

"if current tests continue to yeild so few results, we will have no chouce tmbut to switch to more violent methoods. my theories of the regenerative abilities have already been proven accurate." i froze up hearing this and looked towards his office. i could faintly make out Kerians figure approaching the door and my stomach dropped as i looked to the labs exit that was at least another 20 feet away.

"testing still must be conducted to see if subject is a acceptable sorce for-" he stopped suddenly as he stepped into the lab and looked around.

I sat hidden behind a counter as my heart raced in my chest.

kerian switched off his recorder and hummed as he stepped further into the room, towards the counter. I squeezed my eyes shut afraid he would catch me but as he approached a distinct meow drew his attention back towards his office.

turning back kerian saw none other than s-32 sitting a top of his desk. they stared at one another with mutual digust until subject-32 stood up to strech and started crumbling the paper beneath his paws while digging his claws into them.

"stop!?" kerian rushed back into the office to chase off the cat. s-32 hissed as he ran to the other side of the desk facing off against kerian. I took the distraction as my chance to run and quickly rushed out of the lab without being seen.

"stupid animal-" kerian started but, S-32 suddenly jumped down and phased through the wall leaving the room, confusing kerian.

he paused before looking back into the lab and stepping out of the office to look around.

quickly making my way into the observation control room I was glad there weren't any guards standing outside. Since the vault was sealed they would have no reason to stand here and I didn't have to worry about being caught.

with kerians key card in hand i activated the lock mechanism for the vault door within the observation room. I stared into the black void within as the door slid open. my stomach twisted in uncertainty as I stood there watching.

glowing white eyes appeared in the darkness staring right back at me as I moved towards the airlock. Those piercing eyes followed my movements as he stepped out of the vault and the dark mist that usually surrounded him spilled out along the floor.

is waiting patiently for me to pass through to the other side. "You came." his voice spoke up in the back of my mind.

"did you think I wouldn't?" I asked as I stepped towards him.

he paused, looking me over with an unreadable expression. "I had some doubts..."

"Why is that?"

"because... that man seemed to hold sway over you before. I thought he might've stopped you." He said, sounding a bit disheartened.

'He must be talking about kerian...' "I've recently come to realize Kerian isn't who I thought he was. we were not as close as I had imagined, I think part of me that wished someone would care made me think he was someone else." I admitted, lowered my head.

S-59 leaned down and cupped the side of my head with his clawed hands to lift my chin. closing his eyes he leaned in, pressing his forehead against mine. "I will happily be whoever and whatever you desire ava."

I touched his hand and smiled, leaning into his touch. "You don't need to change for me. I'm here because I've realized who you really are- because I accept what you are."

his eyes opened once again as he gazed at me with a gentle expression. "I'm glad..." he relaxed a bit but I could still see something was bothering him. "Ava, this plan of yours, it will not endanger you will it?"

The question caught me a bit off guard as I looked down. "no, at least I don't think so. the whole idea of to get a better idea as to how your core works. If I can find an alternative to using it without harming you or removing it then I can try to convince the director to stop with these violent experiments. but that means I also need your full cooperation, and most of all your trust. I don't tell anyone about your core or anything like that, to avoid them coming after you but that means you also have to play nice no matter what happens. if I show them you are willing to cooperate and work with us then maybe they'll see-" i stopped, seeing the saddened look in his eyes.

instinctively I knew he wasn't very hopeful, he didn't believe this would work.

I knew I was grasping at straws but how else was I supposed to help him? freeing him wasn't an option. they would gun us down before he could ever reach the outside. I'm not sure exactly where his core might be but getting shredded by bullets was bound to kill if not severely hurt him. He can't escape this place alone so the only option we have is this.

"I do not wish for you to get hurt Ava, so as long as you promise that neither of us shall be harmed with this plan of yours then I shall help...I will escape here eventually so do not risk your life doing this."

I nodded in understanding. I couldn't tell hmif he was just trying to reassure me that he would get out somehow because he didn't want me to stress over it or he had some other plan, but I didn't matter. right now this was the most peaceful option we had. if we take things one step at a time then we can do it, we have to...

"I'm ready." I looked back into his eyes confidently.

S-59 stood up straighter, staring down at me before striding back into his vault. my eyes watched as his form was swallowed by the darkness and I stepped closer.

reaching out towards it, I felt his hand take mine and I stepped inside.

chapter 26

- -

(WARNING: this is it this is your one and only final warning! this chapter is practically monster shut! if your not into that then don't read past S-59 showing his core! YOU HAVE BEEN WARNED.)

Complete darkness.

That's all I could see, little to no light filtered in through the doorway behind me and as I looked back I could see why. the entire vault was swirling the same thick dark mist that S-59 conjured up on a regular basis.

The further I stepped into his den the less I could see, and as the doorway I came in from disappeared, my nerves got the better of me.

"i-i can see anything." I spoke up a bit worriedly as I turned my head to look towards s-59.

"You need not fear the dark. I am here with you." He responded calmly.

stumbling a little over my own feet I had to stop as my heart rate started to pick up. "I'm not like you– I can't navigate in complete darkness, I need some kind of light, even just a little bit...please, I can't do this in pitch black darkness."

the creature holding my hand chittered before moving around me. I could feel him stepping in front of me and tilted my head up as his glowing white eyes came into view. I nearly stopped breathing as he pressed his forehead to mine and stared deeply into my eyes.

something touched the side of my face and pulled my glasses off before I could stop it. "h-hey!" I tried to grab them back but one of his clawed hands cupped the side of my head and turned my face back to his. "Look at me ava."

his voice whispered against my mind and I felt a strange sensation through-out my entire body as I stared into his white soulless eyes.

"I'm going to show you where I come from." He spoke up once more, pulling his face away from mine. I couldn't understand what he meant by that until a soft blue glowing light appeared above my head.

looking up I watched as glowing blue dots slowly appeared all across the ceiling. I watched in awe as s-59's dark mist slowly faded away around us revealing the room around us, only it wasn't a room, it was a cave, illumi-nated by hundreds of bioluminescent cave worms all across the ceiling.

I spun around looking at it all in amazement. The cave was small and there was only one noticeable entrance, a dark tunnel that had previously been behind me, where the door into the observation room should have been.

as I took everything I was struggling to comprehend what was happening and how we had gotten here. all the vaults were supposed to be concrete rooms with the few necessities that any creatures might have needed, built into the walls, not cave Systems. and we had hardly taken more than ten steps into the room, where's the vault doorway?!

"h-how is this possible? Is this real?" I turned back to look at subject-59 as he stood off to the side watching me.

"no, not anymore at least… This is merely an illusion I have created. We are still within the concrete vault but you cannot see it. my abilities extend past that of regeneration, under certain circumstances I am able to trick the human mind into seeing what I want it to." he stepped around me to approach the cave wall and touch it.

"This is a mock visual of the place I once called home many, many years ago." He lowered his head sadly, seemingly missing his old home.

"This small space does not do it justice visually, nor physically." His head turned back towards me.

I looked around the cave in wonder. in the far corner was a bed of moss and fur blankets that almost looked human-made. approaching the bedding i reached out touching to touch it. my eyes widened at the soft and amazing texture of the moss and fur. "it even feels real! This is amazing!"

I looked back and had to trail my gaze up, seeing S-59 now standing close beside me. crouching down he reached out to grab the furs lifting them up to inspect them.

"I wish I could have shown you the real thing, but this space is so different from the actual room, making it harder to contort. The blankets the facility has given me are closer in texture to moss and furs than the concrete is, so I've merely changed its appearance. I have limits to what I can do, and the brain isn't always so easy to trick."

a smile pulled at my lips as I looked at him. "Thank you for showing me this."

"I figured it would be better than the stone walls and pitch black darkness you are so afraid of." We both stood up and I chuckled a little.

"yeah well if you couldn't see in the dark I'm sure you'd feel the same." I reached up to touch 59's cheek and he closed his eyes, leaning into my touch.

"Do you wish to proceed now?" he asked curiously and I could feel my cheeks turning pink.

"i- suppose so. where do you want to start?" I let my hand fall to my side and 59 stepped closer.

"I shall reveal myself to you and then you shall reveal yourself to me." He nuzzled my head affectionately.

"okay." I cupped his face and slowly he moved us back to the mossy bedding. He had me sit atop the plush nest before pulling away to sit back on all fours. with one clawed hand he reached up to his throat, grasping at it, narrowing his eyes the seams of his mouth appeared.

he seemed to struggle a bit, squeezing his eyes shut seemingly uncomfortable as his mouth opened up.

I inhaled sharply as I could make out a faint light from within his mouth as he opened it up further than I thought possible. underneath his skin I could see a faint glow and as his tonugue unfurled, completely extending I could peer into his throat where some glowing veins splintered off from some kind of strange glowing organ in the back of his throat.

I stared in shock at the glowing pulling growth that was unlike anything I had ever seen before. It held the same white glow as S-59's eyes and was integrated almost completely into his flesh.

"m-may i?" I hesitantly asked, a bit intimidated by his fully extended mouth.

"you may." He spoke up without any sort of muscle reflex from his throat or mouth.

Inching closer I inspected how his 'core' pulsed with a white glow and the veins attached to it spread throughout his body almost like it was part of his nervous system. s-59's atom anatomy was far different from any animal or humans but I couldn't hardly fathom how this strange glowing organ functioned.

I decided not to try sticking my hand into his mouth to touch it and instead moved around him to inspect his throat from the outside. reaching out I traced my fingers across the glowing marks on his neck left by the veins within.

S-59 shuddered from my feather-light touch as he sat perfectly still, allowing me to examine him. "This is unlike anything I've ever seen."

pulling away to look back into his mouth he started to slowly close it, allowing everything to settle back into place. I watched as the glowing core practically disappeared in the far back of his throat.

"it is not what you expected..." he said.

"no, not in the slightest, I almost expected something akin to a heart or crystal orb! but, that– core, it looks like some kind of strange growth. I have a feeling that it's more akin to your central nervous system than some random organ..."

he shook his head as his body shuddered, and he slowly relaxed once more. "Exposing my core in such a way feels strange, I'm not sure I like it." He admitted.

giving him a smile i reached out and gently touched his cheek, tracing my thumb over the seam of his mouth. "Thank you for showing me even though it might not have been pleasant."

He eyed me for a moment as his mouth closed up almost all the way but stayed partially open, showing the seams and a few teeth. "You've gotten your examination, Now it is my turn."

S-59 krept forward bringing his face close to mine and I leaned back until my back hit his bedding. I placed my hands on his chest nervously as he practically crawled over me.

"Do not be afraid, I will not hurt you." He leaned in, nuzzling my cheek with his face as one of his hands cupped the other side of my head.

"i-im not afraid of you hurting me. I've just... this is new to me."

"This is new to me as well. I've never exposed my core in such a way and I've never been so close to a human." He admitted.

my breath hitched in my throat as his tongue slipped out of his mouth and lightly teased my collarbone and shoulder, in an exploratory nature before trailing up the side of my neck and behind my ear. "but I am looking forward to it."

I shuddered at the feeling. leaning into his hand as he went. feeling his claws come up towards my shirt I quickly grabbed his wrist to stop him from tearing it off like he had done before. "wait!"

he pulled back a little and looked at me questioningly as I sat up. "don't destroy my clothes, I don't want anyone to know I was in here. I can't leave with my clothes shredded to pieces."

S-59 huffed a bit but didn't protest. "Then will you remove them?"

I nodded before slowly slipping off my lab coat and grabbing the hem of my shirt to lift it up over my head. Once my shirt was removed and I set it aside I gasped, feeling One of his clawed hands gently trace across my front.

watching on confused, he seemed a bit saddened as he stared at my abdomen. "Are you okay?" I asked, snapping out of whatever daze he was in.

hesitating for a moment he pulled his hand away and shook his head. "I am fine."

waiting for a moment I then worked to remove the rest of my scrubs, pushing them down as I shimmied them off my legs. S-59 practically purred once they were off and gently pushed me back down with one clawed hand against my collarbone. seeing how impatient he looked I didn't protest.

looking over my body in fascination, goosebumps crawled along my skin in a blazing trail and he blinded his hand down my front, over my breast and down to my underwear.

heat rushed to my cheeks as I turned my head away out of shyness. his and trailed down my thigh and leg, I couldn't help but notice how his skin was so cool almost like velvet. "You are soft no matter where I touch you." he continued to run his hands all across my body and slowly my head turned back to face him.

clearing my throat a bit his gaze moved back up to my face. "Is it alright if I touch you as well?" I asked meekly.

he tilted his head before leaning in closer and grabbing one of my wrists before placing my hand against his chest. "You may."

slowly I traced my hands across his chest and down his stomach, intrigued by how smooth yet firm his body was. "I'm curious, Why did you want to do this? if you've never really been interested in humans before?" I looked up into his glowing white eyes as he stared down at me.

"curiosity."

my hands stopped for a moment in surprise from the familiar response. "curiosity, and because I think I'm starting to understand it…"

"understand what?" my eyes followed him as he moved down my body. trailing his hand that had been holding my wrist down my stomach to the inside of my thigh.

"Why he bonded himself to a human." closing his eyes he rested his head atop of my stomach, seemingly happy and content.

my heart skipped a beat as I watched him. hesitantly I brought my hand to the back of his head and ran my fingers through his dark hair.

After a short while he opened his eyes and tilted his head to look at me. "Ava, I want to feel all of you, taste all of you, I wish for us to become one. so that I may know what it's like to be human."

I stopped petting 59's head, a bit surprised by his words. "i-i don't understand?" he pushed himself upright as his hand cupped my face. "Are you asking to bond with me?! isn't that dangerous?!"

a deep bellow rumbled within his chest as he traced his claws down my neck to then suddenly grope my breast, in turn making me gasp. "Eventually, yes, but for now I merely want your body and mind. anything that you can give, i wish to take."

his mouth split open once more and I squeaked as his tongue slipped underneath my bra to coil around my other breast.

my face flushed red as I grabbed at his hair as he licked at my nipple and squeezed my other breast within his grasp.

"ahh-!" suddenly his tail coiled all the way up my legs he pulled his mouth away from my chest to move lower.

my eyes widened as he used his tail to spread my legs, and grabbed my panties. pulling them aside, exposing my core to his gaze.

He hummed, while looking at my heat before opening his mouth further. "what're you–" I gasped, and my entire body tensed as he dragged his tongue through my folds slowly.

a raging inferno swirled inside of me as he did it again, and his tail pulled my leg up higher, giving him better access. the tip of his tongue teased my opening and I could already guess his intentions as it started pushing its way in. "h-hold on!" I tried to grab at his head as he brought his face closer allowing his tongue to slip in deeper and deeper.

my protests were cut off by my own moans as I arched my back and fisted his hair. the fleshy muscle writhed and squirmed tasting every inch of my inner walls as it pushed deeper. He was far too impatient to wait for me.

his hot breath fanned across the inside of my legs as he came dangerously close to my skin with his sharp teeth.

as his tongue pressed against my g-spot and licked at my cervix I whined and unintentionally bucked my hips, as black spots started to dance across my vision.

looking down at S-59 my eyes were unfocused as he stared back at me while feasting upon the area between my legs, being careful of his own fangs. "You taste delectable Ava." his voice whispered in the back of my mind sending shivers down my spine.

he teased and pressed against my g-spot again, forcing another cry to escape me as I threw my head back. The pleasure was nearly overwhelming and I couldn't understand why it felt so damn good. but in the heat of the moment I couldn't care. as long as he didn't stop.

a purr vibrated throughout his chest and mouth, as he continued to caress my insides and taste me in ways no other could. S-59 continued to watch me squirm atop his bedding, gripping the blankets in white knuckle fists, as he did this. He seemed more interested in my reactions than anything else.

It didn't take long before I felt myself coming undone, and black dots took over my vision. He must've felt it as well as my inner walls tightened and he gripped my legs tighter to push his tongue as deep as it could go. I cried out pitifully as my hands pulled on the blankets and he lifted up the lower half of my body off the bed.

"beautiful," He mused quietly while his tongue violently writhed inside of me drawing my orgasm out even longer.

once my body was spent. my legs trembled, and the energy and tension slipped away as my chest heaved. He slowed his movements. my entire body shuddered As his tongue eventually retracted back into his mouth, pulling a string of either saliva or my arousal with it... possibly both.

"I should have done this sooner." He purred as the seams of his mouth disappeared.

my head felt muddled as I lay there staring at the sparking glow worms across the ceiling in a daze. I hardly even acknowledged Subject-59 turning me over to where I was face down, or how his claws lightly prodded my overestimated pussy.

taking a shaky breath I closed my eyes and gripped the blankets, but not nearly as tightly as before. I just wanted to curl up into the soft blankets and fall asleep.

"Ava." S-59 pressed his front against my back and chittered as his face nuzzled the side of my neck lovingly. The ticklish sensation made me squirm a bit and I felt one of his hands grip mine as he entwined our fingers.

He then wrapped his other arm around my waist holding me close before grinding against me.

something slick and firm pressed between my legs and I opened my eyes confused and still a bit dazed from my orgasm as it slid back and forth between my folds.

becoming increasingly more away as it moved and S-59 continued to nuzzle and hold me. I realized that wasn't simply his tail because it was still coiled around my leg.

Both my curiosity and nervousness pushed me to attempt getting a look at this new appendage because of the overall feel of its shape and size but with him laying on top of me it was practically impossible.

"Wait, is that your reproductive organ?" I asked meekly, getting a pleased purr from 59 in response. 'I don't even remember ever seeing such a thing before, is he somehow able to hide it?'

"yes..." his voice whispered against the back of my mind. I felt him pull back and the appendages tip poke at my opening as worry washed over me like a bucket of cold water. 'it's too big.'

"that won't fit!" I squirmed to try and break free and S-59 merely cooed as he held me more firmly against himself hiding his face in my neck.

"it will, you will take all of it into your womb as we will become one." He stated happily.

His slick appendage started pushing inside of me, stretching my insides far more than his whole 2-foot long tongue. "no you don't understand–!"

gripping the blankets even tighter I whimpered as he pushed deeper and my body struggled to accommodate him. "just a little more Ava." I trembled as his tongue licked the shell of my ear.

I hadn't seen his cock beforehand but as he pushed it deeper and deeper I knew it wasn't normal, it was bigger– and shaped differently. 'I shouldn't have just accepted this– my body's not built to accommodate him. I wasn't sure how he had planned to through with this but I should've thought about it more thoroughly!'

Even though I knew he was possibly destroying me from the inside, I could feel no pain. I should've been in agony but all I felt was pleasure as he buried himself all the way into my womb.

A deep coo sounded from S-59 as he gently cupped the area right below my belly where a small bulge stuck out from within. "We are one Ava."

shakily I put my hand over his, feeling the bump. "h-how is this possible?" I panted.

"Just enjoy it, little human."

The moment he started grinding into me, stirring up my insides, I moaned, hardly capable of thinking rationally anymore. 'why, Why does it feel so good?!'

The grinding quickly turned to slow deep thrusts as growls rumbled in S-59's chest. his tongue snaked out to trail across my cheek and and down my neck as he grew much bolder with his advances.

"You feel exquisite…" he purred against my mind. groaning I could feel him grind into me as his tongue encircled my neck. he didn't stop, didn't relent for even a moment as he pumped into me growing in speed as the minutes passed by.

keeping me held firmly with one arm his thrusting became much faster and my mind felt dizzy with each passing second as he ravaged me like an animal in heat. "s-slow down– if you keep going like this- I'm gonna faint!" I gasped.

59 pulled his tongue back as he nuzzled the side of my head. "I can't help myself. your insides are so warm and tight. I want to bury myself as far as I can inside– I want to fill you..." He chittered happily as he continued rutting into me like it was his last day on earth and my thoughts became muddled and incoherent from the overwhelming pleasure.

I felt myself quickly approaching my climax and my eyes started to roll back as he became more frantic with his thrusts. "Ava!" He bellowed as I squirmed beneath him clawing at the blankets desperate to hold on.

Hot breath fanned across the back of my neck and I could see Stars bursting right before my eyes as I came undone with a cry. S-59's claws dug into my skin drawing rivets of blood as he growled and I felt the part of him that was inside me throb and pulse as warmth flooded my womb.

my eyes practically rolled into the back of my head and my vision turned black as my orgasm hit its peak. I couldn't even feel pain from him gripping me so tightly or as he bit into my shoulder. The pleasure was so over-whelming, to the point tears formed in my eyes.

"MINE." His deep possessive voice rang in my mind as I felt myself slipping away in the darkness.

I tried to fight those hands clawing at my consciousness as they dragged me down, I knew I couldn't stay here but my strength was slipping away and the pleasure was just too much for me to handle.

So as my eyes closed all I could comprehend was S-59's tongue licking my cheek while my body became limp in his arms. and his voice whispering against my mind once more.

"You belong to me now, Ava."

(note: congrats, we all need therapy now.)

chapter 27

(note: ended up changing this to chapter 27 because what i had posted previously was actually meant to be chapter 28, i just kinda rushed it and fucked up... Enjoy!)

"Ava" a voice called out to me.

groaning, I opened my eyes to the soft blue glow of the dimly lit cave. burying my face into the blankets a clawed hand gently combed through my hair as hot breath fanned across the back of my neck.

"Ava~" the voice purred again as something licked the shell of my ear. looking back I groggily looked up to see S-59 hovering over me with a very pleased look.

"you're finally awake... I worried I might have been to rough, and had hurt you." He leaned down nuzzling my head.

sitting up I rubbed the sleepiness from my eyes. "finally? How long was I out?"

"not long... I would have let you sleep longer if I knew you did not have to leave." He sounded a bit saddened by that as he gazed at me. Turning onto my back I reached up to run my hands through his hair making him purr.

"You want me to stay longer don't you..."

"If I could have it my way, I would never let you leave..." He admitted.

smiling I cupped his face with both hands before pulling him closer. kissing him over the mouth his entire body nearly slumped over on top of mine with a steady purr rumbling within his chest.

He rested his head against my chest and closed his eyes as I rubbed his head. "Sorry but If anyone finds me with kerians ID card and I get caught, things won't turn out well for either of us..."

S-59 opened his eyes and sat up, climbing off of me. "i understand i wouldnt dare risk endangering you, but still, every time we part I fear something may happen to you, I fear losing you. Despite what I am, I cannot fathom the thought-"

tilting my head I watched him confused. "What do you mean 'despite what you are'?" I asked worriedly.

he turned gaze away, almost seeming ashamed of what he would say next. "You are such a beautiful being Ava, kind and pure of heart, I know you wish for me- you think of me as something more than what I am, you believe you can change me but I am and always shall be a monster. it is In my nature, it's part of my core- my very being. I will do anything to keep you safe and by my side, even if it means destroying everything to do so.

my heart swelled hearing this and I quickly wrapped my arms around his neck to hug 59. One clawed hand cupped the back of my head while the other covered my backside as he held me close.

"You are not a monster, I don't care if no one else sees it because you will always be more to me. In my eyes you will always be you, and I will always love you."

he seemed to relax and melt into the hold, nuzzling the side of my head as he held me close. I smiled and we stayed like that for a long moment until s-59's entire body seemed to tense and he lifted his head, seeming to be on high alert.

Confused by the reaction I looked up at him but he seemed to be in some kind of daze as he stared off at nothing in particular and his grip on me loosened.

I followed his gaze but could see nothing but darkness through the doorway that led back into the observation room. "What is it?" I spoke up.

snapping out of it he shook his head, seeming just as confused before looking down at me. He was silent for a moment but soon relaxed. "It was nothing."

I didn't quite believe him but didn't push for answers. I trusted him to tell me if something was wrong.

___5 days later___

sitting inside S-59's observation chamber never felt more awkward. He was unusually distracted and seemed to fall into a trance every once in a while.

even now as I sat in front of him instead of giving me his full attention he was blankly staring towards the far end of the room where the main vault door that leads into the facility hallways stood.

That door has never opened before and he's never paid mind to it in all our other sessions so why is he so hyper focused on it now?

glancing back towards the glass wall past the dark mist I could see the usual party of scientists going about their observations but kerian wasn't here. It was strange considering he always attended these sessions, but I didn't get the chance to question it before being ushered into the room. I tried performing like usual for the sake of keeping up appearances but s-59 hardly responded.

had kerian been here he probably would've pulled me from the room already because we weren't getting anything.

sighing I looked back to the creature sitting before me, still just blankly staring off into space. scooting closer I reached out and touched his tail.

his head snapped to mine as if surprised to see me and my face twisted in worry. He's been like this the past two sessions. 'What is happening?'

"Are you okay?"

he glanced to the vault door across the room once more before returning his attention to me. "I am fine."

"you're acting strange. you have been for days."

lifting his gaze to me he reached out and cupped the side of my face, but didn't say anything. He seemed to be in a daze, lost in his own thoughts as he stared at me.

living my hand to his I grabbed it and leaned into his touch. "talk to me?" I practically asked.

he seemed to hesitate for a moment before finally saying something. "how many others are there..."

my brows knitted together in confusion.

"others?"

he nodded, letting his hand fall to his side. "Yes, others like me. how many creatures with cores reside within this facility."

my eyes widened a little hearing him ask this. I glanced towards the glass wall where the other scientists were watching but he quickly cupped my face again, turning my head to look only at him. "tell me Ava."

Why was he suddenly asking this? What am I supposed to say? Whenever he asked questions I shouldn't answer, Kerian would cut us off and demand we move on. He usually controlled our conversations to some extent, to avoid unnecessary babble and get the info he wanted. this seemed like something he wouldn't allow me to answer but he's not here right now...

"i- there's 17 here. but hundreds more at other facilities across the globe...why do you want to know that?"

He didn't respond to my question and turned his eyes to the floor.

After a moment he lifted his head and looked to the glass wall with a glare. I followed his gaze to see Kerian walking into the control room. He spoke with two other scientists before turning his attention to us and stepping up towards the glass.

"that man... he is one who has power over others of your kind." Those words sounded more like a fact s-59 was trying to verify than a question and I felt unnerved by s-59's strangeness today.

"yes... he's in charge of the labs and science division. He's close with the director of this facility and handles most matters when the director isn't around."

S-59 suddenly stood up before stalking towards the glass wall, openly exposing himself to the view of everyone on the other side. I watched on unsure what was happening as he approached them, with his eyes locked onto kerian.

the scientists either backed away in fear or

watched on in shock and amazement by S-59's sudden boldness.

the doctor tensed as well, seeming unnerved but didn't back down or back away from the glass wall. in fact he openly glares back at subject-59 as he stared down at him.

"what are you doing?" I whispered to S-59. he did not respond and continued to growl down at kerian.

"he watches, but not with the same curiosity as others. there is a deep hostility in his eyes..."

getting off the ground I looked between kerian and S-59 worriedly. I couldn't understand what was happening right now, or why he was acting this way. "he believes your dangerous, that all creatures like you are-"

s-59 all but snarled as the seams of his mouth appeared. "He knows."

'what?' S-59 then suddenly clawed at the glass wall, scaring most of the scientists in the lab and even making kerian falter ever so slightly. His sudden attack left four long jagged marks across the glass's surface as he seethed.

"what are you doing!?" I rushed towards and grabbed his arm but he only continued to snarl at an alarmed kerian. it was as if he was in another trance and couldn't see me.

"Ava, remove yourself from the observation room." kerians voice came in over the ear piece.

I hesitated, looking between the two of them before letting go of 59's arm. He did not look at me once as I made my way towards the airlock.

Once I was back in the control room I walked over to kerian who was still standing before s-59.

The mist beyond the glass wall did little to obscure the angry creature.

"what is happening?" I breathed while watching s-59 glower at us through the glass.

"It's not just him, all of the subjects have been acting strangely, staring at nothing in particular. idly standing in a trance...once extremely hostile entities act like little more than dolls in human presences, it's been like this all week. but subject-59 is the first one to show any kind of emotion such as anger.." kerian spoke up.

I looked at kerian, eyes wide but he didn't dare to look away from the creature in front of him. as if it would openly invite 59 to attack. 'all of them?' refocusing my attention to 59, I could feel in my gut that something was wrong.

after a few moments Kerian finally looked away and gestured to one of the others in the room. "seal the blast doors, the chances of it returning to its vault are little to none while it's riled up."

they nodded before activating the blast doors to close across the glass wall, putting s-59 off from view.

"What's happening to them?" I asked quietly.

kerian turned away before walking towards the exit. He hardly acknowledged me and ignored my question completely leaving me to wonder. I shouldn't be surprised but I hated not knowing anything and being left in the dark.

S-59 said 'he knows' but what exactly does that mean?! I felt helpless and completely isolated just standing there as everyone carried on with their work.

turning away I walked towards the exit to leave as well, seeing as I couldn't do anything else.

as I reached the door and it opened for me however I could hear s-59s voice whispering against my mind. "Avoid the others."

pausing I looked back at the glass wall that was blocked by the blast shield. I could almost imagine seeing him there, watching me as I turned and walked out the door.

'Was that a warning?'

chapter 28

(note: this chapter has had major changes. please re-read!!!)

–1 week later–

The sound of a throat being cleared dragged me out of my daze as I lifted my head to see none other than Kerian looking at me from across his desk.

"you've been zoning out a lot these past few days. Did something happen outside the labs?"

blinking a few times I shook my head to clear it before responding. "no, nothing." I turned my head away, feeling overwhelmed by the awkward standstill.

Kerian hummed before deciding to move on to the matter at hand. flipping through some papers he spoke up without looking at me. "Is there anything you can think of– any reason for why the subject will not interact with you?" He asked.

"no."

Kerian proceeded to tap his pen against his desk as he watched me. Today was another failed test. S-59 had isolated himself within his vault refusing to come out or speak to me. I was just as confused by the strange behavior as the rest of the scientists.

Kerian seemed particularly irritated over the sudden change with s-59 and all the other subjects but refused to say anything about it. Sometimes I'd see him pacing back and forth and he always became frustrated when 59 refused to come out of his vault.

He has been beyond busy with all of this going on but seems particularly bothered by s-59. all the other subjects have gone into a trance but 59... he seems to be an abnormality with the recent change. along with subject 32 who has practically gone missing.

disappointed in the answer, Kerian leaned back in his chair, before standing up.

lifting my gaze watched kerian, as he stepped around his desk to stand before me. "Ava, I do not want to be enemies, I know you see these creatures as more than just monsters but they cannot be trusted. I want to make a deal with you. I know you don't agree with everything that we've been doing and you don't want to be here anymore so how about this, you help me accomplish our mission and I will get you out of here... I mean it, work with me and I can free you. you are the only person capable of getting that thing to talk or cooperate. we need you to work with us." He reached out his hand expectedly but all I could do was stare at his palm.

'free me? Is this really the tactic he's going to use? bargaining my freedom?' looking up at kerian his deep blue eyes were cold and held no compassion. he's completely heartless, and manipulative, why should I trust him?

After a few moments of silence, when I didn't take his hand he lowered it, balling it into a fist briefly before stuffing both hands in his pockets and leaning against his desk.

"I see..." he mumbled in a disappointed tone. He stared at me for a long moment as we sat there in awkward silence. "I can't force you to cooperate, that much is clear and I have a feeling if you learned the truth you would deny it and continue on as you are...you are a stubborn woman."

glaring at kerian I bit my tongue. I can't say anything, I can't expose what I already know or even hint to the fact I may know about their true goals. it would put s-59 in danger...

"You are dismissed." He turned away, walking back behind his desk to sit down.

getting up from my seat I made my way out of the lab without looking back. I needed to find some way to speak with S-59 alone. It was the only way I would get any answers and figure out why he's been so unresponsive.

Continuing to walk down the hall I passed numerous guards and scientists but paid them no mind because I was so caught up in my thoughts.

I'm doing the right thing, it doesn't matter that 59's not human, he doesn't deserve to be treated like this... I've seen his kindness and how gentle he can be. He just wants to be left alone! Why can't they see that? if he was free he would just hide away from the world where no one could bother him. How does that make him so dangerous?!

I stopped in my tracks feeling a bit defeated. I know my plan won't work, not with kerian being in charge. There's so many secrets being kept from me from both sides and it's all just too much to bare...

someone suddenly shoved me out of the way and I yelped as I stumbled and hit the wall. rubbing my shoulder I looked over to see none other than jade smirking down at me.

"Keep staring off into space and they might classify you as a monster too—speaking of, I've heard the monster you're infatuated with has lost interest in you. can't say I'm surprised you were never all that interesting to begin with. your so timid and weak he probably doesn't think you a viable source of food."

I glared back at jade before getting back up to my feet. "You don't know anything about him."

she hummed before shrugging. "oh? What's this? Is the useless intern baring her fangs for once?"

"just leave me alone jade I don't have time for this…" I turned to walk away. much to her surprise. but instead of continuing on her way she just smiled and crossed her arm.

"Yes, I'm sure you're quite busy preparing for your demotion now that the doctor has decided to replace you." she mused.

I immediately stopped in my tracks. I knew she was just trying to get under my skin. I know that i should just keep walking but jades words left an unsettling feeling in my gut.

"seeing how you've failed to deliver results in the past two weeks and how the creature refuses to even acknowledge you now, the doc has assigned me with the new task of communicating with it. Unlike you I'll be getting all the information and data we need. and we will learn so much more from that monster than you ever could hope to dream."

My eyes widened as her words registered in my mind. kerian is going to send jade in there whine subject-59 is acting out of place?! that's suicide!

she smirked before turning to walk away. "don't feel bad, maybe they'll set you up with one of the hellhounds instead."

snapping out of my shock I quickly rushed after her. "You shouldn't do this jade, it's dangerous! subject-59 is– he's not in the right state of mind!"

he scoffed and rolled her eyes. "Is that really the best excuse you could come up with? don't you get it?! you're not special Ava. you may have fooled the doc and that creature before with your silly tactics but your times up you've failed. and by tomorrow you'll be little more than trash in the garbage." with that jade continued on her way leaving me to stand in the hall.

I looked at my hand feeling anxious over the entire situation. 's-59 probably won't come out of his vault. if they try to force him or jade intrudes into his territory he could turn aggressive– I don't want anyone to get hurt. I know what he is and what he's capable of, but I can't let him go back to that kind of life, I can't see him turn into a mindless killer. I don't want to see that kind gentle soul of his disappear.

he's not a killer, he just wants to be left alone... to exist in peace.

turning back down the hall I made my way to my quarters. the more I thought about it and the more scenarios that ran through my head, the worse my anxiety became.

sitting down on my bed, my heart clenched as another possibility came to mind. What if I do lose him? That idea made me sick to my stomach.

no matter what happens I just hope they don't hurt him.

—3 days later—

Today was the day of jades test with s-59. I had been dreading this ever since she told me about it and ended up losing sleep.

invited or not I wasn't going to just sit by and idly let things turn out in ruin. kerian was sending jade to her death much like how they tried to do with me. I can't just turn a blind eye to this.

Upon entering the control room I found all the usual watchers there as well as kerian. He was standing before the glass staring into the room where jade was already beginning the experiment.

rushing up towards the glass beside him he turned his head to look at me a bit surprised by my appearance. "You shouldn't do this." I said while watching the vault and jade intently.

Kerian was quiet for a moment as he looked at me before returning his attention towards the room before us. "how else am i supposed to convince you these creatures are nothing but savages?"

my blood ran cold at kierans words and i turned towards him shocked. he seemed completely unphased. "Is that why you are doing this? to try and prove a point? to make me fear him?! She could die in there!" I snapped at him but he didn't react.

"weren't you the one saying subject-59 isn't some monster that kills people? if he's as docile as you say then I see no issue here... After all he didn't kill you right?"

Balling my fists I angrily glared at kerian. He's putting other people's lives on the line to try and convince me to help him?!

jade stepped towards the open vault door that swirled with dark mist, and confidently stood before it. clearing her voice she spoke up. "subject-59, my name is jade kenslow! I am your new communication companion, please come out and show yourself!" She shouted.

silence was the only response to her order as the dark mist didn't even stir. jade glowered at the darkness before repeating herself once again. still nothing. she grew even more frustrated.

"subject-59! I demand that you show yourself at once!" the black mist moved, ever so slightly spilling out onto the floor but s-59 still did not appear.

I could feel goosebumps run across my skin as an unsettling feeling set in my stomach. bits and pieces of strange visions leaked into my mind as I watched jade continue to try and get s-59 to come out.

the observation room. blood, the bodies and remains of dead scientists and guards. the black sample box. Were these the memories of S-59 erased? Why am I suddenly getting them back?

I shook my head and backed away as the hair on the back of my neck stood up. I could practically sense the malace radiating from the vault on the other side of the glass wall.

Kerian looked at me intrigued but continued to keep quiet. He turned his attention back to the room as S-59's eyes became visible and he glared at jade.

it was getting hard to breathe. I didn't want to see this, I don't want to see him kill anyone for a sick man's twisted goals!

snatching Kerians ID card from his pocket I rushed towards the airlock and saved the card to open the door. Two guards rushed after me but couldn't reach me before the door shut and the decontamination started.

as more dark mist spilled out into the observation room, jade backed up and smiled. "Good now be a good creature, come out and reveal yourself!"

a growl could be heard from S-59 as he stepped out of the vault on all fours, partially obscured by the mist. his full attention was locked on jade as his tail whipped around behind him and he stepped towards her with a predatory stance. She seemed to hesitate and back away slightly.

as the seams of his mouth opened up her confidence turned to disgust and she backed away even further.

Once the airlock finished I ran towards them. S-59's body tensed and his claws flexed, as he got ready to pounce but before he could I jumped in front of jade with my arms out. "stop!"

I saw little to no recognition in his eyes as he looked past me like I didn't even exist. this was what I was afraid of, 59 losing himself. I always knew it was impossible to completely tame him, and to convince the others. As selfish as it was, I just didn't want to lose him. the one person who cared for me, who saw me. If he became a mindless killing machine I'd never get to hear his purrs or see the calm and serene look in his eyes ever again.

He may be dangerous but this isn't who he is.

Even now in this seemingly unstable state of mind he seemed to hesitate and did not lunge to maim and kill.

Jade grabbed my arm turning me to face her before angrily shouting at me. "What the hell do you think you're doing!" her grip was tight and she did not relent on her hold of me as I tried to pull away.

"How dare you come in here and try to ruin this for me! I always knew you were a pathetic rat!"

The creature behind me growled and slowly circled around us without me or jade noticing as I tried to pull free from her. "jade let go! I'm trying to help!"

her hand released my arm but my head suddenly snapped to the side and I stumbled back, falling to the floor as her other hand smacked me across the face.

I was briefly stunned by the hit but didn't even get a moment of respite when Subject-59 suddenly snarled, grabbing both our attention. his tail knocked jade halfway across the room as he screeched angrily in her direction ready to charge, and multiple guards filed in through the airlock.

at this rate, they'll shoot him!

"no, stop!" I jumped up and grabbed his arm, forcing him to halt in his advance and growl. "Please, this isn't you!"

I pleaded with the monster before me, my heart racing as his eyes narrowed and he glared down at me. The way he was acting was similar to when he attacked me, he seemed almost feral at the time like he was in some sort of trance, like some kind of defense mechanism...I need to calm him down!

jade groaned in pain before nearly sitting up and crawling backwards, away from us.

he growled towards her again, ready to lunge once more but I kept myself latched onto his arm. "Please don't do it." I quietly begged.

this time he didn't take his eyes off her. jade fled the room through the airlock as the guards stood on standby at the door aiming their guns towards S-59. "don't shoot!" I warned them before looking back up at s-59

"go back to your vault, please no one's going to bother you anymore so don't attack them..."

his mouth slowly closed up as the growling died down and he seemed to be struggling to control himself as he backed away. He gazed at me for a moment without saying a word before retreating into his vault, out of sight.

worry consumed me as I watched him disappear into the darkness, and the guards came over to usher me out of the room.

I left the observation room and saw two nurses checking up on the frightened jade. looking over to kerian our eyes met and I simply glared at him before walking towards the door.

his hand grabbed my arm to stop me and I angrily pulled it away before turning to face the doctor. "Ava–"

"don't you ever do something like this again!" He looked at me surprised as I stood there fuming. "If you try to use these sick tactics on me I'll make sure you never accomplish your goals, and I will never help you!" I angrily snapped before turning and going straight for the door, I didn't bother to look back as I left the room.

even with everything that has happened up until now, between this test, jade, the lost memory, only one thing occupied my mind. the fear of losing S-59.

chapter 29

----

3 days later–

I stood there anxiously waiting in the hall, glancing at my watch to check the time. Oct. 22nd 11:45pm. Night had fallen over six hours ago, so most of the scientists should be asleep by now.

I had hoped that tonight would be my chance to sneak into the labs but as I peeked around the corner I saw two guards standing outside the observation control room, one of which I recognized...Matt.

internally I cursed whatever deity might be watching over me. "Of all the people, why did it have to be him?' I continued to watch them from afar and listen in on their conversations.

"damn I hate night shifts." Matt's partner groaned while leaning against the wall. "Tell me about it..." he responded. "I wish they would just exterminate this creature already, it does nothing but cause problems."

"doc treats this damn thing like a vip or some shit, even when it goes off and kills people they do nothing about it." the other guard mused.

"What're you talking about?" Matt asked curiously.

"Well I've seen them exterminate other monsters for less before, just last week a plant creature bit one of the scientists, they fucking incinerated that damn thing without a second thought."

Matt hummed before looking up towards the ceiling in boredom.

Matt pulled out a pack of cigarettes, grabbed one and started patting himself looking for a lighter.

"tsk you really gotta do that while I'm here?" his partner hissed.

"fuck off, if we are gonna be stuck here another 8 hours I deserve some respite." Matt snapped back. "I don't get why they even have us standing out here anyways."

"It's because that fucking thing in there." the guy gestures towards sub-ject-59's vault door. "somehow fucks with the cameras. they are practically useless. and after attacking jade they want to make sure it doesn't fucking try breaking out or some shit."

"what fucking luck...where the hell is my lighter?" Matt cursed as he con-tinued to look for his lighter.

"At least our troubles are almost over, we won't have to put up with this thing for much longer and can return to normal protocol" the man sighed.

"How so?" Matt questioned.

"Buddy of mine overheard the doc talking to someone over the phone, with all the creature's suddenly acting out of whack they are wanting to terminate his project. with how dangerous this creature is i don't doubt they'll probably put it down as well."

My blood ran cold after hearing what the guard just said. 'they...are going to kill him?!'

"Good riddance, these freaky monsters need to be eradicated all together, maybe then the world can go back to the way it's supposed to be!" Matt chuckled.

'They can't– they can't really do this?! no, thinking they can't and they won't...I'm only fooling myself with those ideals. there's nothing the foundation won't do.

sliding down to the floor, I sat against the wall at a complete loss. What am I gonna do? I can't let them kill him...I need to tell him, get him out of here somehow!

"I'm going to take a piss." The other man walked away down the hall leaving Matt alone.

"fucking hell!" Matt cursed finding no lighter to speak of.

I banged my head back against the wall quietly, closing my eyes in defeat. I need to get inside. I need to talk to 59 but How am I supposed to get past matt?! I need to get in that lab–!

sitting there leaning against the wall I felt a chill crawl up my spine and the faintest sound of his voice calling out to minfrom down the hall, away from the lab.

standing up my feet nearly moved on their own as I quietly made my way towards an empty lab room. glancing around I saw nothing but equipment and empty desks.

Why did I come in here?

"Ava~" the voice called out again and my attention was drawn up towards a vent in the far back of the lab.

stepping over to the vent I grabbed the sides of the metal grate and tried to pull it off. to my surprise it popped off quite easily, and I set it to the side.

peering into the dark tunnel before me I could practically feel s-59 calling out to me from within.

I chewed my lip while looking at the tight space before sighing. "I suppose I could fit…"

pulling off my lab coat I inevitably crawled inside and followed the voice that called out to me.

After worming my way through the tight space I finally managed to get to the lab and push open the metal grate.

as I crawled out of the vent I came face to face with a very familiar figure and my eyes widened in surprise as he meowed innocently.

"32? What are you doing here? Where have you been?!" I questioned the sneaky little feline. He merely stepped over and ruled up against my leg before trotting over towards the glass wall and phasing through to enter S-59's containment chamber. He then paused and looked back at me as if waiting for me to follow.

past him was 59's open vault door where dark mist continued to endlessly swirl inside of. walking towards the airlock I used a borrowed ID card to open it up and step inside. 32 patiently waited for me before entering the vault.

I briefly hesitated before stepping inside. The mist surrounded me almost instantly in its cold embrace, and all the light from the other room disappeared.

putting my arms out in front of me I slowly stepped forward and called out to him. "59?"

my foot caught on something and I shrieked as I fell forward ready to break my fall with my arms outstretched but something coiled around my abdomen, breaking my fall before pulling me up and against a hard body.

a deep rumble of a purr resonated from within and I looked up to see those white eyes staring down at me. "Ava~" his voice rumbled in my mind before something wet and slick trailed up the side of my neck.

shuddering I put my hands up against his chest to push him back a little. "I can't see anything."

After a moment our surroundings started to swirl as the mist seemingly disappeared, turning into the cave s-59 had shown me before, lit up in a dim blue glow.

S-59 was standing over me with his tail coiled around my body keeping me close while also holding me upright. his clawed hand was reaching for my face as he leaned in closer, extending his tongue. He seemed to be in a daze of some sort as he licked my lips, seeking entry and I almost gave in.

a meow from the other end of the room seemed to halt his advance and I glanced over to see 32 sitting there watching us. s-59 pulled back looking towards the spectral cat for a moment before relinquishing his hold on me.

"I know!" He growled before grabbing at his head and shaking it. After a moment he looked back at me and sat back on his haunches.

"I'm sorry ava...I am not myself right now."

I looked at the creature before me in concern before stepping closer and cupping his face. "What's going on? what's happening to you?"

he closed his eyes leaning into my touch as 32 got up and came over to us.

"It's– complicated." 59 responded.

"Yeah I can see that... you're acting completely abnormal, one moment you're refusing to talk or acknowledge me, the next you're acting overly aggressive, and now you are ready to practically jump my bones. Tell me what's happening."

He opened his eyes to gaze at me lazily before looking towards the cat. They both stared at one another as if having some kind of internal conversation that I couldn't hear. 59's mood just soured even more and he turned away from us both, grabbing his head to mope.

"I cant– I don't want you to hate me!" 59 practically whined as he clawed at his head. He almost seemed to be in pain.

walking up behind him I grabbed his hand and touched his shoulder to pull his attention towards me. "I could never hate you! Please just tell me what's happening to you. Why are you acting out like this?!

"its...its like before. when I felt the need to fall into a deep sleep. back then I didn't understand the feeling and tried to avoid it, tried to resist, but eventually I succumbed to it and went into hibernation." He started before turning to look at me with a blank stare. Suddenly he stood up again towering over me.

I had to crane my head back to look him in the face as he lifted his hand.

"But this time it's different, I can feel it, even if I don't completely understand it," He reached towards me and I didn't move as his clawed hand nearly encircled my neck, but he kept himself from touching me. "What it wants me to do–"

S-32 started growling, making 59 pull his hand away and look at him before turning his gaze to his claws. "It's not safe for you to be here..." he said sadly.

"I'm not leaving until I get some definite answers! I'm tired of being left in the dark! So please, tell me what is going to happen!"

He cupped the side of my face gently before leaning in and pressing his forehead against mine. "You should go..."

"I'm not leaving like this!" I argued.

"Ava..."

"they are going to kill you!" I snapped. with tears stinging my eyes. He didn't say a word and merely stared at me. "they are giving up on trying to get your core– which means you'll be exterminated soon! I don't want to lose you! I don't want to lose the person I have left! I have no friends, no family, no home! nothing! I've already lost everything once. Please, I can't lose you too..."

tears streamed down my face and 59 pulled me against his body, cradling the back of my head.

"you will not lose me Ava, i said i will keep you safe, and I plan to keep that promise. The balance is shifting within the world and I am afraid that you might be hurt in the coming conflict. This is why I need you to trust me... do as I say. so that I do not hurt you again."

looking up at 59 I felt uneasy by his choice of words. "conflict?"

he hesitated before responding. "The humans could not contain us all forever."

I understood that, I knew it was true but it was still hard to accept. S-59, no, all of the creature's were bound to break free eventually. but when they break free, when they all escape this facility, then what? will they return to hibernation and disappear from the world again? will A.c.o.r.n. try to hunt them down?

"Will I ever see you again?" he chittered quietly before nuzzling the side of my face.

"yes. I will come back for you..."

nodding I stepped away wiping my eyes. "Go now, stay safe until the time comes and keep the specter close." as if in cue S-32 meowed before jumping up on my shoulders.

I looked over subject-59 and gave him a small sad smile before turning and walking out of the vault. 32 purred and nuzzled my face to cheer me up but I still couldn't stop myself from looking back at the vault before leaving the way I came.

—10 minutes prior—

"damn it, if all the nights to lose my lighter" Matt moped while looking around the empty halls. He was bored out of his mind and annoyed to have been given a night shift at the last minute today.

his eyes moved to the door beside him that led into the lab. What were the chances someone left a lighter or something capable of starting a small flame in there? with no one around, it wouldn't hurt to check...

pulling out his keycard, Matt scanned it on the door and entered the control room. glancing around he looked for anything that could light a cigarette or even a possible coat that might have been left behind by the scientists.

with little luck he found nothing and silently cursed once again. as his eyes scanned the room they stopped on the glass wall before him and he peered through it staring at the dark void within the vault beyond.

The mere sight gave him the creeps as he stepped a bit closer. The darkness was unnatural and made him uncomfortable the longer he looked at it.

"fucking freaky." turning away he headed for the door only to hear something across the room. looking over towards the source of the sound, it seemed like something was in the vent. grabbing his gun he quickly ducked behind a counter and waited for whatever was coming.

The metal grate popped off and a petite woman crawled out of the hole before dusting herself off and looking around.

Matt's eyes widened as he recognized her. Ava.

watching on in curiosity he heard a meow and saw that weird ghost cat creature pop up in front of her. she greeted it before it suddenly entered the containment chamber and turned to look at her as if waiting.

Matt watched on in secret as the woman made her way to the airlock, and used a stolen keycard to enter. She went inside the containment room, following the cat before disappearing into the test subject's vault.

Once she was out of sight he stood up and thought about how she went inside so calmly. exactly how close was she to that monster that she felt the need to sneak in here after hours?!.

the more he thought about it the more he smiled, with a plan forming in his mind.

"I bet the doc would love to hear about your little excursions Ava..."

chapter 30

Lying in bed all I could do was sit there and stare at the ceiling in deep thought as hours ticked by.

I tried to sleep but I couldn't shake the feeling of unease that had been plaguing me since I came back to my room last night.

there's no doubt about it anymore. subject-59 plans to break out soon, and escape this facility for good. people will die, that's a fact that can't be denied. I wish it didn't have to end like this but there's nothing I can do.

besides... if he doesn't break free along with the other anomalies then he'll die. His death is an outcome far worse than the destruction of this facility.

closing my eyes I tried to push away my guilty conscience. 'This is for the best, I know it is.'

a small meow drew my attention and I opened my eyes to see s-32 sitting before me on the bed. with a sad smile I reached out to pet him much to his approval. "I suppose you're going to keep watch over me while he is busy?"

s-32 just purred in response as I continued to pet him. 'I wonder where s-59 will go once he escapes? I should get out of here as soon as possible too. He said he will come back for me but I don't want to risk him getting caught once again. if I was outside it would be easier and safer to find one another.

At least outside he can be at peace without having to worry about guards or scientists coming after him. Maybe one day humans and anomalies could learn to co-exist.

"imagine the possibilities..." I whispered to s-32.

a knock on the door startled s-32 and he quickly hid under the bed. 'Who could that be?' sitting up I got out of bed and opened the door to be greeted by a guard.

"Miss Ava, kerian has requested your presence at the lab for a quick test."

my mood immediately soured hearing this. "Of course he did." turning around I grabbed my coat off the back of my chair and looked to 32 with a smile. "I'll be back in a few." I whispered.

putting on my coat I followed the guard to the lab.

Upon entering the control room I noticed an increased number of guards as well as the capture team getting prepared to enter the containment chamber.

my stomach twisted into a knot as I stopped and looked around before my eyes landed on kerian standing before the glass wall. fear and worry began taking over my senses as the worst thought possible came to mind.

'they can't possibly be planning to exterminate him right now– can they?!'

hesitantly I stepped towards him and he continued to just stand there staring ahead, peering into the dark entrance of 59's vault.

"D-did something happen?" I asked quietly.

Kerian turned his cold gaze towards me and I immediately felt unnerved.

"there's been a new...development with the project. a possible solution to the problems we've had with subject-59's experiment." he responded plainly before glancing towards the guards and capture team who started entering the chamber.

I watched them as well, getting more anxious by the second. "What are you doing..."

" The board of directors wants everything to be shut down and for the bunkers to be repurposed for what's to come. but I still have one last card to play in all of this and refuse to give up my life's work."

"I told you I'm not helping you with anything..." Kerian turned back to the glass wall and we watched as the soldiers inside surrounded the vault entrance with pole snares and electric prods.

"what– what are you doing!? what are they doing?!" I moved to grab his arm but was suddenly stopped as a guard grabbed my wrist. looking over a sickening feeling washed over me at the familiar face of the man holding me.

Matt.

as I tried to pull my arm away he quickly restrained me, none to gently pulling one arm behind my back and wrapping his arm around my neck, holding me to his front with a snicker. I shrieked in response but my struggles were quickly halted as he twisted my arm painfully. "Where do you think you're going?!" Matt said in my ear, getting uncomfortably close.

"let go of me!" I shouted but Matt refused to relent in his hold.

Kerian sighed as he turned to us and looked on with disappointment. "You don't understand how important this is to us and humanity as a whole..."

"good?! How is torturing a creature who wants nothing more than to be left alone, so you can't get his core, good?!"

"Ava, obtaining this monster's core could change Everything. If we can extract it then we can gain control over it. Complete control. but this is just the beginning! If we learn how to tame a monster like this then we can do so with others, more powerful ones! we can modify them, create our own force of creatures to counter the rest–"

"What's the point!?" I cut in and Matt squeezed my neck for interrupting but kerian signaled for him to stop and let me speak. glaring at kerian I practically growled, still trying to get free.

"You want to make weapons out of them?! for what purpose?! to shed more blood!? to make things worse between humans and these anomalies!? Why do this at all?! they've been lying dormant for hundreds if not thousands of years! Why kick the hornet's nest!?"

Kerian watched me for a long moment before responding. "I've already told you. to save humanity."

I just looked at him like he was mad. 'Save humanity!? how is this–'

"enough talking let's begin." kerian spoke up.

"Yes sir." Matt responded happily before walking us towards the glass wall and making me kneel, before cuffing my hands in front of me.

as he let me go I looked back at them confused as kerian gave the capture team a signal to get ready.

"What are you going to do?" I questioned.

"Initially with the recent changes happening with each of the subjects I had assumed S-59's interest in you had gone away almost completely. that was until Sergeant Matthew witnessed you sneaking into the creature's vault late last night."

I paled in realization. "Doc loved hearing how you snuck in and used a stolen keycard to get into the observation chamber. not only that but how you so willingly just walked into the vault..."

"sergeant..." kerian spoke up in a scolding tone. "enough messing around."

"yeah, yeah just trying to have some fun..." the sound of something buzzing behind me caught my attention and i looked over only for Matt to roughly grab me by the hair stic a earpiece in my ear. "now be a good girl and tell it to come out, or else..."

Matt then held up a taser before me and my eyes widened fearfully. 'They are going to use me to get to his core!?' gritting my teeth I kept my mouth shut refusing to speak. 'I'm not going to help them with this!'

Kerian rolled his eyes before grabbing the ear piece and stepping closer to the glass. "Subject-59 I advise you to come out of your chamber, I'm sure you're watching us right now and you can see we have Miss Ava here. cooperate and reveal yourself so we may speak." he demanded.

looking into the observation room I internally pleaded for him not to listen, for him to not show himself under any circumstances. He's safer in the vault; he can protect himself better and keep the guards out.

After a minute of silence, Matt tightened his grip on my hair and my face twisted in pain as I tried not to make a sound.

Unfortunately that seemed to be enough to bother 59 as a deep growl came from the vault and his eyes appeared in the doorway. mist spilled out across the floor as the soldiers in the room tensed and Matt kept his hold on me.

slowly he stalked out of the vault and looked around at all the soldiers who surrounded him before focusing his attention on the three of us.

his eyes narrowed as his tail whipped around behind him angrily. "Unlike the others of your kind you are still somewhat able to rationalize and think albeit less than usual." kerian mused. "I'll make you a deal, your cooperation for her life. seeing that you two seem to be so close–"

"Don't listen to him! go back to the vault! don't do anything he says!" I shouted loud enough for the mic in kerians earpiece to pick up. Matt immediately turned on the taser and jabbed it into my side.

my body immediately jolted and my muscles locked as electricity shot through me. my scream came out choked as my body spasmed and I couldn't move. a cry left my lips as it finally ended and Matt let my body collapse onto the floor.

S-59 screeched, knocking back four of the several armed men in the room to rush forward and slam against the glass.

my heart felt like it would burst from my chest as I tried to catch my breath and recover from the shock I just experienced. "get up!" Matt grabbed my arm pulling me to sit upright as I lifted my head to see 59 angrily scratching at the glass and turning to screech at the capture team as they tried to restrain him.

'please just get out of there.' I silently begged with tears in my eyes.

"subject-59 if you do not cooperate, you will both suffer the consequences! you may be able to recover quickly from injuries but humans are not so strong. Ava is no exception." Kerian lifted his hand and once again Matt stabbed the metal prongs of the taser into my neck.

crying out in pain as my body locked up again and seized. s-59 screeched even louder, banging against the glass until it cracked. my eyes started to roll into the back of my head when kerian finally lowered his hand letting Matt pull the taser away.

I slumped over, unable to hold myself up as my vision blurred and head spun from the prolonged shock. Only then did s-59 stop raging within the observation room and reluctantly let the capture team snare his arms, legs, tail, and neck. He was still growling and pulling against the restraints but not enough to break free.

"Do you understand now?" kerian asked, fully prepared to give the go-ahead to Matt again.

Matt was crouched down behind me as I laid on the floor unwilling to move as fresh tears fell from my eyes and I watched 59 struggle to hold himself back for my sake. he chuckled before harshly pulling me up off the floor to hold me against him with his arm while grabbing my jaw forcing me to look up at 59 who's eyes briefly moved to mine.

"Go on, give him your best puppy eyes. show em how scared and helpless you are... just like you did with me, that day at the pool." Matt whispered into my ear while squeezing my body firmly against his.

I shut my eyes as tears streamed down my cheeks and I grit my teeth.

"you know what I want... your core, your power for her life. The choice is yours." Kerian said coldly.

59's arms that were once tense and straining against the restraints finally went lax as the capture team pulled him back away from the glass. I could only watch as he gave up the fight and let them do as they pleased.

After a moment he opened up his mouth, further than before just as he had done for me that night, exposing his core to the world. the pulsating organ in the back of his throat glowed brightly and kerian stepped closer in awe at the sight.

The capture team was quick to pin him face down with the pole snares and other restraints as a scientist pulled out a box of equipment and pulled out some kind of syringe gun.

his mouth closed and he didn't even fight back as they pinned his head down like a white animal and a few men climbed over top to hold him. 59 did nothing to stop them, said nothing... his eyes just stared back at me as I sat there helpless.

pressing the gun to the back of his neck the scientist pulled the trigger and the needle pierced through flesh. s-59 seemed to instinctively jolt and start thrashing as his mouth opened and he screamed in pain, but they had him pinned down, completely restricting his movements.

I watched in horror as the vial on the syringe was slowly filled with a glowing white liquid from his core. Once it was filled the scientists jumped off and rushed to leave while 59 still thrashed trying desperately to break free.

my chest constricted and my heart ached as he fought, digging his claws into the concrete. Once the scientist was out of the room he brought Kerian the vial, handing it over like a precious treasure.

"finally..." Kerian smiled ever so slightly as he held the glowing vial up to look at the swirling substance inside.

squeezing my eyes shut I could feel anger bubbling up inside of me and before I knew It I was lashing out as well.

biting Matt's hand I forced him to release me and try to pull away as I drew blood. twisting around I grabbed his gun out of his holster and kerian turned to look at us surprised as I aimed the weapon at him then pulled the trigger.

chapter 31

My head throbbed in pain as consciousness came back to me. as I attempted to open my eyes, blinding lights only made it worse as I attempted to squeeze them shut and lift my hand to block it from my face.

only my arms wouldn't move, they were being held down by something. Turning my head away from the blinding light I winced as another pain shot through my neck.

Slowly I came to realize my entire body was a bit sore.

"finally awake?" a voice spoke up and I opened my eyes. through blurred vision I could see someone standing across the room.

I blinked a few times trying to get a better look but soon realized my glasses were missing. looking down much to my discomfort due to the pain in my neck, I found myself bound to an examination table.

'what? h-how did I get here?!'

The figure across from me set their equipment aside before stepping over and pulling over a chair. I looked at them fearfully as he became much clearer in my eyes and sat down crossing his arms and legs.

Kerian.

"You'll be lucky if you don't have a concussion. you were unconscious for nearly 36 hours... "

His shirt was covered in blood with a very apparent hole In the center of it but he didn't see the least bit phased.

I could only stare at him in shock as he watched me.

I Killed him. I watched kerian fall as I pulled the trigger and the shot went through his chest! how– how is he alive?!

"That was a bold move Ava, reckless but bold. you're lucky the guards didn't shoot you and matt knocked you out. well– maybe not lucky enough..."

"h-how–"

"How am I alive? hmm you were already out when it happened so it's no surprise you're in shock. that shot should've killed me, you caused some severe damage and punctured a lung. no medical staff in this facility would've been able to save me, and even if they had I would've been put in a hospital bed on a ventilator... but it just so happened I had the one thing that could save my life right in my hands."

kerian suddenly held up a glowing vial with a third of its contents missing. "wonderous...isn't it?" He mused.

"I've yet to test its full capabilities but its composition is unlike anything humanity has ever seen. such a small amount was able to completely heal me from what should have been fatal wounds, but not only that, it's made me stronger. possibly even extending my life far past normal humans. I took a major risk injecting myself with this substance for there was no telling what would've happened when I did..."

"y-you..." tears started forming in the corners of my eyes as I glared angrily at kerian. "what about s-59...what did you do to him!?" I asked with a choked sob.

Kerian eyed me carefully before standing to walk away. "The creature is still alive, although greatly weakened it is slowly recovering from the harvesting. we did not fully extract its core for the sake of our experiment, we still need it alive after all. with time it should be able to regrow– at least that's the theory."

'he's alive...' I felt a weight fade from my chest as I lay there.

kerian opened up a bulletproof glass case and set the vial carefully inside before locking it up.

"it's strange... even with so little exposure to the creature's essence. I am experiencing things I do not quite understand." he turned back towards me, and walked over to stand at my side.

"not only can I sense the creature but I can somehow...feel it. it's faint but I can sense its anger, it's pain, but the most intriguing part is its affection. Kerian suddenly reached for my face and my breathing hitched as he touched my cheek. "Each time I look at you it's as if it's peering through my eyes and it's emotions course through me, it cares for you deeply."

my eyes widened as I looked at kerian, it didn't feel like the doctor was touching me, it felt like 59's hand was on my cheek, and his eyes were the ones looking down at me. It was so faint and hard to imagine but I could tell he was there.

"The bond between you two is much deeper than I initially thought, I must admit I was mistaken. I never imagined these creatures to be capable of falling in love with a human, but this has proven that it is indeed possible."

a mix of emotions washed over me hearing kerians words. hearing that 59 loves me wasn't something I ever expected to hear even though I already knew it to be true.

like flicking a switch however kerians gaze turned cold as he pulled his hand away to stuff it in his pocket as he seemed to force 59's influence away. "which is precisely why you're still alive."

dread seeped into my bones as kerian looked at me with an interest far more sinister than subject-59 could ever manage.

"With you and the creature's essence I have no doubt in my mind that I'll be able to control that monster and bend to my every whim. I've already figured out how to block it out of my mind. It's only a matter of time before I'm able to control it with a snap of my fingers and learn how to use its power. it's a shame you aren't more obedient ava, my entire plan was to get the creature attached to you and have you control it while i directed you from the sidelines, you could have spearheaded this project had you only listened. Now you're nothing more than another lab rat." he sighed before walking away towards the door.

gritting my teeth I snapped at the doctor, thrashing around in my bindings. "You're a sick! you treat us like guinea pigs and talk about saving the world! The only thing the world needs saving from is people like you!"

he paused in his stride to glance back at me unamused. "Considering you're no longer an employee here, it shouldn't matter what I tell you anymore." he mumbled quietly.

"Ava tell me do you have any ideas as to why these creatures started waking up in the first place? why were they dormant all these years and now they suddenly start appearing across the world?"

I glared at Kerian, confused as to where he was going with this.

"Your beloved monster clearly knows what his purpose is, all of them do whether they are intelligent or not. They all have once single purpose one drive that connects them all...

Destroying Humanity."

'w-what?'

"Do you get it now? Do you understand what they are? What A.C.O.R. N.'s mission is? That creature you love so much exists for the sole purpose of killing off the human race. They are the world's very own sleeper cells meant to restore balance. A.C.O.R.N is the seed of humanity,a last resort to find a way to save us from being completely annihilated. it would be impossible to uncover all the creature's scattered across the glow and elim-inate them before they decide to turn so it was decided that we had to find a way to fight back once they were all awoken. That is the entire point of this experiment!"

I could hardly believe what Kerian was telling me but the more I thought about it the more it made sense, with 59's strange actions and recent change in behavior... 'but then why– why did he–'

"You could've helped us pave the road to a better future for the human race. instead you've made yourself into another nameless casualty..." the doctor sighed before walking out the door. "I hope it was worth it."

the door shut leaving me isolated within the lab with nothing more than my own thoughts.

I don't know what to think anymore. He was meant to play a part in the end of the world yet he is trying to spare me from it at the same time... how am I supposed to believe any of this? What am I supposed to do?

tears streamed down my cheeks as I stared at the ceiling numbly.

I still love him...

a familiar meow from across the room snapped me out of my thoughts and I looked over to see S-32 sitting on a counter watching me.

kerians words replayed in my mind about s-59 being in pain and how all the creature's had a part to play in this...

it wasn't by choice. He wasn't choosing to do this, that's why he wanted to keep me at a distance. He can't control it; he only wants to keep me safe.

I know what I have to do.

as if on cue s-32 grabbed a scalpel off a metal tray on the counter and jumped down before bringing it over to me, and setting it in my hand.

using the sharpened blade I carefully cut through the strap holding my wrist. Once it snapped I could move my arm and finish freeing myself from the other straps tying me down.

climbing off the table I winced holding my side where I was tased. my entire body ached but the two places Matt had tased me throbbed in pain. 32 watched me, seeming a bit worried but I gave him a small smile and pat on the head in reassurance and slid the scalpel in my pocket.

looking across the room, my eyes locked onto the glass case with the glowing vial of 59's core essence. 'I have to get it back to him.'

stepping over to the case I tried to pry it open despite knowing how pointless it was with the fingerprint lock. When that didn't work I grabbed a chair and tried banging it against the glass to no avail, it hardly scratched it.

"dammit! how am I going to get it..." I huffed as I glared at the box.

s-32 happily jumped up onto the counter and rubbed up against my arm with a purr before stepping up to the box. with ease he phased through it, grabbed the vial then phased out and plopped it into my hand with an all too pleased look.

With a huge smile I picked up the cuddly cat and gave him a big hug. "You're the best!" setting him down i rushed over to kerians office and searched through his desk drawers for a spare keycard to no avail. "shit i'll have to figure something else out..."

picking it up I took a deep breath trying to mentally prepare myself. 'I can do this.'

Suddenly the entire room trembled slightly and I looked around confused. "What was that?" s-32 seemed to grow uneasy and meowed before going towards the door and looking back at me as if to say we need to leave.

I nodded and we quickly exited the lab. outside, numerous scientists were standing around murmuring about the strange shaking while some guards rushed down the halls headed for the upper floors.

s-32 quickly trotted down the hall towards 59's vault and I did my best to follow him without drawing attention to myself.

as we passed a set of guards, one of them seemed to stop in their tracks as they recognized me and I moved faster as he called out telling me to wait.

I didn't listen and started speed walking down the hall only for that dame guard to run up and grab my arm. "Hold it!" He snapped as I tried to pull my arm away.

s-32 suddenly ran over and hissed at the man. the man yelled in surprise releasing my arm as 32 latched onto his leg with his claws and bit him through his pants. The guard tried helplessly to shake off the feral acting cat and stumbled back, falling to the floor.

taking the distraction as my chance to get away, I made a mad dash down the hall away from the guard.

When I looked back I failed to see someone turning around the corner and clashed with them head on. she screamed as we both were knocked off balance, papers the woman was holding went flying and I shielded the vial in my hand with my arm as I hit the ground.

ignoring my sore body I sat up a bit panicked and looked at the vial to make sure it didn't break. Once I saw it hadn't been damaged I sighed in relief.

my relief was short lived however at the sound of a familiar voice. "fucking dammit Ava!? Are you blind!?" Jade snapped at me as I looked up at her surprised. her eyes moved to the glowing vial and her anger turned to confusion at the sight of it.

quickly jumping to my feet I ran away past her and she yelled after me. "wait! get back here you idiot!"

—-

as jade got back to get feet groaning in anger. Matt ended up catching sight of her picking up papers off the floor and came over to see what the problem was. "You good."

"Does it look like I'm good?!" jade snapped at him.

he rolled his eyes before helping her to pick up her stuff. "What happened?"

"that dumb girl ran into me while blindly sprinting down the hall not looking where she was going!"

Matt's face twisted into confusion until he glanced up and saw an all too familiar face staring back at him from down the hall in front of the elevators.

eyes widening he dropped jades papers and grabbed his taser before running after her. The elevator doors opened and Ava quickly fled inside and pressed the button for the doors to close as Matt ran at her.

Ava glared back at him, clutching the vial close to her chest as the doors shut before he could reach her. Matt slammed against the doors before cursing and turning to shout at the nearest guard, barking out orders to shut down the lower sector.

—

Once the doors closed I felt I could breathe again as my heart pounded in my chest. my eyes moved to the vial in my handillas if I was holding 59 himself. 'i promise I'll keep you safe...'

as the doors opened I made my way to the vault. Once the black numbers 5 and 9 came into view I smiled.

"Hold it!" a man shouted. spinning around I saw three armed guards with guns running up behind me before aiming at me. "put your hands up!!!"

my eyes widened and I backed away panicked only to hear more soldiers come from the other end of the hall. "stop right there!"

looking back and forth between the two sets of guards I found myself completely trapped right in front of 59's vault. the entrance to the control room lay just a few feet past the guards but I had no way to get past them or get inside.

"give it up Ava. there is nowhere for you to go." kerians voice spoke up from behind. Turning to face him he stepped past the guards ordering them not to shoot while glaring at me. "What were you planning to do exactly? free the subject? you can't do that without my ID card. Kerian waved his card in front of me before rolling his eyes.

you are out of options Ava, so just give up already... spare yourself the pain...”

as he said that Matt arrived with his taser in hand. He grinned before stepping past the other guards and kerian to walk towards me. “hand it over and I'll go easy on ya this time–”

I looked around desperately, trying to find a way out of this. my gaze landed on the vial in my hands and only one option came to mind as I glared up at Matt and kerian.

“I'll never give in to the likes of you.”

kerian narrowed his eyes at me and mat stepped closer only to stop as the entire facility started to violently shake. the overhead lights flickered before going out. alarms started blaring, flashing in red and yellow hues as the emergency lights flicked on. Matt lunged for me only to stumble and fall as I dodged out of the way, throwing myself back against the vault door as the shaking continued. Kerian was quick to brace himself against the wall while the other guards struggled to keep balance as well.

my eyes met kerians and as I opened the vial he shouted for me to stop as I brought it to my lips and drank it.

Once it was empty I dropped the vial and covered my mouth. The shaking faded away and I could feel a burning sensation growing inside of me. grabbing at my throat it became worse by the second and I found myself falling to my knees and clutching at my chest painfully.

it was hard to breathe and my entire body was burning up from the inside out. I was lifted off the ground as kerian grabbed me by my shirt and shouted in my face. “What have you done!?”

my vision blurred as a sharp pain stabbed through my mind and I screamed, grabbing at my head, squeezing my eyes shut.

suddenly all at once everything just stopped.

the pain, the alarms, the shouting.

opening my eyes I found myself standing in a vacant room alone. lowering my hands from my head I looked around finding no entrances or exits, just four blank walls. 'Where am i?'

"Ava"

I jumped a bit startled as subject-59 suddenly appeared behind me. Turning and looking up at him I could tell he wasn't doing well. He looked drained, weaker than normal.

I stood there frozen, unsure what to say or even do, other than blame myself for all of this. I couldn't tell if what I was seeing was real or not as we stood there in front of one another.

After a moment I managed to muster up a reasonable question. "What is this?"

"a place, deep inside of your mind. you consumed a decent amount of my essence, bringing both our consciousnesses here." I looked around the space after his explanation. "Why did you do it?" his question caught me off guard.

I looked at him unsure, as to what he was talking about. 'is he asking why I took his essence?'

"i– it was the only way I could possibly save you, if I didn't then the doctor would've taken it back and used it against you, to control you. I couldn't just let him do that."

s-59 stepped closer before pressing his head against mine tiredly. "Ava... doing this– you're threading our souls together. you'll bind yourself to me and I to you."

smiling I reached up to cup his face lovingly.

"If that's what it takes to save you then that's a price I'm willing to pay."

he gazed at me quietly as his hand covered one of mine on the side of his face and he leaned into my touch. "Are you sure this is what you want, despite knowing what I'll do? despite everything?"

leaning in, I pressed my forehead against his this time. "I'll be your strength this time and help you escape, so you don't have to suffer anymore."

his eyes closed as he relaxed and black mist filled the room around us, within seconds I was snapped back to reality gasping for air as the doctor violently shook me and shouted. "what have you done!?!"

matt and the guards were still recovering behind him as the alarms rang out.

grabbing the blade out of my pocket I stabbed him in the arm and snatched his ID card. He pushed me away with a shout and grabbed his arm in pain before removing the scalpel and angrily tossing it away.

but as he looked back up at me slumped against the wall holding his ID his anger disappeared and he froze, not willing to make any sudden movements.

My entire body was trembling and felt weak as a side effect from drinking 59's core, but I still managed to stand myself upright and look at the man before me with a blank expression.

"it's over." I whispered.

lifting the card it brushed against the scanner on the wall and beeped.

chapter 32

(warning: lots of gore in this one but some very much needed payback
gets delt! if you're squeamish you can skip this chapter completely!
there's not much story relevance!)

Red warning lights flashed throughout the halls painting the surrounding
areas in a deep crimson glow.

a loud and intense alarm blared as the vault doors lock mechanism came
undone and the seal broke. a hiss of air escaped as the doors separated and
slowly opened allowing the dark mist to pour out all across the floor.

The guards redirected their weapons from the girl to the dark doorway as
the alarm continued to blare and the gap grew wider.

Matt stepped back a few paces watching along with everyone else. the
doctor openly glared at the doorway before backing away and turning to
run down the hall. Matt watched surprised and called after him only to be
cut off by a loud screech that made anyone within proximity of the vault
cover their ears.

Ava stumbled away, using the wall as support before falling to her knees. she was clutching at her chest in pain while panting and seemed to be struggling after consuming whatever she drank.

Once the screeching stopped the soldier recovered and Matt looked to the woman across from him as he took a step forward to apprehend her something lashed out from within the vault knocking him back.

he hit the wall as the rest of the guards momentarily froze in shock before aiming their guns at the darkness. a set of glowing white eyes could be seen from within the doorway as a deep growl resonated from within.

Matt groaned as he looked up to see those white eyes staring back at him. The creature within, stepped out of the vault slowly, looming over each and every person like an omen of death. its tail whipped around wildly behind it as the dark mist filled the room making everything harder to see.

as it's mouth opened up Matt swore it had somehow grown three times its normal size. no, this couldn't be that same monster right? this thing was different! not only was it bigger but its limbs looked distorted, it had another set of arms and two new sets of haunting glowing eyes! this couldn't possibly be the same creature!

Matt pressed himself further against the wall and looked around to the other guards. some of them were backing away, two ending up dropping their weapons and either just stood there watching the thing before them or collapsed. Why weren't they shooting it?!

Matt also took note of the fact Ava was suddenly gone. 'that fucking bitch ran away just like the doc!'

a chill crawled across Matt's spine drawing his attention back to the creature before him as it crouched down and looked him right in the eye. Only then did a deep voice speak to him from the back of his mind as the creature said one singular word, causing the blood to drain from his face.

"RUN"

as it pulled away one of the guards suddenly screamed and started shooting wildly with no sense of direction as to where he was aiming. the creature snarled and practically moved like a shadow within the mist as it went after one of the guards who was just standing there frozen in fear.

Matt watched in horror as blood splatter the wall beside him and he could faintly make out the creature tearing off someone's arm. another man screamed only for his voice to get cut off as something pierced through his body and he was thrown across the hall like a ragdoll.

more gunfire sounded from across the hall as one of the guards suddenly started gunning down his companion. even after the man collapsed dead on the floor he wouldn't stop shooting the body.

another gut screamed before running away disappearing into the mist. it was as if everyone had lost their mind. Matt heard a wet crunch and gurgling sound as the monster killed someone else and finally snapped out of his shock. "fuck this!!"

getting up to his feet he ran away from the slaughter without looking back. somehow the mist seemed to have spread down the halls of the facility and panic ensued everywhere. as he passed another lab some sort of dog creature crashed through a glass window, tearing into one of the resident scientists.

stopping in his tracks Matt backed away and turned down another hall. 'What the hell is happening?! fuck fuck fuck!' as he turned another corner he stopped in his tracks at the sound of a familiar voice, and looking into a room he found his companion Sarah trying to fend off a small reptile-like bird creature with blade-like wings as it screeched and jumped at her.

she waved a baton at it as it screeched at her angrily and two more appeared, covered in blood from one of their victims. Once she saw Matt in the hallway her eyes widened and she started begging for help. "matt! Please help!" cursing her grabbed his pistol and charged forward to help only to stop in his tracks as he noticed several more of the same creatures feeding off a body on the other side of the room. After a moment they stopped and turned their attention to the girl and him. one hissed and flew at him while the others cornered Sarah, backing her into the wall.

three jumped at her at the same time and she managed to knock one back but the other two latched onto her arm and leg and started tearing into her with their tiny mouths. she screamed and tried to pull them off only to end up hurting herself in the process as their blade-like feathers cut her hands. "Matt!!!" the rest of the birdlike creatures squealing before pouncing and attacking the woman.

one lunged for the man but he quickly shot, and killed it instantly before shooting two others who were on top of Sarah. She screamed and cried as they continued to attack her ruthlessly and Matt tried to aim at them, unable to get any clear shots. "fuck!" he lowered his gun, backing away unable to do anything but watch as they killed his friend.

As he backed out of the room he heard more screams down the hall, and looked to see a plant monster of some kind killing anyone within its vicinity as it made its way through the hall. 'I have to get out of here! I have to find somewhere to hide somewhere there aren't so many people!'

turning his back on his companion and the rest of the civilians he ran through the halls trying to avoid any monsters he saw. as he turned a corner he caught sight of subject-32 carrying an ID card.

He watched as the creepy ghost cat jumped up and managed to get the card close enough to a scanner for it to beep and open up another creature's vault door. some sort of bug-like monster clawed at the door as it slowly opened, impatient to escape its confines.

subject-32 looked up at the man knowingly with a glare and he felt rage bubbling up inside of him. "damn you!" raising his gun he shot at the cat only for it to phase through the wall, disappearing from sight.

The creature in the vault squirmed and managed to get half of its body out the door as it continued to open and Matt was forced to turn another direction and run.

'Why is this happening to us?! What did we ever do to deserve this!' He managed to find a secluded area away from all the bloodshed and hid in one of the lounges in the recreational area, trying to catch his breath.

he hid behind a wall and slumped to the floor, panting as he tried to hide.

screams and gunfire could be heard down the halls as monsters and people alike were killing each other. cursing Matt banged on the concrete wall behind him trying to vent his frustration as guilt and anger flooded his system. This was completely unfair why, just why was this–

His thoughts were halted as he caught a glimpse of a familiar figure snaking towards the showers, trying to escape the bloodshed.

Ava.

like a switch being flicked all Man could see was red.

It's all because of her. This was Her fault! she must've conspired to do this, to get back at him and the others for messing around with her. yes. That had to be why this was happening! it's all because that fucking bitch planned for this!

pushing himself to his feet, Matt went after the wretched woman, following her through the shower room and to one of the pool rooms. there was no one around, so it was the ideal hiding place for a rat like her to hide in.

slamming open the door to the room she was in, Matt felt some form of sick satisfaction as he startled her. He almost smiled, seeing her doe eyes go wide and her form back up into a wall.

"you. this is all happening because of you!" he shouted and tossed his gun aside before stomping towards the defenseless woman. Before she could slip away he grabbed her by the arm and harshly threw her to the ground before lunging and wrapping his hands around her neck.

Her choked cries did little more than anger him more as she struggled and whimpered trying to break free, but her attempts were futile. Matt was stronger, bigger. He could hardly even feel her useless attempts to escape, and it made him feel good.

"this is all your fucking fault! Why did you do it huh?! Why did you decide to turn into a goddamn traitor!" He squeezed her neck harder and felt like he might just break it as she struggled to breathe.

"Is it because of what I did that night? because I followed you in here?! I did that because I pitied your worthless existence– I was going to help you but no, you were too self-righteous and thought you were too good for the likes of me!!"

Suddenly Ava stopped struggling. Matt noticed her expression go blank and felt a chill crawl up his spine as that same voice from earlier spoke up in the back of his mind once more.

"Is that how you see it? How you see yourself? you believe your actions were Justified?... Pathetic."

Ava disappeared right before Matt's eyes, turning into nothing more than a towel roll. confused, Matt jumped up to his feet and backed away only to bump into something behind him.

shouting in fright he spun around to find that same creature that Ava had free'd looming over him. He backed away fearfully into the wall much like Ava had done as his eyes widened and questions raced in his mind.

"You think of yourself as some kind of saint, that you were 'helping' her when in truth you were only trying to hurt her and make her feel small so you could feel bigger." the voice spoke in his mind again, laced with venom.

the creature stalked forward, as the seams of its mouth opened up and its eyes narrowed. "Humans like you think that what is happening is due to the faults of others, of innocents. you fail to see that you've all brought this upon yourselves. you blame her for confiding in a creature like me and refuse to acknowledge the fact this is happening because of what you did. you turned your backs on one of your own and now they have turned their back on you, yet you still deny your part in all of this!" subject-59 hissed angrily.

Matt slumped to the ground, stricken with fear as the monster before him reached forward with its claws grabbing him by the neck.

"I'm sorry! please– stop this!"

"did you stop when she begged?" 59 growled.

too words escaped Matt's mouth in response to the question, for he knew the answer was no.

"Then why should i?" 59 glared at Matt as he released his neck and backed away slightly. relief and confusion washed over the man briefly before the creature's clawed hand swiped at him and everything went dark.

Matt screamed as he was knocked to the side and his entire face radiated with pain. He could feel blood running down his face but he couldn't see. bringing his hands up to his face he could feel blood trailing down from where his eyes should have been. his Anguished whaling filled the room as he tried to crawl away only to be grabbed by the back on his head by the monster.

"consider this death a mercy to your disgusting existence." Matt then found his head encompassed by water. as his head was forced into the pool. forgetting all about the pain of having his eyes clawed out he started struggling to get free from the monster's grasp as water filled every opening.

gurgled screams were muffled by the pool as he thrashed around trying to get free but subject-59 would not let him go until all movement from the man's body ceased and the struggling stopped completely.

Only then did he release the dead human, letting their body fall into the water. He waited a moment longer watching as Ava's assailant floated lifelessly in the pool, the illusions he created for the wordless sack of me he killed only proved that the human was responsible for most of Ava's pain. he doubted she would agree with his methods of vengeance but that was one thing that separated the two. She was everything he was not.

the man would never have shown mercy to her had he truly cornered her once again. That was why 59 needed to end his life once and for all.

turning away to go after the next one, subject-59 stalked through the halls shrouded in darkness. Despite his body thrusting with the need to kill more he had a specific target in mind and simply passed by the fleeing humans with little care.

he would let the others deal with the rest of the facilities humans, there was little need for him to waste his time going after them. as long as no one got in his way then he didn't bother attacking.

his newfound connection to Ava somehow made it easier for him to control his own urges. He no longer felt the insatiable need to kill at random, instead he was focusing his attention on those that had wronged them...

He had taken Ava to safety after being released from containment and knew the specter would keep the others like him away from her while she recovered. so now he just needed to find the last person on his list of targets.

not only for the sake of revenge, but to take back what was stolen from him, and to end this once and for all...

chapter 33

The fleeing doctor could hear the sound of screaming and gunfire all around him. subject-59 was not the only one free'd from his vault. the more he thought about it the angrier he became.

this wasn't how it was supposed to go. His life's research on these creatures was supposed to help the human race, to allow them to fight back. turn nature against itself and give them a fighting chance. So why... Why was everything crumbling down all around him?!

The entire facility shook once more, nearly knocking the man off balance as he got to his lab. What was causing these tremors?! Was he already too late? Has the cleansing already begun? locking down his lab and closing the doors, the doctor made his way over to his office.

If he could contact someone from outside then maybe he can get reinforcements into the facility and stop this outbreak.

picking up the phone he attempted to contact someone to no avail. no matter how many times it rang, no one picked up. 'Why is no one at headquarters answering?!'

opening his laptop the doc's eyes widened at the sight before him. an emergency signal had been sent out from HQ warning all the facilities to lock down. This system alert came over 45 minutes ago, he had been so preoccupied with his newfound discovery that he never saw it.

sitting down in his chair the doctor stared at the screen in disbelief. He had run out of time far sooner than he thought. He believed had more time to work on his project, and to gain control over subject-59 but in reality he was too late, the end had already begun when the creature's all started acting strange.

'I should've known.' he buried his face in his hands while leaning against his desk.

the surface must be in absolute disarray, far worse than this facility.

lowering his hands from his face he looked to the papers on his desk and stood up. 'No. this isn't the end. I haven't failed yet! I still have all my research and myself, part of 59's core is still inside of me– I can find other subjects to experiment on, ones that are stronger, and easier to control!"

The doctor's body was proof of something! if he couldn't control the creatures, perhaps he could find another method. perhaps they can combat the monster's with abilities of their own?

He quickly started gathering papers into a briefcase and even started forwarding any information he could on the computers, to HQ. "Soon enough the creature's in this facility will rush to the surface to escape and continue their massacre. Once it's safer in the halls and things have calmed down I can make a distress call and get picked up. then with my research I can go elsewhere and–"

he stopped as the lights in his lab and office suddenly flickered and went out encasing the rooms in darkness. kerian could somehow sense him coming...

setting the briefcase down quietly he stood still waiting, and watching the doorway. slowly he made his way out of his office and peered into the lab, looking for any signs of it.

Only then did he notice how quiet it had gotten out in the halls. stepping towards the glass windows that peered out, all he could see was a black void. like the room itself had been swallowed whole.

dread seeped into his bones as he looked at his own reflection in the glass. an all too familiar dark figure was standing there behind him menacingly.

panicked he spun around to face the monster only to be greeted by the sight of...Ava?

"Were you planning to escape and run away?" She questioned. looking at her more closely the doctor noticed her eyes were now silver in color? No. This wasn't Ava...

her voice and expression was far too cold to belong to that of the girl. she tilted her head to the side while keeping her hands clasped behind her back.

"Did you think you could get away with everything so easily? after what you did?" she questioned, stepping forward, forcing the doctor to step back. his once calm and focused persona faltered as his back came in contact with the wall behind him.

The glass window behind him did not mirror Ava's form in its reflection. It only showed the large demonic figure of the doctor's prized test subject.

the doctor couldn't respond and just glared at the woman before him. Had it actually been Her he would not have been so worried. He could've used her as a hostage to escape even, but he doubted 59 would even allow such.

The moment she opened his vault, it was over.

she smiled before speaking up again. "something wrong? you seemed so confident before, any time I saw you but now you're no better than any other cowardly human in this facility!"

he grit his teeth. Why is it doing this? Why is it taunting him instead of just killing?! "What do you want from me?" the doctor finally spoke up.

"What do I want from you?" She asked, seemingly confused.

"yes! What do you want from me!? what reason do you have for playing these games!"

within the blink of an eye she grabbed him by the neck slamming him back into the wall. The reinforced glass window cracked as subject-59 pinned him against it with an unreadable expression.

"I want you to suffer for the torment you put me and the others through... I want you to feel as weak, helpless, scared and pathetic as you made Her feel. I want you to realize that you brought all of this death and destruction upon yourselves. You humans never seem to understand that you are to blame for all the terrible things that happen. you are never willing to accept that you were possibly wrong and that you are the monsters."

the lights in the room buzzed and flickered overhead causing subject-59's form to change between his own self and Ava.

the hand around the doctor's neck tightened as he struggled, and he was lifted off the ground. "You seem to believe you're free of the consequences of your actions. I'm here to show you just how wrong you are."

The man struggled against the hand that held him, feeling claws digging into his skin as he tried helplessly to break free.

"Do it then! kill me already!"

Ava's form disappeared completely, replaced by subject-59's as he leaned in closer and spoke up within the back of kerians head. "Kill you? no, I have a much worse fate in mind..."

the seams of his mouth opened up and the man's eyes widened in horror at the sight as 59 leaned in closer to his face. "I believe you have something that belongs to me..."

————————

–Ava–

flashing lights, blaring sirens, the sound of gunfire and screaming. I could only remember bits and pieces once the vault opened.

Besides that, it was just pain radiating from my chest in waves. it felt like something was sinking its claws into my very heart, making it hard to breathe.

ever so faintly I remember seeing subject-59 standing over me. I remember hearing him call out my name as he gently nudged me. then it was all black for a while.

when I briefly came too again, I was being carried, cradled against my monster's chest as he took me through the halls. my head was swimming and I couldn't understand what was happening as screams sounded from all around us.

Before I knew It I was being laid back in my bed as his voice called out to me. "Stay here, I'll come back once I've taken care of things..."

besides hearing that and seeing 59's face I couldn't remember much else as I awoke.

blinking I found my room dark as an eerie silence filled the space. sitting upright I was a bit surprised to be back in my room, in bed. my memory felt fuzzy as it slowly came back and I groaned, grabbing my head in pain from the headache it gave me.

finding I was completely alone in my room and the outside seemed quiet, I climbed out of bed and peeked out the door.

The hall was in complete disarray and completely silent. the lights seemed to have gone out, leaving me in the dark. hesitantly I stepped out, and made my way through the halls in search of someone.

I felt uneasy being alone.

as I made my way through the desolate facility. I came across numerous signs of fighting and bloodshed. broken flickering lights, bloodstains all across the halls, bullet casings and papers scattered across the floor, claw marks and bullet holes on the walls. but otherwise it was quiet.

The silence was what made the whole situation unbearable.

hugging myself I pushed forward in search of 32 or 59. if the massacre was over then shouldn't they have been here with me? What if they got hurt?

turning a corner my heart nearly left out of my chest at the sight of a hellhound in the middle of the hall. it was lying on the ground in a pool of its own blood, unmoving but the sight still shook me.

around it were the bodies of at least 3 dead guards.

slowly and cautiously I made my way past the scene trying to keep my gaze from straying towards the bodies. as I passed an open door something lunged out and grabbed my arm making me scream.

"ava!" a terrified jade sobbed, while latched onto me as I stood there dumbfounded trying to calm my racing heart.

jade cried, while desperately clinging to me. her hair was in disarray and he had a few scrapes on her arms and legs but otherwise she seemed unscathed, she must've been hiding in the closet while the massacre was going on.

I managed to pry her off by grabbing her by the shoulders as she continued to sob. "everyone's gone! everyone's dead!"

I almost felt bad for the woman despite the things she did to me. She was a complete mess now and seemed like little more than a lost child at this point. she was no longer the stuck up bully I had known before. somehow I didn't fear or hate her anymore, the only thing I felt towards the woman was pity.

Even still I couldn't offer her any words of comfort and could only stand there awkwardly as she hugged me and cried some more. After a few minutes she finally calmed down enough to pull away, whining her eyes and nose on her sleeve as she sniffed. "I thought I was the only person left..."

Those words left a pang in my chest as I looked around at the empty rooms. I could understand her fear of that all too well. Being alone in a place like this was terrifying, that's why I wanted to find 59 or 32 as soon as possible. "Look, we can't stay here, it's not safe." almost immediately she grabbed my arm again.

"Please don't leave me Ava! i'm sorry for all the mean things i said before!" She begged.

I tried my best to push her off as gently as possible. again. "I'm not! but we need to move and find help! I'm sure there's probably others still around hiding as well."

she sniffed again, calming down once more. "okay." she nodded.

With a sigh I continued my search with a very jumpy and frightened jade on my tail.

As we went we were careful about making too much noise and tried to be as subtle as possible. Jade and I both avoided looking at any of the remains we passed by whether they were human or not. with each dead creature found however I feared the worst for subject-59.

for some reason any time he came to mind, I could feel something strange in my chest. like a shadow of another heartbeat over my own. I couldn't understand or make out what it was but it was kind of comforting...

"Where are we going?" jade whispered and I briefly glanced back at her. I know if I tell her she wouldn't be all too pleased with the answer.

"We are looking for help." I replied.

"help? shouldn't we be trying to find our way to the main level so we can get out of here? surely then we can call a phone and get rescued!"

Her idea was quite logical but the last thing I wanted was to get picked up by 'Acorn' soldiers.

"We can do that after I find my friends." I said while peeking around a corner down a darkened hallway. something felt off about it.

"friends?..." she paused for a minute before grabbing my arm. "Ava! Please tell me you're not dragging us down here in search of that monster!" She exclaimed, none too quietly.

I quickly hushed her and shrugged her off. "He's not a monster jade and he's a lot safer than any guard or soldier would be! you remember how the doctor and guards let you go into that chamber while he was unstable! they knew what would happen! he could've killed you and none of them would've bat an eye– they did the same thing with me."

"You're crazy! The fact it almost killed us is plenty of reason not to go searching for that thing! you think it's gonna risk its life protecting us from the other creatures?! it's probably killed more people than the hellhounds!" She snapped.

I glared back at jade. "he's not an it or thing! you don't know him like I do, he's our best bet so stop yelling and–"

a scuttling sound and deep croaking interrupted us as a giant centipede-like creature came around the corner, crawling along the ceiling. The both of us froze in fear and drool dripped from its fangs and its long antennae started feeling around the air.

subject-67 why did it have to be subject-67...

more croaking came from the giant bug as it crept closer, trying to seek us out. It was mostly blind due to previous testing and experimentation but that didn't make it any less dangerous.

Under normal circumstances I might've felt bad for the creature because of all the things it's been through but right now I can't trust that it would show the same sympathy for us.

"jade, just don't move, I don't think he can see us if we–" before I could finish what I was saying I was shoved forward, towards the creature by the woman behind me. I yelped as I fell on some broken glass and looked back to see jade running in the opposite direction.

instead of attacking me like she expected the giant bug screeched and chased after her fleeing form, crawling across the ceiling. Jade screamed as it caught up to her and struck forward grabbing her around the waist with its fang-like pieces. they cut into her stomach as he squirmed and screamed trying to get free.

the creature readjusted, grabbing hold of her legs with its own front ones to keep her from escaping.

I could only watch in horror as it did so and she looked up fearfully before reaching her hand out toward me. "Ava please!!"

s-67 removed its pincers from around her waist and moved to get a better angle and grab her head between its fangs.

I quickly looked away as it finished jade off and her arms fell limply to her side. I didn't dare look back as 67 started happily consuming his meal.

with subject 67 well distracted I crawled away far out of sight and sat up against a wall. tears clouded my vision as I grabbed my head and pulled my legs up to my chest.

ch 34- The end is only the beginning

'It's not my fault– it's not my fault– it's not my fault!' I repeated to myself quietly while taking a moment to recover.

pushing myself up I quickly and quietly escaped from the area and headed for the elevators, as guilt twisted in my stomach. After getting a short distance away I ended up emptying out my stomach much to my own displeasure.

'Jade was always cruel, but did she really deserve such a brutal death!? I don't know anymore...' I knew this would happen, I knew people would die– but seeing it happen right in front of me? seeing the death and destruction I caused... I'm having a harder time coping than I thought I would.

After taking a few minutes to calm down I continued pushing forward, the further I went, the worse I felt, and the guiltier my consciousness became.

'so many lives...so much death and destruction. I just want to find 32 and 59 and get out of this place, I just want to leave it all behind and forget about everything!'

Eventually, I came to the end of the hallway and saw the elevator doors attempting to close but some kind of dark mass on the ground was blocking them from closing. They opened and tried to close repeatedly as I tried my best to navigate forward in the dimly lit hall.

As I stepped closer I could make out the mass lying in the doorway of the elevator was the upper half of a soldier's body, his lower half was obscured by the darkness of the elevator as he just lay there unmoving.

I stopped in my tracks feeling the hair on the back of my neck standing on end as I covered my mouth and turned my head away. 'I can't do it. I can't keep going like this–'

A vine-like tendril snaked out of the darkness and coiled around the corpse, dragging it Inside out of sight. I heard a sickening squelch and slowly looked back to the elevator as the doors opened up completely due to something moving inside.

vines started creeping through the doorway spreading out from the elevator and slithering along the walls and floor. As they came towards me like snakes seeking out prey I backed away only for my heel to catch on something making me shriek and fall back.

When my hand came in contact with something wet I lifted it up to see dark red all across my arm and palm. Refocusing my eyes I found that the thing that I had fallen on was another body.

As something coiled around my leg, I returned my attention to what was before me and could see the vines were now right on top of me, with one gripping my ankle in a tight squeeze.

Feeling panic take over I kicked at the vine helplessly, making it tighten its grip as more closed in.

A dozen of the plant-like tendrils coiled around the body beside me, dragging it towards the elevator and another gripped onto my wrist before I felt myself being pulled along as well.

"No no! Stop!" I struggled to pull free and thrashed around desperately trying to break free as I was pulled towards the dark elevator shaft. my struggles seemed futile as more Vines wrapped around my body restraining me further, until I could hardly move my arms and legs anymore.

Squeezing my eyes shut I quietly begged for someone to help, for all of this to just stop.

an angry snarl from across the hall had me lifting my head to see a dark figure rush past me and dive straight Into the darkened elevator.

The vines coiled around me stopped as snarls, hissing and thuds could be heard from within the small space. As the vines around me loosened I managed to free one of my arms and tried to pull the rest off of my body so I could get free.

The struggle from within the elevator continued for a moment more before everything went silent and the vines completely went slack.

With my arms free I tried my best to untangle my legs as tears burned my eyes and I continued to panic. Only when a deep bellowing sound came from the elevator did I pause and look up.

as 59 crawled out of the darkened space towards me, I felt relief and my shoulders sagged.

He took notice of the blood on my clothes and quickly rushed over, tearing the vines off of me. "Ava! Are you hurt?!" I quickly wrapped my arms around him in a hug as he sat there somewhat shocked.

"N-no, im fine its not my blood..." I squeezed him tighter and his body seemed to relax as he wrapped his arms around my frame to hold me close.

"Ava...you shouldn't be here." He scolded quietly.

"I know. I'm sorry, I just didn't want to be alone– I couldn't help it."

s-59 chittered quietly as he nuzzled the side of my head, only then did I notice my glasses were missing, but I could see perfectly fine. "It's probably because of the bond. I have also been anxious about not being near you, but now I feel more at ease, just having you in my arms. still, you should have waited for me to come back, this place is still crawling with dangers."

pulling back some he looked over me carefully, seeming displeased with my bloody clothes, despite the fact he also had dried blood on his face and claws.

"is– is it over?" I asked quietly. He turned his head away to look at our surroundings before narrowing his eyes.

"For now... No humans are left here, but a few lingering creatures are roaming about. I had planned to chase them out of the building so it would be safe for you to come out but I have not had the chance."

59 then suddenly turned his attention to the wall and narrowed his eyes in displeasure. Following his gaze I saw 32 appearing through a wall. He looked at the both of us and his ears folded back as he faced 59. they clearly weren't happy with each other.

"something wrong?"

"he was supposed to stay with you, protect you while I handled every-thing."

"It's not his fault, things didn't go exactly to plan, and if he hadn't helped in the ways he did I'm sure things would've turned out much worse," I argued. 59 merely looked at me before relaxing and pulling me in close once more.

"as long as you are unharmed."

I gave a small smile and hugged him back for a long moment, taking comfort in his presence. being here with him, being in his arms I felt whole, I felt calm and safe. But I still couldn't help but worry about one last thing...

"is– the doctor– does he still have part of your core?..." I spoke up a bit afraid of the answer.

59 held me tighter, cradling the back of my head as we both stood there.

"No." I peeked up at my companion and he turned his gaze down to me. "That man is no more, and my core has been restored. you need not worry about any of that anymore." he finished.

I just nodded in understanding. I wasn't surprised that he went after the doctor, I had expected as much... it doesn't matter to me what happened to him as long as we could finally leave in peace.

"We should get out here, there's no telling when reinforcements might arrive to take back the facility. we can take the elevator up to the surface and–" I pulled away to go to the elevator but 59 grabbed my wrist to stop me.

"We cannot leave Ava..."

Confused, I stopped and faced him once more. "What are you talking about?! we have to leave, the whole point of breaking out was so that you and the other creatures could escape this lab and be free! we've already wasted too much time if they send soldiers here–"

"Ava it's far too dangerous outside for you, it's best we stay here... we will clear this building of any other creatures and block the entrance so none try to enter."

my stomach sank at his words. "What are you talking about? How– why is it more dangerous outside?" He crouched down seemingly trying to make himself smaller. "What do you mean its not safe for me??" I asked quietly, although I felt I already knew the answer.

59 didn't respond as 32 sat beside him looking between the two of us remorsefully.

"It's already started?" I said feeling unsure of myself. still no response from them.

my mind was racing with the pressure and shock of it all. The doctor told me how things would end, I knew it was true I understood that it would happen eventually but– time seemed to stand still as i stood there frozen.

"Your kind has already started killing off the population outside, haven't they?" i said more to myself than asked. "Then the outside world..." my voice trailed off as my mind raced with all the possible scenarios.

staring at the elevator i took a deep breath. "I have to see it."

s-59 lifted his head surprised as I walked towards the elevator and quickly ran up beside me. "Ava you don't need to–"

"I have to see it for myself if I don't..." i wasnt sure what else to say. He stared at me for a long moment before relenting. The three of us made our way to the surface floor of the bunker, the main door into the facility cracked open when we got there and I could smell smoke and blood in the air, making my stomach churn in disgust.

I know I wouldn't like what I would see outside. I knew things would never be the same but if I didn't see it myself, i would never be able to accept it...

It took me a moment to compose myself before I approached the door and reached for it. Neither of the two creatures tried to stop me as I pushed it open and was blinded by the outside light.

———

Gasping, I jolted upright in my bed, startling subject 32. he jumped back a ways away with his tail down and ears back as I tried to calm my racing heart.

seeing my distress he slowly approached me tilting his head to the side as I grabbed at my hair.

"That... all of that was real?" I muttered quietly. "that couldn't have been...that wasn't real!?" I felt my mind practically splitting in two from the newfound memories. 'But were they really my memories? or was it all just something my mind came up with?! if that was real then none of this is!? But then why have I forgotten!? why couldn't I remember any of it!'

"you already know why Ava." I looked across my room to see an eyeless Matt standing in the far corner. "You wanted this!" turning around I could see Jade standing at the foot of my bed with sarah close behind her, jade's stomach was practically cut open just as it had been when subject 67 attacked her.

I shook my head scooting back on my bed as Matt walked across the room to stand next to them. "y-your not...how–"

"Because." another voice spoke up from beside me and I immediately froze, not willing to face the figure sitting next to me. "the human mind knows when something is wrong with it." the doctor's voice whispered in my ear.

gripping my bedsheets I grabbed at my head and started hyperventilating.

s-32 lowered himself to the bed like a scolded pup regretting a bad decision, as I looked at my shaking hands. "You know what you must do." all four figures spoke up.

my eyes widened before i jumped out of bed I rushed out of my room and started sprinting down the hall. The three figures disappeared as s-32 watched me run away.

"There's no going back after this!" Matt's voice taunted as he seemed to follow me down the halls. "nothing is going to change!~" Jade said as she appeared in the doorways of each room I passed.

Despite their words, I just kept running, ignoring their presences.

I wouldn't let them stop me, or let their words sway me. I need to get answers– I need to put an end to this.

I made my way to 59's Vault with the intent of opening it. I had to know, I had to see if it's all true–

as I went I didn't see a single person pass me by, there was no one in the halls, no one in the labs. this place should've been crawling with people but it was completely empty...

"Because you killed them all." Matt taunted.

"no! I didn't!" I shook my head denying his poisonous lies. i never meant for any of this...

Once the vault door was in sight I slowed from a run to a walk and quickly removed my ID card. walking up to the looming blast doors I shakily scanned my ID over the scanner with Matt and Jade at my sides, looming over me.

the scanner beeped, only for the light to flash red and deny me access. "no, no no no!!" I banged my fist against the scanner, swiping my card over and over, desperate to get access. "open damn you! you have to open!! I have to see!"

tears stung the corners of my eyes as I shouted and banged on the door feeling completely hysterical, it was as if I was trapped and completely unable to escape as the two ghosts on my shoulders continued to whisper poisoned words into my ears, drowning me in my own uncertainty and fear.

I was about to slam my fist against the door again only for a hand to grab my wrist and spin me around. I looked up a bit shocked to see none other than kerian looking at me with so much pain, distraught, and worry in his eyes.

Jade and Matt seemed to completely disappear as we both stood there looking at one another in bewilderment.

"Ava..."

he sounded so tired... so defeated. but still pulled me in for a hug, cupping the back of my head as he did so. "please. you're hurting yourself..." he pleaded.

I didn't say a word and just trembled in his arms trying to calm my breathing. Once I managed to somehow get a hold of myself, I placed my hands on his chest and pushed him back.

"Who are you?" I asked. kerian merely stared at me, seemingly unable to bring himself to answer. he lowered his head in shame before looking at his hand in deep thought. After a moment he sighed deeply and looked me in the eyes.

"Ill show you, ill do whatever you want me to, tell you what to know, but only if you calm down and promise not to hurt yourself!" he tried to step closer and reach for me but i was quick to sidestep away.

"K-keep your distance!" i ordered and he hesitantly obliged.

"Im not going to hurt you ava, i promise." he reassured before pulling out his ID carn and holding it out to me.

Hesitantly i took the card and looked at kerian skeptically as he took a few steps back to give me some space. Looking over the card for a moment I turned and scanned it.

The lights above flashed red and a deep horn sounded warning of the vault door opening as it cracked and the seal came undone. I waited with baited breath for the doors to part enough to let light in so I could see what was inside. Kerian stood back quietly waiting behind me, saying nothing.

Once they were about halfway open I could see clearly inside of the concrete room. It was empty.

I wasn't sure what to think, say, or even do anymore. The vault being empty meant that all those memories were real, that this was all fake, the life I had been living was make-believe...

"Do you understand now?" 59's voice spoke up from behind me. Turning I looked back at him, no longer seeing him in human form. He stood there quietly watching me as the surrounding space dissolved back to its original form as well.

"Why... Why are we still here? Why have we been living like this?" I looked up at him.

"When you stepped outside that day and witnessed the destruction and death, you changed... it was subtle but over time you grew sadder and struggled to cope with the events that took place. The idea of being the only human left seemed to weigh heavily on your mind dragging you deeper into a pit of despair." as he spoke more memories flashed before my eyes, memories of how I struggled through isolation and the shock of what happened.

"Slowly your state of mind declined and you started seeing things that weren't there... they were symptoms of PTSD as you called it. I tried to help, tried to make it easier for you, but it all just became too much to handle. your mind was tearing you apart. so after a few weeks you gave up the fight and told me you just wanted to forget about all of it..."

I could remember that night, sitting in bed hugging my knees. He was there with me, just waiting and watching, confused and worried. He didn't know what to do or how to help, he was just as lost as me.

I had looked at him while my mind started contemplating the idea of ending it all. I could hardly live with myself and it felt like I was losing my mind. but as I looked at him I knew I couldn't just leave, not after everything we had been through.

So I came up with another idea...

"I asked you to do this... to erase my memory." I nearly faltered as I stood there and had to lean against the wall to keep myself upright.

"yes. you told me that with time you may be able to recover, that your mind would adjust and you would be able to come back to me eventually... I didn't want to do it but I felt as if I had no other choice, I couldn't stand seeing you suffering anymore so I buried it all. all the memories of me, the people who hurt you, the events that took place. I made you forget all of it, it wasn't easy at first. when you awoke with no memory of me you were terrified at the mere sight of me. so I did it again, and that time I made myself look human to hopefully gain your trust, but as I told you what happened you still reacted negatively. so I did it again...and AGAIN. so many times I had to start over until I managed to finally find a balance and make everything seem 'normal' for you.

With all the failed attempts I learned how to change your surroundings and make you more comfortable. I used a familiar form I knew you once liked and made it my own so that I could stay close to you. With the memories and knowledge I acquired I was able to more effectively mimic human interactions and shape our surroundings to better fit us both. To my surprise, It was working. you were happy again even though you were blissfully unaware of the True state of the facility and outside world. but none of that mattered because in the past few months that was the first time I had seen you happy.

Unfortunately over time your mind registered inconsistencies within the illusions I created and once more you started to grow worse, you became paranoid and fearful. I tried to help you through it and fix my mistakes but that only made things worse. You started to fear Me. so once again I started all over, and over, and over. for years I worked to perfect this reality in hopes of one day you would finally be able to accept the truth...

At one point things were going well, you had been living like this for such a long time that the specter thought it might be time to put an end to the charade. I was hesitant, I was afraid of how you might react but I had grown numb to the feeling and process of starting everything all over again. when he brought back your memories, y-you..." he stopped and I looked back to see him covering his face with one clawed hand as he tried to compose himself.

"You told me you were fine, you smiled and hugged me... I knew it wasn't true I knew you weren't the same, but I was too happy to care, I thought I had finally gotten you back. that same night you tried to— you nearly died." he said with a shudder before sinking down towards the floor.

"After that I've been unwilling to let you gain your memories back. I've been too afraid of that happening again…I'd rather live in this illusion with you than risk losing you like that again. That's why I did all of this, why things are this way. but no matter how many times I erase your memories, no matter how I change things to make it better. you always start to remember!! this time being one of the shortest times between wipes yet–" he looked at his hands before lifting his head to gaze at me. He was miserable, he was suffering, and struggling to cope with everything, because of me.

"Ava, I just don't want to lose you." He moved closer hesitantly reaching out, seemingly afraid of how I would react if he touched me.

I grabbed his hand in my own, bringing it up to my face so I could rest my head against his palm. This seemed to comfort him as he moved in closer and held me, during his face in the side of my neck.

"kerian?" I spoke up, grabbing his attention. "How long has it been?"

calling him subject-59 didn't seem right anymore. not after all the stuff we had been through. He may somewhat look like the doctor but they were nothing alike, and after calling him kerian for so long, I'm not sure any other name would fit him. it was part of who he was now.

he seemed to freeze up at the question. seemingly afraid to answer. "15 years…"

hearing his response, i took a deep breath and held him tighter trying my best to stay calm.

pulling back a little he didn't try to stop me as I looked around at our surroundings. The facility was still in disarray although it seemed he had tried to clean the place up to the best of his ability.

I started walking down the hall and he quietly followed, seeming unsure of my intentions as I went.

For 15 years we have been living like this...I understand now. everything makes sense...along with my memories from before I could faintly remember our time together during those years. all the struggles and loving memories between us. even if they weren't completely real they were still a huge part of our lives.

I looked at my hand as I thought more about it. 15 years and I haven't aged hardly at all, I knew the bond probably was the reason my eyesight was fixed but was it truly capable of extending my life?

passing by the cafeteria I checked the coffee to see it was long since expired. no wonder it tasted horrible, im lucky this stuff hasn't made me sick... continuing on I went back to my room to see the Calendar was on the ground with the day things changed circled repeatedly. How many times have I gone through this process? pick up the calendar. I felt Kerian come up behind me.

"Ava?"

I turned to face him, he was watching me closely with worry still plaguing him. reaching up I cupped his face and he closed his eyes, relishing in my touch.

"I'm not going to hurt myself again. I promise." I reassured him with a small sad smile.

He relaxed a bit and opened his eyes to gaze at me. "But you aren't better are you?" He asked. my smile fell as I looked past him to see the four dark figures that haunted me standing quietly across the room. closing my eyes with a sigh I willed them to disappear and they vanished once I opened my eyes once more.

"No, I'm not." I knew they weren't real, but their presences made it clear I still wasn't any better. I couldn't stay like this for long, my mind would eventually bring them back along with all the negative thoughts and other hallucinations it had created before.

Kerian nodded in understanding, leaning his head against mine as we both quietly stood there.

"Ava?" He spoke up. "Can we just lay together for a bit?" he asked solemnly.

squeezing him tighter I nodded before pulling him back over towards the bed. We both crawled atop the mattress and Kerian practically curled himself around me, holding me close as his tail hung off the end of the bed.

As his eyes started to close I brushed my thumb over his cheek and started lulling him to sleep.

"I'm sorry for putting you through this. but can you wait for me just a bit longer?" I Asked quietly.

I wasn't sure how long it would take, how long he would force himself to endure living like this but It wasn't time, i wasn't ready to move on. I wouldn't be able to leave the facility and live out there... not yet. I still had a long way to go to recover, and I knew he wouldn't let me go so easily. so the only choice we had was to start over again and hope one day I'll be able to heal.

pulling me closer with his arms around me and one hand cupping the back of my head he nuzzled my face affectionately. "You need not ask. no matter how many times it takes, no matter what becomes of us or the world above, I will be here with you each time you close your eyes and open them again. I'll be by your side no matter where you go, and I will help you through this..."

"I will wait an eternity for you Ava."

closing my eyes I hugged him back tightly. "I know you will."

————

opening my eyes I was startled awake with a gasp, by a hand on my shoulder. "hey, hey! I'm sorry! I didn't mean to startle you, you were out like a light... Are you okay?" a voice spoke up beside me with a chuckle.

groaning, I rubbed my eyes and looked down to see I was sitting at my desk. "y-yeah i think so?" I replied wearily.

as someone stepped around in front of me I raised my head to see a familiar face and silver eyes smiling down at me. "Come on, you shouldn't be sleeping at your desk... how about we go get some drinks?" he held out his hand and I stared at it blankly for a moment before taking it.

"Are you sure you're alright? you keep zoning out." blinking a few times I shook my head and got to my feet. before rubbing my temples.

"Yeah I'm fine, just a strange dream is all."

"a dream? about what?" I looked back at kerian as he tilted his head. I tried to think about what I had been dreaming about but for some reason I couldn't. looking around confused, something felt strange but I couldn't quite put my finger on it.

my eyes moved to my glasses on my desk and I merely stood there, staring at them until kerian spoke up again, snapping out of my daze. "Ava? What kind of dream was it?"

"I don't remember..."

((The End))

(maybe...)

(note: wow OK this story came out a lot longer than expected and changed A LOT from the initial plot I had planned! I'm hoping this ending ties up all the loose ends and explains a few things. It's not quite the happy ending I know we all want but that's because... well, read the epilogue and you'll see I enjoyed writing this story quite a bit and hope this ending isn't as shity as I feel it is. (I hate this chapter idk why, may make some changes to it later)

IF YOU HAVE ANY QUESTIONS please feel free to ask in the comments!!! I'll explain everything to the best of my ability! whether it be a question about the characters themselves or a specific scene that you didn't understand! anyways thank you all for reading and please stay tuned for the epilogue!!! I think you'll like it)

Experiment-000

S irens screamed out in the air as screeching and gunfire drowned out their warring cries.

The smell of smoke, gunpowder and the iron stench of blood was thick in the streets of the city as a woman carrying a small child in her arms ran through the aftermath of a bloody fight between monster and man alike.

with her hand on the back of the child's head she kept their head down to spare them from the gruesome sight of dozens of bodies littering the street, painting the pale sidewalks red.

She ran past numerous monsters feasting upon their fresh kills and carefully navigated through the road filled with abandoned cars.

as one such flying creature tore an arm off a dead corpse, it lifted her head and noticed her fleeing. with an angry screech the birdlike monster flapped its wings ready to take off into the air only to be gunned down by a barrage of bullets.

the woman gasped, ducking down in fright as she looked back to see armed militants shooting every creature on sight.

turning a corner she rushed down an alleyway out of sight to stop for a moment and catch her breath. Looking back at the street she came from, she could hear the soldiers shouting as some new creatures came charging down the streets in swarms towards them.

an orange glow of fire lit up the alley as one of the soldiers blasted the creature's with a flamethrower, burning everything in his path.

fearfully the woman looked around for a place to hide away from the conflict and out of sight. seeing a cracked door of a house, she quickly went over to it, running across another street and opened it up, entering the abandoned building with no one inside.

shutting the door behind her she made her way to the back of the house away from the windows and doors as more gunfire and screeching roared outside. finding a basement door she hesitantly moved down below keeping an eye out for any possible dangers.

Once she was sure no one or nothing was there she found a dark corner behind some shelves, an old cabinet hidden away out of sight from the stairs.

Kneeling down, the woman pried the child from her front and set her down with a blanket inside the cabinet before cupping the young girl's face in her hands.

The small child had a head of messy black hair and violet eyes, that looked up at the woman, confused. the woman before her flinched at the sound of something exploding outside and cast a sideways glance to the stairs afraid of something possibly finding them.

When she turned her attention back to the child she gave her a small sad smile as her irises glowed with a strange blue hue. "I'm sorry my darling…"

The child just looked at the woman innocently, and confused as she leaned in, pecking a kiss on her forehead.

The sound of something breaking into the house upstairs above them startled the woman and she quickly pulled away. shutting the doors of the cabinet with the child inside.

The little girl watched absently through a Crack in the cabinet doors as the woman left the basement.

she flinched and whimpered at the sound of roaring upstairs followed by gunfire as light flashed from up top. The body of a strange creature tumbled down the stairs after being gunned down and more fighting ensued above as the little girl clutched her blanket fearfully hiding away out of sight.

moments later the fighting ceased within the house but she could still hear the distant battles from outside, as the city burned and the war between humans and creatures alike raged on.

At some point the child ended up drifting off until morning. When she awoke within the small cabinet, everything was silent. there was no more gunfire, no more sirens, everything was just silent.

pushing the cabinet doors open the small girl crawled out of the dark space and looked around for the woman who left her there, confused.

a creaking sound drew her attention to the stairs as a giant, spider-like creature started creeping down the steps. she stood frozen as it came down into the basement quietly and crawled across the wall. mosses and mushrooms grew all along the top of its legs and back almost like a natural camouflage but they did little to hide the horrifying appearance of its face as it scanned the room and found her standing there frozen in fear.

a strange clicking, sounded from the creature as it krept closer to the small girl. she couldn't look away as it moved towards her, raising its front claws to reach out and nearly touch her before it was suddenly blasted with gunfire. The creature screamed in agony and spun around as bullets pelted its abdomen from the stairwell.

the young girl ducked down fearfully covering her head as the man on the stairs shooting the monster, emptied his clip.

three soldiers fully decked in gear rushed down the stairs behind him and blasted the creature as well, shredding it apart with their bullets until it was on the ground writhing in pain.

They surrounded it with their weapons up as it twitched a few times and stopped moving completely, legs curling in like a normal dead spider's would.

one of the soldiers touched the earpiece on their ear stating the house was cleared of hostiles.

Another man dressed in similar attire to theirs came down the stairs looking over the dead monster curiously. When he noticed the small girl hiding behind a shelving unit he tilted his head and removed the mask on his face.

one of the armed soldiers came up beside him with his weapon ready as he approached the child and kneeled down. "

"a survivor?" He said a bit confused and surprised. as the little girl looked up at him with tears streaming down her face. You poor thing..." he mused as the girl wailed.

He hesitantly reached out and picked her up in his arms as he stood.

"sir?" one of the soldiers spoke up as the man wiped the tears from the child's face and let her cling to him as she cried.

suddenly they all froze at the sound of a distant screech from outside.

"bring the truck around to the front..." he ordered. one of the soldiers nodded before using his coms to contact someone outside the house.

"shhh, there there, you're okay, hush now." The man bounced the small girl in his arms as he patted her back doing his best to soothe her. turning back to the other soldiers and the dead monster he contemplated for a moment before turning to go back up the stairs. "Get the samples we came for and let's return to base."

With that he took the girl up the stairs running his hand over her head as she sniffed and cried from the fright she had experienced. The inside of the house was an absolute war zone as at least three different monster corpses littered the living and dining area as well as 5 dead soldiers.

The man quickly buried the girl's face in his shoulder to keep her from looking, and to muffle her cries as he made his way through the house and back outside. Once they were out the door the girl looked up to see the streets a mess with a few fires still blazing and pillars of smoke rising into the air in the distance.

as a military truck pulled up the man carrying her gave out some orders as he climbed into the back seat with her and buckled her in. "There, now you see? no reason to cry, we're gonna go somewhere nice and safe away from all the scary monsters, ok?." the man smiled warmly at her, wiping some tears off her cheek with his thumb.

He then turned to the driver with a serious face. "get us back to the outpost immediately."

"Yes sir." the driver responded before pushing through the street.

looking out the windows of the vehicle, There were collapsed skyscrapers and dead monsters and humans alike everywhere. along with one of the fallen buildings was a massive creature bigger than anything anyone had ever seen before, lying dead against a large building.

as the girl sniffed and wiped her face with her hands, the man beside her wrapped his.arm around her and pulled her close so that she was laying her head on his lap. "good thing we found you..." He smiled down at her before looking ahead.

the small girl curled up against him in the seat as the truck drove through the destroyed city headed to some unknown location.

Her eyes grew heavy and she did her best to fight off sleep as the truck bounced a little as they drove over debris littering the streets. the man beside her hummed quietly while rubbing her back, lulling her further into the depths of sleep.

She wanted to know where the woman went but after everything she had gone through in the past few hours she couldn't resist the urge to close her eyes and doze off as the world continued to burn around her.

(note: DUN DUN DUUUUUN that's right there's a 2nd book! hooray! time for another monsterxhuman romance! because what do we do when we finish one book? we torture ourselves by starting another! huzzah!

Anyways, thank you all so much! So thankful to all of you who followed along this journey and story of Ava and I hope to see you all in book 2!

I know you're all curious as to what the original initial plot for s-59 was so I'll give a basic rundown for you guys.---

much like how the story did in fact go ava awakes in the facility going about her daily routine and life. as she goes about normally she experiences hallucinations and keeps hearing strange voices but any time these things happen her loving and Strang boyfriend kerian pops up and they suddenly stop for a short time. but as the days go by these things keep getting worse and she keeps having visions of the vault door to s-59's vault.

but in the original plot I never planned to go through and show her all memories of what actually happened to ava and how she got to where she was, instead she would have found signs from her past memory wipes such as notes and other hints that things weren't as they seemed. initially she grows to not trust her boyfriend and tries to keep her distance from him, he doesn't like it and becomes pushy trying to stay close to her making her trust him even less.

as she goes along having these dreams of a creature (s-59) trapped in the vault speaking to her begging to be free'd. her boyfriend keeps her away from the vault and seems to always be around when strange things happen. she slowly starts noticing inconsistencies with her coworkers and also finds some of them seem to know things that she's only told to her bf or her bf knows things she's only told her friends.

becoming paranoid she starts to believe she's going crazy and at some point she does finally manage to get to the vault and open it. when it's opened she finds it empty and her bf appears behind her as the monster from her dreams. Only then does she remember what she had done in the past. She released the creature believing it was good and in turn it slaughtered everyone. she was spared by it because she let it go free and it became unhealthy obsessed with her wanting to keep her as his own. She couldn't handle the trauma and grief and lost her mind.

The creature didn't want to let her go so it wiped her memories to keep her with it for the rest of eternity.